CHICAGO PUBLIC LIBRARY
CONRAD SULZER REGIONAL LIBRARY
4455 N. LINCOLN
CHICAGO, IL 60625

P9-DOA-914

MAY 2009

THE
Unnameables

THE
Unnameables

Ellen Booraem

HARCOURT, INC.

Orlando   Austin   New York   San Diego   London

Copyright © 2008 by Ellen Booraem

All rights reserved. No part of this publication may be reproduced
or transmitted in any form or by any means, electronic or mechanical,
including photocopy, recording, or any information storage and retrieval
system, without permission in writing from the publisher.

Requests for permission to make copies of any part of the
work should be submitted online at www.harcourt.com/contact
or mailed to the following address: Permissions Department,
Houghton Mifflin Harcourt Publishing Company,
6277 Sea Harbor Drive, Orlando, Florida 32887-6777.

www.HarcourtBooks.com

Library of Congress Cataloging-in-Publication Data
Booraem, Ellen.
The unnameables/Ellen Booraem.
p. cm.
Summary: On an island in whose strict society only useful objects
are named and the unnamed are ignored or forbidden, thirteen-year-old
Medford encounters an unusual and powerful creature, half-man, half-goat,
and together they attempt to bring some changes to the community.
[1. Utopias—Fiction.   2. Satyrs (Greek mythology)—Fiction.
3. Friendship—Fiction.   4. Change—Fiction.]   I. Title.
PZ7.B646145Un   2008
[Fic]—dc22   2007048844
ISBN 978-0-15-206368-9

Text set in Adobe Jenson Pro
Map illustrations by Jeffery C. Mathison
Designed by Linda Lockowitz

First edition
A C E G H F D B

Printed in the United States of America

R0421014018

CHICAGO PUBLIC LIBRARY
CONRAD SULZER REGIONAL LIBRARY
4455 N. LINCOLN
CHICAGO, IL 60625

For Rob,
who gave me the Goatman
and the courage to write about him

Contents

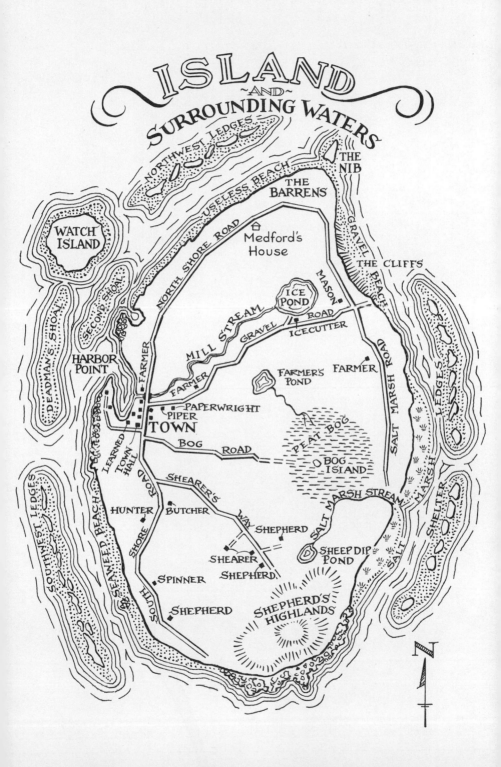

Prologue

IT IS AN ORDERLY ISLAND. Anyone can see that, even from a distance.

Fields of late hay, oats, and barley wait for harvest, sown arrow-straight and weeded to stay that way.

The houses are squared and repaired, their biggest windows facing south to catch the sun. The roof shingles line up like crow flight, a chimney emerging neatly from every roof. Firewood is perfectly stacked and entirely covered.

But out here over the ocean, between the orderly island and the mainland miles away, the seabirds are in chaos.

They flap. They squawk. Spare feathers whip away in a vortex.

The wind is out of the west.

But then it switches around and comes from the north.

Then south, then east. Then again from the west.

Down on the water, a tiny sailboat rocks amid frothy waves. Despite the keening of the wind even a bird can hear the *whap-whap-whap* of the sail as it wheels around.

A man is clinging to the sides of the boat for dear life. He shouts something, tries to gesture. But the wind grabs his words and swoops off with them. He attaches himself to the gunwales again and closes his eyes.

The man's robe is purple and far from clean, the sea-birds notice. Not what they're used to in this part of the world.

His dingy white sash crosses from right shoulder to left hip. The sun glints dully off a pair of droopy horns on his head. The horns have tarnished golden balls attached to their tips.

A black-and-white dog cowers in the bow of the boat, wet and shaking. She lifts her head and howls, the way anyone does when she has taken up with a horned man who can't sail.

Could such a miserable, wind-tormented boat really be heading for that sunny, orderly island?

Not yet.

Not for nearly a year.

Don't worry, though. It'll get there.

THE
Unnameables

Town

TANNERY · SAWYER TANNER · GRAVEL ROAD · PICK[...] · NORTH SHORE ROAD · FORGE · COOK'S · OVEN HOUSE · GRIST MILL · MILL STREAM · CARTWRIGHT SHOP · SAWMILL · POTTER CARPENTER · FISHERS LANE · BAITSHE[...] LANE · HARBORSIDE ROAD · POTTERY · POTTER'S LANE

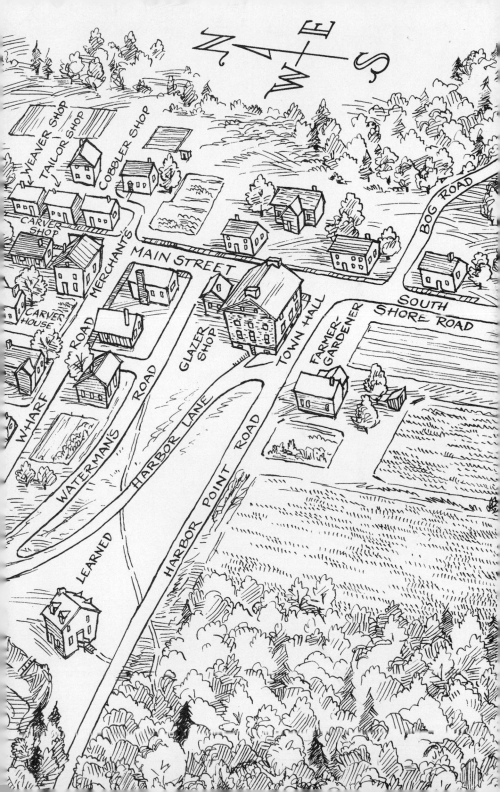

CHAPTER ONE

❧

Cropfodder

A Pumpkyn may remayne Wholesome the Winter through.
Gut the Fruit, then cut in Pieces and String it. 'Twill drie
lyke Apples.

—*A Frugall Compendium of Home Arts and Farme
Chores by Capability C. Craft (1680), as Amended and
Annotated by the Island Council of Names (1718–1809)*

W HEN MEDFORD thought about it later, that day in
Hunter's Moon was a good example of Before.
Before Transition.
Before the Goatman.
Before life changed forever.
Before, before, before.
He and Prudence Carpenter were on the beach, watch-
ing the Farmers gather seaweed for winter mulch. Grover
Gardener, Councilor for Physick, was there, too, hands
red with sea slime. So was anyone whose kitchen gar-
den needed mulching, which was almost everybody. That
morning's sky, the departing birds, and Emery Farmer's

1

bones had announced that seaweed gathering soon would be a chore rather than a pleasure.

You'd gather the seaweed anyway, of course, pleasure or no. Seaweed was Useful and that was that. The Book even named specific types: Cropfodder, the kind most people were after today; Windbegone, which Grover gave to patients who had digestive troubles; Bone-mend, which he dried for chewing when you'd broken your leg.

Medford and Prudy were ignoring seaweed. It was still Before, and they were being Useless. *Run, run when young,* the Book said. *Later in the day, settle and stay.* Time enough to be Useful after Transition.

They were knee-deep in sea-foam, bare feet numb, clothes salt-spattered. Waves hissed in over the sand, then sighed back out again. The sun-drenched air was warm but sharp. The winter winds had come early this year, whipping up the waves. Two weeks from now the sea would be stone gray and the monthly Mainland Trade would be over until spring. Boats would hunker down on shore and people would eat salted Common Fish.

Medford stood still and let the retreating water slip over and around his frozen feet. It ate away the sand at his heels until he teetered and almost fell over. Fifty feet out, a Nameless brown bird made a clumsy splash landing in the water while a Nameless gray bird swooped over its head, laughing. Medford flailed his skinny arms to keep his balance, laughing himself, his scraggly brown hair wild in the breeze.

Skinny and lanky and practically Nameless, he had a lot in common with that brown bird.

Seabirds had no names, regardless of color. *No Use, no Name,* the Book said. And names were what mattered here, thirty-five chilly miles east of Mainland. Mainland maps called the place Fools' Haven. But the people who lived on it called it Island.

Island was ten miles long, north to south, and seven miles wide, west to east. Its principal town, on the western shore closest to Mainland, was called Town. The town hall was called Town Hall and said so on a plaque over the door. Town Hall was on the main street, which was called Main Street.

Islanders liked names that said exactly what a thing—or a person—was or did, and nothing less.

Islanders liked things (and people) to do what their names said they would. Nothing more.

Islanders who fished were called Fisher. Others had names like Carpenter, Merchant, Tailor, and Miller. So what would you expect of a thirteen-year-old foundling called Medford Runyuin?

Not much.

In fact, you might want to keep your eye on him. And you'd be right, but so far Medford was the only one who knew that for sure.

Beside him, Prudy plunged her hand into a retreating wave, one blond braid dipping into the water. "Ooo, look," she said, something in her hand. When a new wave hit she swooshed the thing around to get the sand off.

It turned out to be a Baitsnail shell three inches long, glistening white with pale pink stripes, its tail a perfect funnel, not a chip on it.

"'Tis the best yet," Prudy said.

"Let's see it," Medford said, holding out his hand.

The stripes spiraled into a point at the top. The inside of the shell had its own design, fainter and more delicate. If this were a piece of wood, he'd know just the right blade and just the right amount of pressure that would bring out those spirals, make them—

He shuddered and dropped the shell into Prudy's hand as if it burned his fingers.

Unnameable thoughts again.

The Book never defined Unnameable. It just figured you knew. Medford did know, but he forgot sometimes. He shook the unwanted thoughts out of his head, breathing deep for calm as the Book suggested.

The calm didn't last. It never did.

"Med-ford Run-you-in," called a hated voice from behind him. But he and Prudy had been the only young ones on the beach when they'd arrived. He'd checked, first thing.

"Run-you-in, let's run you out," the voice said. Other voices snickered, although it could just have been the waves.

Medford decided to ignore them. He didn't turn

around. He pretended he didn't know anyone named Arvid Tanner, and he could tell Prudy was doing the same. She was examining her new shell as if it had a Use.

"Been sawing your hair off with your knife again, I see," Arvid's voice said, closer and louder. "Raggedy Runyuin." Those were definitely other voices, laughing.

Yet again, Medford considered growing his hair into a pigtail. Medford's foster father, Boyce Carver, always said a pigtail tickled his neck and the stray hairs got in his eyes when he was working. A pigtail probably would tickle. But it might be better, just for a little while, to look like everyone else.

"Ain't you scared, standing in the water like that?" a second voice churgled. That was Hazel Forester, who found it difficult to talk without giggling. He imagined her chins wobbling. "You might get drownded like your parents."

"Who sails without a chart?" Arvid said. "Nameless Mainlanders, that's who."

"Raggedy don't care about duh wahder." This from Arvid's brother, Fordy, who always sounded as if he had a cold in his nose. "He'd just wash back id od a plank like he did the first tibe."

Someone splashed water onto Medford's back. "Plank Baby, Plank Baby," Fordy chanted. Another splash.

It sounded like just the three of them but that was enough. Arvid had an unfailing sense of what would hurt most, whether it was a finger between the ribs or a tale flung across three rows of desks in Book Learning. Fordy and Hazel either led the admiring laughter or blocked the way so you couldn't run.

"I heard what you and Run-you-out get up to on that secret island of yours, Prudy." Arvid again. "Hazel says her ma'd never let her sneak off like that with a raggedy, Nameless—"

Prudy whirled and kicked water in Arvid's long, freckled face. It was a good, soaking splash, one in a thousand, and when he turned away to wipe the salt out of his eyes she kicked him in the seat of his linsey-woolsey knee breeches.

Several things happened then.

Arvid fell nose-down just after a wave went out and didn't quite get up in time to miss the next wave coming in. It slapped him in the face and he went down again. Now it was Prudy laughing.

Hazel Forester balled up her fists and headed for Prudy. Medford balled up his fists and stepped in front of Prudy. Prudy stepped out from behind him, stuck her new shell in her pocket, and balled up a fist or two herself.

Fordy helped his brother up, hand already clenched.

It had never come to blows before but this might be the time. Medford hoped he'd know what to do.

"Prudence!"

As if they were connected by fishing line, everybody's hands dropped to their sides.

Prudy's father, Twig, grabbed her arm and pulled her to shore. "Explain," Twig said.

"They called Medford Nameless and Plank Baby and said we're up to something bad on our island."

"Many say the same," said Arvid's father, hovering nearby. He had a nose for secrets, eyes for shame, and always a tale to tell, not necessarily true.

"I thank thee, Dexter," Twig said. "Go away, if it please thee."

"My son be blameless, Master Carpenter."

"Take Arvid with you, if you please. Your horses need tending." Sure enough, Dexter's team was meandering forward with its load of Cropfodder.

"Hauling Creatures they're called, to be by the Book," Dexter said, his face a model of virtue.

"Looks like they be hauling too soon, by the Book or no." Twig was among those who ignored the Beast and Domestic Creature Classification of 1853, which in addition to other innovations renamed horses as Hauling Creatures and cows as Greater Horned Milk Creatures. The Shepherds had always ignored it because they could hardly call themselves Shepherd if sheep were Fleece Creatures. Others just thought the new names were too hard to use.

At the moment, Medford thought, Twig Carpenter was simply trying to annoy Dexter Tanner. It worked, as always. Dexter turned his back on Twig and gestured angrily to Arvid, Fordy, and Hazel, who slogged out of the waves and down the beach to rejoin the seaweed gatherers.

"More trouble for young Master Runyuin," Dexter said

in the tender, saddened tone with which he savored bad news. "Well, they do say, once a Runyuin never a Carver." He stalked off after Arvid and his cronies.

"Tanners breathe in poisons, Medford," Twig said. "Then they talk."

"I'm fine, Twig." Having Prudy's father around made Medford want to put on a brave face. Twig wasn't tall—Medford was taller—but he was broad at the shoulders, sunbrowned and strong, so solid and with such a bounce in his step that he seemed bigger than he was.

"Arvid's going to be a Sawyer, like his ma," Prudy said. She was chewing on one of her blond braids, the way she always did when something made her nervous.

Twig pulled the braid out of her mouth, gave it a little tug. "And Sawyers have sharp edges. We get our lumber from Dulcie Sawyer, girl."

Prudy's back straightened, a sure sign of a fight. "He deserved kicking, Pa."

"Thou shalt tell him sorry," Twig said, using Book Talk so she'd know he meant it.

"But Pa—"

"Thou shalt do it now, Prudence." Twig clamped a hand on her shoulder as if to propel her toward Arvid.

Prudy shrugged her shoulder free. "Aye, Pa."

"Can't do it now," Medford said, trying not to sound relieved. "Arvid's off with his pa." Dexter's horses were struggling toward the South Shore Road, Arvid and Fordy wrestling a slimy mound of seaweed in the back of the wagon. They'd have to have a full-out bath in the kitchen when they got home.

"Thou shalt go to his house this evening," Twig said. Prudy took her new shell out of her pocket and studied it as if she hadn't heard him. Twig patted her shoulder and went back to Emery Farmer's hay cart, which he was helping to load in exchange for transporting his own garden mulch. Prudy plopped down in the dry sand.

"I do name thee Pinky," she said, holding the shell up to the sun and using Book Talk for ceremony. "Pink as the sunrise, pink as Balmweed."

Pink as Prudy. "'Tis a Useless name," Medford said. He sat down next to her. Her hair smelled of sun and cut grass.

"'Tis a Useless Object," she said. "One more to smash at Transition." She pressed her lips together the way she did when she was determined not to cry, and started building a little driftwood house for Pinky. Medford watched, marveling at how she could fit odd bits of wood together so they'd stand up straight.

So Prudy was worried about Transition, too. It was scary, that ceremony at the start of adulthood, when all the Useless things of childhood got smashed underfoot. Medford imagined Prudy's new shell already in pieces, turning to dust under her heel.

Medford didn't have any Useless Objects to destroy

at Transition. Well, he did have some, actually, but he couldn't show them to anyone. Their destruction would have to be secret, like their making.

He would burn them and make no more. He promised himself that.

His biggest fear was that the Council would refuse to change his name. He'd been apprenticing with Boyce for five years but his foster father kept his ideas to himself—it was hard to tell whether he thought Medford deserved to be called Carver.

Prudy went by her father's name, as most young ones did. And she'd decided to take the Carpenter name for good, continue apprenticing with Twig. She expected no arguments. Neither did anyone else in this class of Book Learners. Medford was the only one whose future was in doubt.

A roar among the seaweed gatherers broke into Medford's thoughts.

"Young Master Earnest Carpenter," bellowed the mighty Chandler Fisher, "what ails this motor?" Twig's children both were having a hectic day.

Master Fisher stood knee-deep in seaweed, yanking the start cord of his motorboat engine as the boat drifted toward the rocks. The motor coughed and gave up.

Prudy's older brother, Earnest, watched from the beach, pitchfork in hand, a deceptively witless grin gleaming in a face gone blotchy red. Essence Learned had dropped her pitchfork and was doubled over, screeching with laughter. Medford hadn't seen her laugh like this since she and Earnest went through Transition last spring. She was apprenticing with her dismal father, Deemer Learned, so Medford could understand her darker mood.

It was nice to see her laugh again.

Prudy snorted. "'Tis not funny," she said.

It wasn't as funny as Essence was making it, Medford had to admit. She clutched her middle as if the laughter hurt. She couldn't seem to stop.

"Thou wast fiddling with this contraption after I got here," Chandler hollered, impressive in Book Talk. "What didst thou dislodge, young Nutgatherer?"

"Nothing," Earnest said. "Probably nothing. Almost nothing." He dug his fork into the sand and headed for the boat. His white-blond hair blew free of its pigtail and danced around his face, making him look like a madman. "Well, maybe something."

Nobody knew what to do about Earnest. He spent the workday building things and his free time taking things apart.

"He'll grow out of it," Twig told those who complained. "Probably."

Rrruppp-rrroar! The motor came to life and Earnest waded ashore. "I put that twisty thing back upside down," he yelled to Chandler, who shook his fist at him.

Essence Learned gave Earnest an approving punch, still trembling with laughter. "Just encouraging him," Prudy muttered.

The tide was coming in fast. The sun dipped low. The rocks disappeared under the water and the seaweed began to float. Islanders who had stripped down to their linen shirts (unbleached to save labor) now pulled on vests and sweaters (dyed dark brown to hide the dirt). Chandler churned off toward Town in the overloaded boat.

Earnest poked at the sand with his pitchfork, keeping a shy distance from Essence Learned but watching her out of the corner of his eye. She swung a last forkful of Cropfodder onto her handcart . . . and went rigid.

Her father, his black Council robe flapping and outlandish in the breezy sunshine, was marching down the track to the beach.

Deemer Learned, Councilor for Ethics, acknowledged no one, responded to no cheery call or wave, just headed straight for Essence. His Council tricorn hat looked as if a bird had dropped it on his bald head by mistake.

Prudy brushed the sand off her knee breeches and strolled nearer. Medford followed, although he didn't see why they'd want to get closer to Councilor Deemer Learned.

Four days a week, year-round except during harvest, Island young ones suffered through Book Learning, with lessons ranging from cooking and farming to Island Ethics. They broke free of Councilor Learned only at Transition.

Now the Councilor towered over his only daughter, his robe billowing from his skinny frame. "I have read thy journal, girl," he said.

Essence looked as if she'd been bleached in the sun. "By what right, Pa?"

"I am thy father and thy master. Come."

"I'll stay here and see you later," Essence said, chin up.

"Come."

"Pa, I beg—"

"Come."

Essence stepped over her fallen pitchfork. Without a glance at anyone, she followed her father off the beach and up the sandy track to the road.

Earnest fumbled in his pocket for his tiny screwdriver and his great-grandfather's imported Mainland pocket watch. He liked to take it apart when he was worried.

"That," Earnest said, unscrewing things, "is why I keep no journal."

CHAPTER TWO

ॐ

Book Learning

Merit Glazer, who hath taught our Children from the Book these Ten Years, wishes to change names since he no longer maketh Glass. He shall be Learned now.

—Journal of Ida Waterman, 1790

E SSENCE WAS LATE to Book Learning the next day and her father started the class without her. The auditorium on Town Hall's second floor was even chillier for her absence. The sunlight through the windows seemed weak and cold.

Medford worried that Councilor Learned was going to try to teach all fifty-three students by himself. His temper would be nasty and the younger students, usually taught by Essence as Deemer's apprentice, would be in tears. The New Learners were sitting unnaturally still and silent, hoping Deemer would forget they existed.

Deemer had to carry the Book the few steps from its safe to its lectern all by himself, staggering under the weight. The pupils froze to their hard wooden chairs, not making a sound, hoping he wouldn't drop it. It was anyone's guess what his temper would be like if that happened.

The Book was huge: a foot and a half wide, two feet long, a foot thick. It was the only reason there was Book Learning. The only reason there was anything.

Like all else on Island, the Book had a name: *A Frugall Compendium of Home Arts and Farme Chores by Capability C. Craft (1680), as Amended and Annotated by the Island Council of Names (1718–1809)*.

Perversely, no one ever used the Book's name. They just called it the Book. No one knew who Capability C. Craft had been. Medford thought of him as a talkative version of Boyce, his foster father—clever hands and steady patience with a touch of sturdy, confident Twig Carpenter thrown in.

Deemer eased the Book safely onto the lectern. Only then did Prudy dare to raise her hand. Nobody else bothered because they knew Prudy would do it for them.

"Where be Mistress Learned?" she asked.

"Mistress Learned's whereabouts be no concern of thine," Deemer snapped. "Chalkboards out."

"If she be ailing—"

"Chalkboards out!"

Essence walked through the door just then. Her eyes were red, her usually thin face as puffy as Baker's dough. Her light brown hair was tied back in a lopsided braid. She might actually be ailing, Medford thought.

The New Learners were too afraid of Deemer to cheer out loud when they saw her. They just exhaled as a group and relaxed. Essence gave them a wan smile and headed over to sit with them.

But Deemer slammed his ruler on the lectern, a gesture no one ever ignored. The ruler was a foot and a half long and sturdy, used for measuring things, pointing at things, and skimming the tops of pupils' heads.

"Over there, Mistress Learned," Deemer said. He pointed the ruler at an empty seat in the aisle farthest away from the New Learners, behind Prudy.

"Pa, I would—"

"Councilor Learned to thee. Take thy seat."

Essence obeyed. A New Learner let out a whimper. Deemer ignored the sound and from that moment on he ignored Essence, too. He made Prudy come up to read out the Book's shellfish fritter recipe. Scribbling on their chalkboards, the pupils tried to figure out how to increase the recipe from six servings to fifteen, then decrease it to two.

Deemer stalked among them, criticizing, ruler in hand. He spent an especially long time among the youngest pupils, who hadn't known such ciphering existed until now. By the time he moved on many of them were weeping, just as Medford had feared.

Essence sat at her new desk paying no attention to anything, not even the tears of her New Learners. Fordy Tanner, three seats away in the Middle Learners section, tried to signal her for help with his calculations. She didn't notice, just stared up at the huge map of *Island and Surrounding Waters* on the auditorium's front wall.

When he finished his figures Medford studied the map, too, trying to see what Essence saw. The map showed every stream and pond on Island, the blueberry ground to the north, the mountains to the southeast, even the older houses. Out at sea, dotted lines marked the shoals and ledges that ringed Island at low tide. It took a canny sailor to reach Town Harbor even at high tide—you had to know the ocean bottom like your kitchen floor.

Every time Medford looked at that map—four days a week, year-round except during harvest—his eye went first to Deadman's Shoal, just under a mile out from the harbor. That was where his Mainlander parents had come to grief. One of them, he didn't know which, had tied their infant son to a plank as their sailboat broke apart, and he had floated ashore on the incoming tide.

His parents' bodies followed, days later. When Medford was seven, Arvid and Fordy described that scene in detail as recalled by their father. Medford ran into the woods and got sick. After that he made himself stop reacting and they let it drop.

Papers in his father's pocket had identified them: Curtis and Maybelle Runyuin and their son, Medford. Useless, senseless names, all of them.

Arvid, in the next seat, saw where Medford was looking. "Guess you've still got that plank," Arvid whispered. "Guess you hug it and call it Ma."

Deemer came up behind them and skipped the ruler lightly across Medford's scalp. "No talking. Chalkboards to me, both of you."

It was a simple problem and both Medford and Arvid had the answer right. "Too messy," Deemer said. "Do it over." This was not going to be a good day.

When the time came for Ethics, Deemer called Medford up to read from the back of the Book, where the early Islanders had written in their own rules. Medford always hated his turn at the Ethics lesson. The handwritten text was much harder to read than Capability C. Craft's printed advice up front. Every time Medford paused to figure out a word, Deemer would roll his eyes and Hazel Forester would let out her shrill giggle.

"*Thou art thy Name,*" Medford read out haltingly. "*Let thy Name . . . match thy Use to thy fellows. Do those things which thy Name . . . demands—the Weaver ply her loom, the . . . Tailor his needle. If thy Name demand it not, leave it to thy . . . thy . . . thy Neighbor whose name suits the task.*"

"Clumsy as always," Deemer said. "Discourse upon this, Master . . ."—Deemer paused and smirked at the rest of the class—"Master *Runyuin.* Tell us, what do our forebears—I beg pardon, for of course they be not *thy* forebears at all. What do *our* forebears wish to convey to us in this passage?"

The heavy sarcasm in Deemer's voice, the titters of the other pupils—Medford barely noticed any of it anymore. At least not with the front part of his brain. The back of his brain felt his ears getting hot, a little more cheer ebbing out of him. But that, too, was familiar. All he wanted was to get this over with and sit down.

"The Originals tell us . . ." He stopped to think. The lesson seemed obvious but sometimes it wasn't. "They tell us to do what our name says we should and no more. So if your name be Weaver you should leave the tailoring to the Tailor."

"And thou, boy, thou wilt take care of . . . what? What service wilt thou be to thy fellows?"

"Medford will be a Carver," Prudy burst out. "He'll carve, like Boyce."

"Mistress Carpenter, thou speak with as little wit as thy father. Sit down, boy."

As Medford gratefully took his seat, Arvid whispered, "Run-you-in, run-you-out."

Prudy straightened her back when she heard that. "*He who Ridicules his neighbor's Name*," she whispered, quoting from the Book, "*maketh himself Ridiculous.*"

"Hah," Essence said out loud. "And if 'tis in the Book it must be true."

Deemer slammed his ruler on the lectern. "Enough! Mistress Carpenter, if thou be so eager to instruct, do thou drill the younger students in their letters. I shall test the older students on Edible Herb, Fruit, and Root Classifications."

Everyone stared at Deemer, stunned. Prudy stuck a braid in her mouth. They'd seen this before, someone other than Essence being singled out to teach lessons. Last time it was Earnest, Prudy's older brother, who had asked so many questions about the Originals that Deemer began to tell everyone he had the makings of a Learned.

Earnest was excited at first, working up in the Archives with Essence. Normally, no one but the Learneds got to read the three centuries' worth of journals up there. But the ones Deemer let him read turned out to be a bore. "'Tis all about planting and harvesting and what's for the Trade," Earnest told his parents. "I can hardly keep awake."

Twig and Clarity were happy to hear it. "I don't want my son turning out like that prune-faced fool," Twig said to Clarity, with Medford and Prudy standing right there to hear. "He was ever thus in Book Learning—lurking where he wasn't wanted, seeking what wasn't his."

"He wanted to be like you," Clarity said mildly. "At least he did until he decided to hate the ground you walked on."

"Tuh. Why Ada took up with him I'll never know."

"They both needed to marry," Clarity said. "And you wouldn't look her way."

Twig blushed but Medford thought he seemed rather pleased.

The main result of that conversation was that Medford and Prudy started calling Deemer Old Prune Face behind his back.

In the end, even Deemer had to agree that the Learned life was not for Earnest. In Book Learning, when he asked

Earnest to talk about what he had learned upstairs, Earnest would stand there goggle-eyed and erupt with some unconnected nugget of knowledge. "They planted beets," he'd said once after a long silence.

"Crimson Boiling Root," Councilor Learned instructed him coldly, and it was clear Earnest would become a Carpenter after all. At the annual Transition ceremony the following spring, he put his collection of rusty motor parts into a bag, marched to the wharf with a gaggle of screaming children behind him, and threw the bag into the harbor.

Essence had wept that day as she burned her dead mother's bowls and spoons and took the Learned name for good, as the Council said she must. *Bend thy Will to thy Neighbor's need*, the Book said. Burning her mother's things had been Deemer's idea, and the onlookers had gasped to see such Useful items going up in smoke. "'Tis the Useless dreams of childhood she destroys," Deemer said, although no one actually had dared to ask.

Did Deemer think Prudy would succeed where Earnest had failed?

The silence in the auditorium grew as the Councilor waited for Prudy to obey him. Essence jumped up and ran from the room.

"Mistress Carpenter," Deemer said, "take thy braid from thy mouth and do what I have asked of thee." He flipped through the Book, found the page he wanted. "Master Fordy Tanner, what is the improved name for what the Originals called a carrot?"

Fordy stammered something about stew and the color orange. Medford watched Prudy take the youngest pupils over to a corner and sit with them on the floor. She would make a good teacher—better than Deemer, anyway. But she loved carpentry, working outdoors and nailing things together into logical and Useful shapes.

"Master Runyuin!" Medford came to with a start. Deemer was a step away from Medford's desk, hand raised to whap him across the scalp with the ruler. Among the Middle Learners, Hazel Forester was giggling so hard she could barely keep her seat.

"Welcome back, Master Runyuin," Deemer said, lowering his hand. "I ask again: Why do seabirds have no names?"

"I've wondered that myself," Medford said without thinking.

Hazel fell out of her seat at last. The class gave a shout of laughter that died when they saw Deemer's face. Councilor Learned was smiling, giving the class a rare glimpse of disorderly teeth. Even the dullest pupil could see the malice behind that smile.

Medford didn't see a thing, intent on the thought that had just struck him. "There are so many kinds of seabirds," he said. "We name trees, why not birds?"

"We need to know the difference between the Syrup and Tanningbark trees," Deemer snapped. "Surely Boyce hath taught thee that. There is a Use for such names."

"But seabirds have a Use," Medford persisted.

"Medford," Prudy said from her seat among the New Learners. "Don't."

"Nay, Mistress Carpenter," Deemer said. "Let Master Runyuin proceed if he will." More of his jumbled teeth became visible.

Medford knew he should stop, apologize, subside into his usual defensive stupor. But somehow he couldn't. "I like to watch seabirds," he said, "and sometimes they tell me when weather's coming. The gray ones huddle on the shore and—"

"The seabirds speak to thee, Master Runyuin?"

Arvid snickered.

"Nay," Medford said. "But if you watch them sometimes you can tell—"

Whap! The ruler skimmed across the top of Medford's skull, making his eyes water.

Deemer towered over him, smiling no more. "Always the Runyuin. I said it from the start and I say it still: Book Learning is wasted upon such as thee."

"He ain't wrong, though," said an adult voice from the doorway behind them.

Everyone turned. Ward Constable, one of the pair of large, round brothers who took care of Town Hall and kept the peace, had come in to stoke the woodstove.

"Be about thy business, Master Constable," Deemer said.

Unworried, Ward opened the door to the stove and added a couple of sticks. He placed them exactly right and they caught immediately. "Seen young Raggedy watching the seabirds," Ward told the stove. "You do learn from watching animals."

"Art thou teaching this lesson, Master Constable?"

"Stoking the stove, Master Learned."

"Then do so in silence." Deemer stalked back to the Book and flipped its pages.

"For those less concerned with Nameless beasts," he said, "heed this: *If it hath a Use, give it a Name. Let the Name match the Use. If it hath no Use, it needeth no Name and wilt do thee no Harm. Turn thy Back and 'tis gone.*

"But heed this also." His pewter gray eyes widened and he leaned forward as if to dive into Fordy Tanner's desk. "*The Unnameable is another thing entire. Take care, or thou shalt be Gone.*"

Medford wanted to ask. He had to ask. He would ask. He would ask now.

Fortunately, Prudy got there first. "Master Learned, what *is* the Unnameable?" she asked. "Wilt thou not say it plain?" She used Book Talk to soften the question.

"The Unnameable waits to entrance us, Mistress Carpenter. I can be no plainer."

Medford could see that Prudy didn't think that was very plain at all.

CHAPTER THREE

⚭

Essence Is Gone

Hannah Waterman has asked the Council for a Mainland motorboat to ease the Trade voyage. I like not this challenge to our traditions, not least because the fuel for the smelly thing be one more item we must bring in from Mainland.

—*Journal of Booker Learned, 1945*

A N HOUR PAST DAWN and the air in Boyce's workshop already was sweet with sawdust, coarse with the *swisher-swisher-swish* of two carvers at work.

One Carver and one Runyuin, rather.

Medford and Boyce were silent as always. Nothing to say. Sanding hardly required instruction, after all. Medford started his second Platewood platter for the season's last Mainland Trade as Boyce was finishing his third. They bent over their work, intent, each rough spot a new world to tame and smooth.

Medford was shocked when Boyce set down his platter and sandpaper and said, "Thou must not go to Bog Island again. Least not with Prudy."

Medford kept his sandpaper moving but his attention was on Boyce. "Why not?"

Boyce met Medford's eye and looked away, as he always did when a conversation strayed beyond the polite and the technical. "Just don't go there with her, that's all."

"But why, Boyce?"

"'Tis all I have to say, Medford. Work for another hour, then go outside and run some." He picked up his sandpaper and turned back to his work.

Medford found a spark of courage. "Arvid said something about Bog Island the other day, about Prudy and me being up to something. I need to know what he meant, Boyce. I beg thee."

Boyce set his sandpaper down precisely where it had been when he picked it up. He spoke to the wall. "You are too old to be alone like that anymore."

"Alone like what?"

"People will think you and Prudy are courting."

Medford dropped his sandpaper.

"I don't mean 'tis time for that yet," Boyce continued. "But people wonder about you and they talk. They won't like a Carpenter girl courting a boy with no Useful name. That's all."

"Prudy's my friend." Medford felt like crying but he was too old for that, too. This ache in his throat, the itch behind his eyes . . . none of it was any Use.

"People know that if they ponder on it. But they may not ponder. Thou art almost grown now and thou must be more careful."

"Careful of what?"

"Don't draw attention to thyself. That's all."

Boyce bent over his platter again, his back settling into the slight stoop he'd had ever since Medford could remember. For the hundredth time, Medford wondered whether Boyce would have taken in a plank baby if he'd known his wife would die just three years later.

"I didn't know young ones grew this fast," Boyce had said to Comfort Tailor when she was measuring Medford yet again. "I always figured Alma'd be here and she'd take care of all this."

A loud laugh and a quick hug, that was all Medford had left of Alma Weaver. Maybe she'd talked more than Boyce. Medford couldn't remember.

And yet there were times when he thought Boyce might be proud of him. The day Medford had turned his first Sweetwood bowl, Boyce had treated it as if it were his own, showing Medford how to oil the bowl for long life, buff it to a high polish. He filled it with fish stew to show Medford the beauty of a truly Useful thing.

When something of Medford's traded out—a loom shuttle for Prosper Weaver, a rolling pin for Clayton Baker—Boyce made sure the buyer knew who'd made it and noticed how well it was shaped. Because Boyce was standing right there, people had to smile at Medford and say how well he'd done. He treasured those smiles.

Medford went back to sanding the platter, which had a beauty of its own. As he sanded, his mind's eye transformed the patterns in the wood, made them pictures of real things. He began to see shapes. That big brown circle—didn't that look like Bog Island, the way a bird would see it?

The familiar buzz started at the back and the very bottom of his brain. Or perhaps the top front. Not a buzz, really, more like a rush of air after you opened a window. No, a hum, almost a song. But not a song, not at all. Nothing like a song. More of a tingle.

He envisioned trees, which would take the sharpest of blades to carve. He could color the leaves with berries and—

Unnameable thoughts. Medford shuddered and shoved the platter away from him.

"Go out and run," Boyce said. "I can do this."

Medford left but he didn't run. He wandered down the alley between Boyce's workshop and Clayton Baker's oven house. He thought about hanging around to beg a heel of hot bread. But he found himself heading for the large Pipewood tree next to Boyce's house and sitting down to think things through.

He and Prudy had found their little island five years ago while slogging around Peat Bog getting gloriously muddy. The air had been warm and fragrant, buzzing with insects. They hopped across rosy peat and tea-colored water, from log to hummock to log again, until they reached a place where brambles arched over a log pathway.

The logs led them to a rise of solid ground, a place so beautiful Medford could hardly talk at first. The mossy space in the island's center was still as green as June, shouting back at the blue sky. Brambles and small trees flamed with every color known to autumn.

A pair of fallen trees, pewtered with lichen, made a seat in the sun where Medford and Prudy ate the bread and cheese they'd brought. They talked about the barns she'd build, the perfect bowls he would carve. No one could see them through the brambles, no one could make some sly comment about plank babies or Med-ford Run-you-in.

Since then they'd seen Bog Island in all seasons, even creeping out over icy logs to be dazzled by it in snow. Prudy had woven branches into a three-sided shelter against the wind.

What if they never let him be alone with Prudy ever again? She and her brother, Earnest, were the only people he really talked to. Without them, his tongue would shrivel up. He'd be a moaning, tongueless person sanding platters all day.

The idea of Prudy and him courting was ludicrous, humiliating. What would he say to her when she suggested going to Bog Island? He would have to say why he couldn't. How would he face her after he'd said it?

With a rush of heat he realized that Prudy had known

exactly what Arvid meant yesterday when he spoke of them "sneaking off"—that was why she'd gotten so angry. Maybe he couldn't talk to her at all. Maybe he'd already lost his only friend.

"Medford!" He hadn't heard Prudy's footsteps but she must have been running. She'd spent the last four days teaching the New Learners, Deemer hovering over her. Now she was breathless, glowing with the joy of being outside on a day with no Book Learning. "Medford, come down to the wharf. Something's Nameless."

He ran after her, glad he hadn't had to talk. By the time he reached the wharf, two streets away from Boyce's house, he was winded but braver.

Prudy was on her way down the ramp to the floats below the wharf. At first, everything seemed normal. Cooper Waterman and Adele Fisher sat against wharf pilings splicing rope. A cluster of Fishers had nets spread out for mending. The large motorboat used for the Mainland Trade was rocking at a float beside two fishing sailboats. All as usual.

Except . . . there, down on the float, Deemer Learned lurked like a molting blackbird in his Council garb, as out of place on the waterfront as on the beach. Why did he wear his Council robe all the time? None of the other Councilors did.

Master Learned was in dour conversation with Violet Waterman, whose face was wrinkled up as if she hurt. Essence stood nearby, head high but looking at nothing, holding herself so tense with a face so white and tight she might be ready to split in half. She had a bundle at her feet, wrapped up in Common Stuff with a wooden handle tied on.

Prudy headed for the float like a Honeybug to its hive. "Essence," she said. "What's that bundle for?"

Essence shook her head. Medford had never seen anyone look so scared, even Fidelity Spinner after the Great Northeast Gale took the roof off right over his head.

"Into the boat," Deemer told his daughter. Essence swung her big bundle into the Trade boat, where it toppled into a puddle of seawater and sat there, soaking it up. Deemer ignored it, and ignored Essence as she prepared to step down from the float.

Violet offered her hand. Essence took it and stepped aboard. She lurched onto the aft bench and sat there, ankles crossed, hands folded, eyes down.

"Essence," Prudy tried again, yelling over the engine noise. "Are you going somewheres?" Essence didn't seem to hear her but Deemer gave Prudy a look that should have made her braids smoke.

He stepped down into the boat himself, waving off Violet's hand exactly when the vessel bucked under him. He stumbled across the cockpit and barely saved himself from hurtling over the side. Violet met Prudy's eye and hastily looked away, biting her lip.

Cooper Waterman came down to cast off for his sister, and the boat moved away from the float. Medford and

Prudy watched it churn toward the mouth of the harbor, the motor's drone fading away under the cries of the seabirds.

"Too bad he was in such a hurry," Cooper said. "Should've sent some Trade goods for a Useful trip."

"Where's Essence going?" Medford asked.

Cooper pretended no one had said anything. Medford felt his face go red.

"Cooper," Prudy said, "where's she going?"

"She's gone," Cooper said.

"Gone?"

"Gone to his place." Cooper jerked his head at Medford. "Off to Mainland and won't come back."

Prudy gasped. "Why, in all the Names?"

"Banished 'cording to the Book, that's all Master Learned would say."

The motorboat kept getting smaller and smaller out there on the cold sea. Medford had heard of banishings, of course, but he'd never seen one.

He thought about Essence laughing at Earnest on Seaweed Beach, her kindness to the New Learners. She didn't deserve this.

When would he be old enough to stop wanting to cry?

"What will happen to Essence?" he said. "How will she live?"

This was such an interesting question that Cooper forgot to ignore it. "They'll leave her on the Trade Beach and come back," he said. "Nobody needs to know more than that. And now we'd best be about our Uses, Mistress Carpenter."

He turned toward the ramp but Prudy blocked his path. "Master Waterman, shouldn't there be a . . . a Council discussion or a Town Meeting or—"

"Seems not." Cooper clamped his mouth shut the way only a Waterman could and went back to his splicing.

"*Take care, or* thou *shalt be Gone.*" That was what Deemer said in Book Learning. Could it be this easy? Medford couldn't see the motorboat anymore, but he kept staring at the last place it had been. Maybe it would come back. Maybe this was all a mistake.

His mouth tasted like iron. It was all he could do not to run home and set fire to everything hidden under his bed. How could he have been so foolish?

"Clayton Baker got a Town Meeting when he was in trouble," Prudy said to Medford.

"Clayton Baker? He's still here."

"Aye, but they almost sent him away, Pa said. Couple of winters ago. He made a sugar paste, shaped it like flowers, and put it on muffins. Council said 'twas a waste of time and good sugar. Which was true, of course."

Medford couldn't help agreeing. He liked Clayton's muffins plain.

Essence's boat wasn't coming back in.

"Clayton said he wanted to cheer people up, but they put him out in that little shack on the North Barrens for a week and he almost died, he was so cold and lonely. He promised not to do it anymore, so they let him stay. Pa said Deemer was furious."

"You never told me this before."

"Pa only told me about it last month. Anyways, it didn't seem important. Clayton's still here." Prudy was hugging herself, shivering as if the sun had gone cold.

"'Tis important enough." Nearly banished for sugar flowers. Medford shivered, too. Not that sugared muffins were a good idea—good thing the Council put a stop to that.

How could he get rid of those carved things hidden under his bed?

"Earnest won't like this," Prudy said, as Medford followed her up the ramp.

"Maybe Essence is better off," he said. "Imagine apprenticing with Deemer."

Prudy stumbled as if the words had struck her in the back. He'd forgotten about Deemer making her teach the New Learners. Why didn't he ever think before he spoke?

She faced him at the top of the ramp, the roses gone from her cheeks. "Maybe Essence refused to do it anymore. Maybe that's why she's gone."

"Whatever it was she did, Deemer read about it in her journal." He tried to sound comforting. "You don't keep a journal yet."

"Medford, what if that dried-up old prune says I have to be a Learned now?"

"Your parents won't let that happen, Prudy. They want you to be a Carpenter."

"They couldn't stop it. Earnest would have had to do it if Deemer had said so."

"Then you'll have to say no."

"But maybe that's what Essence did. And look what happened to her."

"Aye." Medford checked the mouth of the harbor again. Still no boat returning.

"Medford, what would make them send her away like this? I have to know."

"According to the Book, Cooper said. Guess she did something Unnameable."

"*The Unnameable is another thing entire*," Prudy quoted. "*Take care, or thou shalt be Gone.* But Old Prune Face never says what the Unnameable is exactly, does he?"

"It must be in the Book somewheres," Medford said.

"So let's find it."

CHAPTER FOUR

❦

Bog Island

In a cold House that ye wish to heat up quick, a Log of
Wood be thy Friend. For Baking and other pursuits requir-
ing a Steady Heat, a Peat Fyre be best.

> —A Frugall Compendium of Home Arts and Farme
> Chores by Capability C. Craft (1680), as Amended and
> Annotated by the Island Council of Names (1718–1809)

FIND IT? FIND IT HOW?" Medford wondered if he
sounded as squeaky to Prudy as he did to himself.

"We'll look at the Book. We can do it right now, whilst
Deemer's away."

Medford swallowed, trying to think. Reading the Book
by yourself wasn't exactly forbidden. But usually you did it
in Book Learning, with Deemer glowering at your back.
After Transition the Council told everyone what the Book
said—and it was usually the Learned Councilor who did
that, too.

"Would the Book be out of the safe when there's no
Book Learning?" Medford said, buying time.

"I think Deemer takes it out every morning in case

the Council needs it." Prudy squinted at the sun. "Dinner hour. No one will be in Town Hall. Come on."

Medford slouched along beside her, hoping to fade into the wooden sidewalk. "Don't draw attention to yourself," Boyce had said. Well, he was trying.

They walked up three blocks from the harbor and turned right at Merchant's General Store, white clapboard like every other building in Town. Freeman Merchant, Councilor for Trade, was standing on the porch, tidy as ever with his watered-back hair, his clean shirt nearly sparkling under his apron. He peered into his pickle barrel, poking into it with a pair of tongs.

"Councilor Trade!" It sounded like a screech bird but actually it was Comfort Tailor, Councilor for Naming, whose haberdashery was across Main Street from the general store. Sure enough, her plump body filled her shop door. Medford and Prudy slowed down so they could listen.

"Aye, Councilor Naming," they heard Freeman call back wearily, trying to fish out the tongs he'd just dropped into the pickle barrel. Once elected, most Councilors proudly used their Council posts as their unofficial last names. The Learneds were the exception, the Learned name being proud enough for anyone.

"May I ask why my fine linen neckerchiefs have returned unpurchased from the Mainland Trade?" Comfort Naming demanded.

"I've told thee before, Councilor, men don't wear linen neckerchiefs over there. They haven't done so for a century." When he was angling to become Councilor Trade, Freeman actually had spent a couple of nights on Mainland, visiting the Traders. He had returned to become the Island expert on the entire rest of the world.

"Thou liest. I was at the Trade just last spring and the motortruck driver had on something like."

"'Twas not the same thing, ma'am, what that driver had on. The Traders don't know what to do with thy neckerchiefs, fine linen or no."

"As ever, sir, thou runnest the Mainland Trade as if 'twere thine own private treasury." Comfort's voice followed Medford and Prudy down the street. "I will bring it up next meeting, see if I don't."

Marvin Glazer was standing outside his workshop, scowling at the sidewalk while Patience Waterman talked into his good ear. "They left just now," Patience said in a low voice, not even noticing as Medford and Prudy sidled past her. "No Town Meeting, no word to nobody. She's gone, my uncle says."

Marvin grunted. "Ain't by the Book," he said.

Patience said something more but Medford couldn't hear it. Prudy stuck a braid in her mouth and speeded up.

Town Hall was Island's only three-story structure, even more imposing because its ground floor actually was a dozen steps up from the sidewalk. Prudy marched up as if she belonged there. Medford slunk up as if he belonged at the bottom of the harbor. "Stop looking so guilty," Prudy hissed. "We're not doing anything wrong."

Once they were inside the door, though, she was just as sneaky as he was. She tiptoed over to the Council office to make sure no one was in there, even peeked into the little room that held the radio, a Mainland contraption used to contact the Traders.

"We'd better leave as soon as someone comes back from dinner," Medford whispered. A Carpenter could be excused a little youthful curiosity, but not a Runyuin.

Upstairs in the auditorium, Medford pulled a stool over to the Book's wooden lectern and began to turn the huge pages. He could feel the centuries that lay on them like dust. There had to be a place that talked about the Unnameable. But how to find it in a book a foot thick?

One of the older, printed pages at the front of the book offered Capability C. Craft's cure for a bad chest cold. Medford remembered it well—he could still smell the cloth, soaked in oil and hot pepper, that Boyce had wrapped around his chest that time.

Another page, handwritten in the back by some early Islander, spelled out the Transition ritual. *The First Daye of the Sowing Moone, bring together in Towne Hall all Children of 14 yeare . . .*

When Prudy took a turn on the stool, she hadn't been up there five minutes when she sucked in her breath. "This may be it," she whispered. "*Thou and the Unnameable*, it says. What a strange way to put it."

"Just read it," Medford whispered, looking over his shoulder.

"*If it hath no Use, it needeth no Name, and wilt do thee no Harm,*" Prudy intoned, her nose two inches from the page. "We know that already. *Turn thy Back and 'tis gone. The Unnameable is another thing entire. Take care, or thou shalt be Gone.*"

"We've heard that, too."

"But there's more," Prudy said. "*Beware, lest thou stare at the Nameless thing for too long. Thou, and only thou, canst Transform the unnamed to the Unnameable. And then in Truth thou shalt be Gone.*"

Downstairs, the front door creaked open. Floorboards squawked and the Council office door closed. "That," Prudy said, heaving the Book shut in defeat, "makes no sense at all."

Sense or no, Medford thought as they crept outside, he'd better stop staring at Nameless things. And the ones under his bed . . . he'd destroy them and make no more.

Medford was so busy thinking about this, walking down the sidewalk at Prudy's side, that he didn't notice when the moment he'd been dreading crept up on him.

"Let's take bread and cheese to Bog Island and talk about all this," Prudy said.

He almost said, "Aye, let's." But then he remembered Boyce, just that morning.

How would he explain to Prudy why he couldn't go

to Bog Island? If the words existed, they weren't anyplace where Medford could reach them.

One more time couldn't possibly hurt, could it? Of course not. He'd think of a way to tell her. Later.

They went to Prudy's house for provisions. Prudy's mother, Clarity Potter, was sitting at the kitchen table, yawning.

"Art thou just getting up?" Prudy asked, the disapproval in her voice verging on Rude Speech to a Parent, expressly forbidden by the Book.

"I worked late last night, dear one," Clarity said, smiling at her sleepily. "Until past four of the clock."

"Why canst thou not work in the day?" Prudy muttered, opening the ice chest to look for cheese.

"*Let not the Sunset curtail thy Usefulness,*" Clarity said. "'Tis in the Book."

"*Rise afore the Sun that thy Day be of Use,*" Prudy retorted. "Here's the bread, Medford. Slice it thick."

"Going to Bog Island?" Clarity asked, as if Prudy hadn't spoken so harshly.

"I . . . I don't know," Medford said. What if Clarity talked to Boyce later and said where they were going?

Prudy shot him a questioning glance. She looked like her mother—pale hair, blue eyes, broad face, rosy softness over stone—but their expressions right now were opposite. Clarity was drowsily sipping milky tea out of a mug she'd made herself, her hair in a loose bun, blotchy red cheeks the only sign that she was not at peace. Prudy chopped cheese with sharp, sullen strokes, back straight, braids aquiver.

"Why are you so angry at her?" Medford asked as they headed down Harborside Road.

"People will talk about the hours she keeps," Prudy said. "'Tis not right."

"She turns out enough pots."

"Not enough for all those hours. She must be slow at night. She's always tired."

"'Tis not worth such a fuss. Let's run." And so they did, all the way to Peat Bog, shaking Prudy out of her bad mood.

They hadn't visited the bog for a couple of weeks. They were shocked to see how many rose- and brass-colored leaves had fallen, floating bright in the dark pools between hummocks of peat and grass. They skittered along their path of fallen logs, then crawled like critters through the bramble archway to solid ground.

Another shock awaited them. The largest tree on Bog Island, some scrawny and Nameless relative of the Sap Tree, had been uprooted in the same winds that had stirred up the waves last week at Seaweed Beach. Dying needles clung sadly to the branches, and the green moss had a ragged black gash where the roots had been.

"Oh, poor tree," Prudy said, patting the trunk.

Medford squatted down next to the hole left by the roots, feeling ridiculously sad. It was a Nameless tree, no

loss to anyone. But the roots looked so forlorn, the rup-
tured earth so painful.

Prudy threw down her food satchel and stood, arms
out, eyes closed, basking in the sun. Medford watched a
worm explore the hole where the tree roots had been. The
worm curled upright and poked its nose at a funny, square
rock half buried to one side.

Medford poked at the rock, too. But it wasn't a rock.
It felt cold, like metal.

He looked closer. It had a lid. "Prudy. There's something buried here." He stepped into the hole, moved the
worm out of his way, and scrabbled at the earth. The thing
proved to be a metal box, black, battered, and scratched,
more than a foot square.

They had to break the lock with a stone. The hinges
broke as the lid creaked open. A strong, musty smell
greeted them.

"Cloth," Prudy whispered, peering in. "Not Common
Stuff, either."

The cloth had so many colors that at first Medford
thought autumn leaves must have fallen into the box.
When he unfolded it, something fell out: a thin book a
foot long, like the one Boyce kept as a journal and Trade
record. Prudy snatched it up.

Medford had eyes only for the cloth. Where would
such colors come from? Who would put them on a piece
of cloth? The threads had been cunningly woven—he

couldn't imagine how—to make a flat representation of a man. Sort of a man.

Not really a man, because he had horns. They drooped from his crown, weighed down by the pewter-colored balls at the tips. But of course it wasn't horns. It was a hat, an outlandish hat.

"Cordella Weaver," Prudy said. "'Tis her journal. In 1830 she wrote it."

It was hard to decipher Cordella's handwriting, faded to light tan. The pages were dusty with mildew. When Prudy turned them, pieces came off in her fingers.

"Careful," Medford said.

"I'll just find the last entry," Prudy said.

She found it near the back of the book, *Third Daye of the Sowing Moon* at the top of the page. She held it close to her nose and squinted at it. "*Merit Learned upbraided me today for Unnameable weaving,*" she read. "Huh. Merit Learned. Sounds just like Prune Face. *Master Learned said I be wasting my time seeking roots and soils for color and the Clothe be not warm nor Useful. I must leave this Island and he will burn my Weavings. One only will I save from the greedy Flames, the one that doth depict my secret Friend from afar. I will Bury it with my Journal.*"

They contemplated the cloth man's droopy hat with the pewter-colored balls on it.

"That explains the funny hat," Medford said. "He's not from here."

"*I would know,*" Prudy read, "*as I tread the unknown*

world beyond the water, that one of my Nameless objects doth survive me. Stay, my creation, and tell our Descendants that Cordella Weaver dwelt here and saw a World in Coloured Thread."

Medford wondered why his heart lifted so when he looked at such Useless stuff.

"Well," Prudy said, standing up. "We know what we must do with this."

"Must do?" Medford couldn't take his eyes off the man in the cloth.

"We'll take it to Deemer Learned. 'Tis an Unnameable, the woman said so herself."

Medford frowned, tried to concentrate. "Deemer Learned."

"Of course. He'll want to burn this."

Medford imagined a hole in the cloth man's chest, expanding into ash. "No," he heard himself say, before his brain knew anything about it. "We'll bury the box again."

He hardly ever disagreed with Prudy. He looked up at her and nearly gasped. She was chewing on a braid—nothing new about that—but her eyes were hard and stern in a way that scared him.

"'Tis an Unnameable," she said. "It scares me. It must be gone."

"If we bury it again 'twill be gone," Medford said. He felt desperate, as if this cloth man was important to him.

"I'll know 'tis here. Every time we come here I'll know." Prudy's voice trembled. "People who make such things would destroy us. They deserve to be gone and their works consigned to fire." She sounded so fierce.

"But you *like* knowing things," Medford said.

"Real things. I like to know . . . things that are Useful to know about. Things that won't . . . make me gone."

"You'll still know about this even if it be burnt."

"I don't want it under my feet. 'Twill talk to me when we're here."

Medford couldn't put it off any longer. "Prudy, Boyce says we can't come here anymore anyways. He says we're too old and people talk." He couldn't look at her. He watched a leaf fall, three leaves, five, six. The season was aging fast.

"My parents don't care. They laughed when I told them what Arvid said."

"Boyce is not laughing. He says not to draw attention to myself."

"Fine." The book thumped into the metal box. "Fine. Bury this object as you like. Or throw it in the bog. I won't stay and watch."

"Prudy." But by the time he was on his feet she was gone.

Medford wrapped the journal in the cloth, repacked the box, got the lid to close as tight as he could. Digging another hole with a stick and throwing in the dirt was like burying a coffin. He planted a mat of moss on top, though he doubted it would take root this late in the season.

"There, Cordella Weaver," he said. "Thy cloth man is safe for another to find."

CHAPTER FIVE

❧

Mistress Learned

Brent Weaver returned from the Trade with a Useful object, a garment like a shirt but knitted of yarn thicker than for hose, lighter than for a cap. Calls it a Sweater. 'Tis warm and keeps out the wet to a goodly extent.

—*Journal of Prosper Glazer, 1900*

O N THE PATH HOME he found Boyce scouting trees for carving stock.

"I just saw Prudy," Boyce said.

"Aye."

"Were you on Bog Island together?"

"I told her we couldn't go again."

"I told thee not to go this time."

"Aye."

They examined opposite tree trunks.

"If thou wilt not do as I ask, I cannot help thee," Boyce said.

"I'm sorry, Boyce. 'Twon't happen again."

"I suppose thou wouldst move to thine own house after Transition."

Would he? Medford hadn't considered such a thing.

"We can talk to the Council about claiming land for thee outside Town. Trade with Twig to build a cabin."

Medford's vision fogged. He blinked back the tears. It was true then. Boyce didn't want him around. "I'm sorry about Bog Island, Boyce," he said again.

"'Tisn't that."

"Would I still work with thee?" His voice didn't shake. He was proud of that.

"Sometimes. But thou wouldst work alone as well and trade through me."

"Will they let me be called Carver?"

Boyce dug the toe of his shoe under a root, pulled up on it. It gave a little but not much. "They ain't quick to embrace new ideas. Nothing against you, Medford."

"Aye. Well, I'll see you at . . . at your house, Boyce."

"See you at the house, boy."

Medford was walking away when Boyce said to a sapling, "Or you could help me scout trees."

Medford just couldn't, not with these tears welling up. "Do you need me to, Boyce? Because I'd rather run some more."

"You run then, boy. I'll get something at Cook's for our supper."

And so Medford ran. Alone. He ran alone the next day, too. And the day after that. When he wasn't outdoors he stayed in Boyce's workshop and sanded until his shoulders ached. He didn't catch sight of Prudy and didn't try to. Best to let time pass, forget Cordella and her cloth man, bury them once and for all.

When Book Learning started up again for the week, he walked into the auditorium to see Prudy standing in front of the lectern, head bowed, while Deemer talked at her, bending in close to her ear.

Prudy's normally rosy cheeks were ashen and she had circles under her eyes like charcoal. Medford wanted to pull her away from Deemer, run with her out the door and back to Bog Island. Instead he walked to his desk and put his dinner satchel inside.

"Master Runyuin," Deemer snapped, "help Mistress Carpenter carry her desk to the New Learners section. They will be her charge from now on."

Prudy didn't look at him, just walked to her desk.

He joined her there. "Prudy," he whispered, "what is happening?"

"Silence!" Deemer slammed his ruler on the lectern.

Prudy spent the day instructing the New Learners. They clustered around her like chicks around a hen, even during the midday dinner. Medford couldn't get near her.

He watched her, though. Sometimes she relaxed, even laughed at the antics of the young ones in her charge. But when the older students were working on their own Deemer would join her, instruct her, chide her for letting the New Learners giggle too much, say he must "rid thee of thy Carpenterish glee." The light would leave her face

and again Medford wanted to take her hand and dash outside.

When Book Learning ended for the day, Medford
waited for Prudy at the door to the auditorium. But
Deemer was with her and she gave Medford a look that
told him to keep his peace. He stepped aside and she followed Deemer up the stairs to the Archives.

They couldn't make her be a Learned. Someone had
to stop it, but Medford didn't know whom he should talk
to. The Council? Prudy's parents?

He tried Boyce first. Boyce didn't even stop sanding
to think about it. "Stay out of this, boy. 'Tis just Deemer
trying to become Twig, same as when they were young
ones."

"But what about Prudy?"

"Leave it be, boy. She won't thank thee for interfering."

Medford left it be for ten minutes. Then he bolted
out to Prudy's house to find Twig and Earnest in the
workshop, glowering at each other from opposite sides
of the huge workbench. When Medford appeared in the
doorway, Earnest turned his back on his father and bent
over the plane he had in his hand, sharpening it with a
whetstone.

Medford wasn't sure what to do or say. You didn't
question adults very often when you grew up on Island.

Twig set his whetstone down on the bench. "How fare
ye, Medford?" he asked. He didn't smile or get up to slap
Medford on the shoulder the way he usually did.

"She doesn't want to be a Learned," Medford said. "She wants to work with you and be a Carpenter."

"'Tis what we wanted for her, Medford," Twig said. "But I have Earnest to work with me and Deemer has no one."

"Aye," Earnest said. *"Bend thy Will to thy Neighbor's need."* He threw his whetstone down so violently that it skipped across the workbench and crashed into a pile of shovels. He jostled past Medford and disappeared.

"She doesn't want to be up there with Deemer all day," Medford said.

"She likes working with the young ones. 'Twill be fine, Medford." But Twig wouldn't look him in the eye.

Clarity arrived as Medford was heading out the gate. She was as pale as Prudy, carrying a basket of vegetables as if it were a basket of anchors. When she saw Medford she put the basket down and threw her arms around him. It was the first time he could remember being hugged, although it felt so familiar he thought Alma must have done it long ago.

"Just be Prudy's friend, Medford," Clarity said. "'Tis all we can do."

Medford didn't get a chance to talk to Prudy alone until four days later, the first day free of Book Learning. Even Deemer knew enough not to keep an apprentice in the Archives all day. Medford was waiting for her when she left Town Hall midafternoon.

Cordella Weaver's cloth man still hung in the air

between them. They couldn't look each other in the eye. But Medford brushed past all that. "How is it?" he asked.

"'Tis fine. 'Twill be fine. I like teaching the young ones." He knew she was saying this as much for her own ears as his.

"What about Deemer and reading in the Archives?"

She pressed her lips together and started walking quickly toward home.

"Prudy?" Medford said, keeping pace with her and trying to look into her face.

"'Tis fine, Medford. Dull as a Mason's morning, reading all that about seeds and harvests and what's in the root cellar for winter. But Master Learned says I must earn the privilege of reading the better journals. I did read about when we got sweaters and our first motorboat."

She stopped walking, looked at him at last. To his surprise, her eyes had brightened. "Some didn't want us to have the motorboats, see, so there was a big fight at Town Meeting. The Learneds said 'twould be the end of us, cutting the Mainland trip to one day and having to bring in the fuel and the parts and such. But more than sixty years have passed and here we be, same as ever. I said that to Master Learned."

"And what did he say?"

"That I should go back to my reading and not make ignorant comments." She grinned, almost like her old self.

"So you're really going to do this? You're going to be a Learned?"

The grin faded. "I have no choice, Medford. All I can do is make the best of it."

They started walking again, slower now. "Will you come to us for supper?" Prudy asked, as if everything was the same as ever.

"I'll have to ask Boyce," Medford said.

"So do it."

So he did.

BY THE TIME winter blasted in from the sea they were fast friends again, although Prudy spent so much time in the Archives that they hardly saw each other. When they were together, there were the following restrictions: They avoided looking each other in the eye when alone. They did not use the words *bury* or *buried*. And they never mentioned Bog Island.

Under Deemer's influence, Prudy started using Book Talk more often. Sometimes even Medford couldn't figure out what she was saying. Everyone put up with it until the day she came down in the morning and told Earnest, "I dost bid thee good morrow, brother." He dragged her outside and put her head under the pump. That took care of Book Talk, but only for a day or two.

Prudy stopped chewing on her braids. (*In the sight of Others, do not gnaw on thy Nails nor the skin of thy Hands,* the Book said. Deemer said this applied to braids as well.) She never crossed her legs. (*When seated, keep thy feet*

Firm and Even.) She rarely laughed (*Show not thy Mirth at any Publick Spectacle*) although she sometimes clapped her hand over her mouth, shoulders trembling. And she no longer allowed anyone to call Deemer Old Prune Face. Medford got sick of sentences that began, "Master Learned says . . ."

For his part, Medford did his best not to attract attention that winter. He grew a pigtail, only to discover that it did, in fact, tickle. So he resumed cutting his hair off with his knife. This somehow attracted even more attention than it had before he grew the pigtail. All of his classmates and most adults called him Raggedy Runyuin now.

Except for the conversation he and Prudy had overheard between Marvin Glazer and Patience Waterman, Medford never heard one person mention Essence's banishment. Even Earnest never spoke her name in public, although Prudy said he'd tried to get Twig to find out why she was gone. "Pa said we'll find out soon enough," Prudy reported. "Earnest isn't speaking to Pa much just now."

In February a blizzard dumped four feet of snow on Island in just over a day. To Medford's relief, Book Learning was canceled for the week it took to pack down the streets and sidewalks. This did Prudy no good at all—it just meant she spent more time up in the Archives with Councilor Learned.

The blizzard was even worse news for others. Old Millicent Tanner, Arvid Tanner's grandmother, was sealed into her cabin by a drift and couldn't get to her woodshed, though it was right outside her back door. She died of the cold before Arvid's father could get to her through the snow.

Councilor Freeman Trade came back from the spring's first Trade voyage with tales of something the Mainland drivers called a snowplow. Instead of packing the snow down on the roads with a team of horses and a heavy roller, Mainlanders attached a sheet of metal to the front of a motortruck and scraped the snow right off the roads. The motortruck was faster than horses and didn't mind being out in the storm, so the roads could be cleared sooner.

"'Twill save lives," Freeman told the Council. "And the spring melt-off won't be so messy with no snowpack to soften up the mud. The snow'd just be gone."

Verity Farmer was not impressed, even though she was Councilor for Island Safety and Welfare as well as Head Councilor.

"With no snow on the roads," she asked, "how would I use my sledge?"

"Thou wouldst use wheels the year round," Freeman said.

"But then I'd have to stay on the plowed road," Councilor Welfare said, her face rock-hard as if Freeman were trying to wheedle more than his share of the wheat stores. Even her hair looked like granite.

"Aye," Freeman said, "but in the spring we would no longer be mired in mud."

Councilor Welfare shook her head. "Nope. Not for me."

"Councilor Trade wishes us to import more parts and fuel," Councilor Naming said. "And what have we to Trade with people who don't even wear neckerchiefs?"

"Councilors," Deemer Learned said, "shall we consult the Book?" He flipped pages back and forth, looking for the right place. "Ah," he said at last. "Here 'tis. *Ye need not fear the New. But ye need not embrace it, neither. Weigh carefully the consequences of Convenience.* I believe our ancestors would have continued as we are. Sledges and sleighs be best in winter."

And with that flat pronouncement, the subject was closed.

As Transition drew near, Boyce appeared before the Council to claim four acres of land for Medford on the North Shore Road an hour's walk from Town. This caused comment, since even on Island fourteen was young to leave home.

"Something wrong with the boy?" Councilor Welfare asked Boyce.

"He's ready to be on his own, Mistress Head." Boyce would not explain further.

Deemer Learned read them what the Book had to say about the Rights and Responsibilities of a Parent or Guardian. (*Question not a Parent's writ, lest thou be Questioned in thy turn.*)

"Ah," said Grover Gardener, Councilor Physick. "Same

passage we heard after thy daughter's departure." Deemer gave Councilor Physick a cold pewter look. The other Councilors hastily dropped the discussion and granted Medford his four acres.

Medford wasn't so sure he was ready to be on his own. He would have to trade carving for lumber, shingles, windows, and other fittings for his cabin, and for Twig's time building it with him. He needed seed for vegetables and pots to cook them in. Everything he would carve for the next year was spoken for.

Transition came. Prudy grimly became a Learned and Arvid became a Sawyer. A Pickler, a Smith, and a Dairyman were created.

Medford held on to hope until the last possible minute. But after everyone else had been granted a permanent name the auditorium went silent and he knew. "As to Master Runyuin," Comfort Naming said, "we need more time to make sure he doth merit the name Carver as his foster father proposes. Return next year and we shall see."

Medford tried to be happy that Boyce had at least proposed the name change.

"Once a Runyuin never a Carver," Arvid whispered from the other side of Prudy and Deemer. Boyce acted as if he hadn't heard but his jaw got angular.

Medford wished he could turn his ears off as they made their way outside. Whispers and chuckles mingled with the creak of floorboards. He knew they were directed at him.

Outside, when her turn came, Prudy stomped Pinky and her other shells into dust. Her braids were arranged in a grown-up knot at her neck. Her back was straight and stiff. She did not cry, just tightened her lips.

Medford didn't cry, either. He had collected Sap Tree cones the day before and now crushed them underfoot, trying to look sad. He saw Boyce give his head a little shake, as if his brains had shifted. He'd never seen Medford with a Sap Tree cone in his hand.

Prudy had never seen Medford pick up any kind of cone. She looked at him as if she'd never met him before. "Why art thou so red?" she asked.

Everyone was watching, so Boyce stuck out his hand for Medford to shake. Clarity hugged him. Twig punched him on one shoulder, Earnest on the other.

"Well," Boyce said. "Best be getting to work on that cabin."

Two months later, when his cabin was almost finished and Boyce was off at the Trade, Medford took his real collection out from under his bed, packed it in two boxes, nailed them shut, and added them to the small pile of possessions headed for his new house.

Again he promised himself he'd destroy the things and make no more. He'd just wait for quieter times.

Really.

๛

CHAPTER SIX

Pinky

My Grandfather talks of the Belt buckles these old Main-landers would wear, decorated with Fancy Shapes that must have increased the work of a foundry Tenfold. If I wasted my time on such Useless decoration, my Family would starve.

—*Journal of Service Smith, 1756*

MEDFORD'S LAST Goatman-free morning was four months after Transition.

It was a warm, breezy day in early autumn, Honey-bugs droning in the Poultice Weed outside his window. Five months before, it would have been a day for running with Prudy. Now it was a workday, another chance to pay down his debt to Twig and the others.

Medford sat on a high stool at his workbench, feet on a rung halfway up the stool. His skinny legs, crooked at the knee, poked way out sideways like wings. He looked exactly like a Nameless brown seabird.

All morning he'd been blamelessly hacking away at a blameless squared-off bowl—*chock-chock*, chisel on Syrup

Tree. But now he noticed a discolored swirl at one end. The sight made him put down his mallet and lean in close.

The swirl was three inches in length, oval, but with a funnel-shaped tail. It had alternating rings of tawny and rose-red wood. Medford poked at it with his forefinger. He smiled for the first time that day.

"Pinky," he whispered. He reached for a smaller chisel.

There was that feeling again, blowing through his brain like a spring morning.

The feeling scared him. It wasn't real, wasn't right, had no Name. He stifled it, tamped it down to a murmur, something he could control.

And then he acted on it. He ignored all messages sent by the better part of his brain. Disgust, for example, because he'd promised himself he'd never do this again. Resignation, because he'd known he would. Terror, because someone might find out.

Joy, because he could do it at all.

He sculpted a Baitsnail shell, with rosy stripes and a funnel-shaped tail, at the bottom of Twig Carpenter's trencher. He made it too big at first, whittled it down until it was perfect. Three hours later a beach of perfect shells covered the bottom of the bowl.

His hands obeyed his thoughts. He used every skill Boyce had taught him and some he'd made up himself: measuring before he cut, correcting mistakes early, exerting the right pressure on the blade. He colored Pinky with berry juice. "Prudy," he said.

He should have stopped to eat his midday dinner. He should have stopped, period. But he didn't.

In early afternoon he carved a clump of Cropfodder at one end of the trencher. Peeking out from under it was the rough shape of a horn with a ball protecting the tip.

Medford chipped away at the horn without thinking, smoothed it out . . . then froze, chisel in midair. What was a horn doing on a beach of shells?

It didn't take long to figure out. It looked just like the hat Cordella Weaver's cloth man was wearing. He'd thought about Cordella's Unnameable Woven Object nearly every day for almost a year. Sometimes it was all he could do not to run back to Bog Island and dig the cloth up to look at it again.

But this thing he'd carved wasn't a hat. Although Medford hadn't spent a lot of time with farm creatures, he knew this was a horn. Definitely a horn.

Outside, the breeze gusted up, rattling the north window in Medford's workshop. Then the gusts of wind were from the south. Then from the east, then the west, then the south again. Then the north again. Medford stood and pushed back his stool. What was this?

From far away, so faint he wouldn't have noticed if he hadn't been paying such attention to the wind, he heard an animal howling in what sounded like despair.

Medford shivered. He stared down at Twig's trencher,

which he had rendered Useless for any purpose he could think of. The wind dwindled to a gentle breeze but he didn't notice. A whole morning gone, and this was all he had to show for it—another Useless, Nameless thing to wrap up in an old shirt and shove under the bed.

An Unnameable thing? Enough to banish him? He wouldn't think about that.

Outside, one of the porch steps—still not quite seasoned—cracked like a whip under somebody's foot.

Medford gasped. He grabbed the object on his workbench, clutched it to his chest, and tried to think of something to do with it.

"Runyuin?" a voice called. Arvid Sawyer. He was the last person Medford wanted to see when he had a Useless (perhaps Unnameable) Object clutched to his chest. Arvid didn't torment Medford as much as he once did—they were getting too old for that. But he was a tale-teller like his father, with just as keen an eye for secrets.

"Raggedy?"

"Ohhh," Medford moaned, louder than he'd intended. He whipped off his shirt, wrapped up the Useless Object, hid it under the workbench.

"Art thou all right in there?" Like Prudy, Arvid talked Book Talk all the time now.

"Aye, Arvid!" Medford yelled. "Do thou take a seat out there in the fresh air. I shall be with thee anon." A little Book Talk never hurt.

Scrawnily bare-chested, Medford darted from his

workshop into the kitchen, rounded the cookstove, and reached for the latch on his bedroom door.

"By the Book, Raggedy, running around without a shirt? 'Tis Harvest Moon, boy." Arvid poked his upper body in through the front door, his feet still on the porch so he wouldn't really be entering without invitation. (*Make not Free with another's Domicile, tho' it be thy Friend's*, the Book said.)

"'Tis warm enough," Medford said, scuttling into his bedroom to pull his second-best shirt out of his clothes chest. Arvid was leaning in, trying to see into the workshop, when Medford charged at him, shirttail flapping, and forced him back out onto the porch.

"At thy hair with thy knife again," Arvid said, settling into a chair. He flipped his own wispy pigtail out from under his collar, where it probably was tickling him. "Cabin's looking good, though, Raggedy. Prudy's pa did thee proud."

Medford, standing there stuffing his shirttail into his knee breeches, felt the guilt prickle up his back. He owed Twig an entire set of trenchers and bowls. He'd done five pieces. The sixth was now a mass of seashells wrapped up in his everyday shirt and stuffed under the workbench.

"Lotta windows, though, hast thou not?"

Medford could imagine what Arvid would say to his father and what Dexter would say at Cook's. "*Two windows onto a covered porch Medford's got. Aye, them Glazers talked him into it, I'm guessing. Surprised at Boyce, letting the boy waste heat like that.*"

Medford opened his mouth to say he'd wanted two windows for light but Arvid spoke first. "Ma needeth tool handles. A dozen of them. Make 'em out of Wheelwood, if thou wouldst. We found some on her back woodlot."

For the blink of an eye, Medford was pleased that Dulcie Sawyer was coming to him rather than ordering through Boyce as usual. But then Arvid craned his neck to look through the door. This was not a good-natured visit.

"Lonesome out here, is it not?" Arvid said, leaning sideways for a better view.

"I like it," Medford said. "'Tis private." Then, since he was a Runyuin and in no position to be rude, he added: "Quieter, you know."

"Oh, aye," Arvid said. He gave up trying to see what Medford had for dishes and sat back in his chair. The conversation died.

"I'm thinking of raising chickens," Medford offered, shifting his weight from one foot to the other.

"Egg Fowl," Arvid said primly. "To be by the Book."

"Aye. That's what I meant." Medford searched for something else to say.

"Guess thou seest not Prudy as once thou did."

Between the Book Talk and the change of topic Medford could barely grasp what Arvid had said. Something about not seeing Prudy much, which was true. Prudy was so different—serious, stern, a little scary. He thought of her now as New Prudy.

"She comes out once a week to visit," he said, trying not to sound defensive. "She and Earnest. And I see her in Town."

"Thou comest not much into Town."

"I go into Town twice a week. I have to give Boyce what I've made." What was Arvid after, anyway? He had some purpose behind the Book Talk.

"She says she doth not see thee much," Arvid said. His face was filling out to match its length. He looked healthy, grown-up, confident. He made Medford feel spindly. "I see her at the sawmill. And at Cook's. She enjoys a tale or two."

And Arvid enjoys a lie or two, Medford thought. Why did he keep talking about Prudy?

Arvid patted the seat of Medford's favorite rocking chair. "Sit down, Runyuin." Who was Arvid to invite him to sit down on his own porch? Medford sat down.

"I know thou wantest what be best for Prudy," Arvid said, making his voice sound deep and adult. "Does her no good, no good at all, spending time with thee way out here, even with her brother. She descends from one of Island's earliest families, Originals. Twig says he worries about her future, especially now that she be Learned."

"Twig never said that," Medford said.

"Well, mayhap he should have. Mayhap Prudy should spend her time with someone more like herself."

Someone with freckles and a wispy pigtail. "Prudy can take care of herself," Medford said. "You know that better than anyone, Arvid." He pictured Arvid facedown in the waves at Seaweed Beach.

Arvid flushed, no doubt picturing the same thing. "We be not young ones anymore, Runyuin. 'Tis time to look ahead, not behind."

Medford stood. "I will make thy tool handles, Arvid. Bring me the Wheelwood and I'll get started." He didn't know when he would make tool handles when he still owed so much carving to so many people. But he would think about that later.

Medford watched Arvid until he disappeared down the woods trail to Town, then went inside to put his everyday shirt back on and kick his bed pillow until it split.

He wrapped the seashell bowl in a rag from an old tunic and stuffed it under the bed with the others. This one he would leave unfinished, he told himself. And soon he'd burn them all.

He knew he wouldn't really. But thinking he would made him feel better, as it had almost every day since Transition.

In spite of Arvid, in spite of the Council, in spite of everyone who wondered where the talent came from, Medford loved carving as if he'd been born to it. He loved the sweet smell of Syrup Tree wood newly split, the heft of the mallet in his hand, the way soft Sapwood and hard, sharp-smelling Tanningbark wood were opposite and yet the same.

But wood wasn't just wood for Medford. It was shapes, waiting to get out.

He didn't know *how* it had started but he did know *when*. He'd been new to the craft, and it had seemed to him that he saw a seabird's wing in the walking stick he was carving. He couldn't help grabbing a knife and seeing if he could bring it out a little. He would never forget the shock and the thrill of seeing that wing, feathers and all, come out of the wood under his hand.

He also remembered what happened next: Boyce's hand lunging into view and wrenching the stick away from him. Boyce broke the stick on his knee. "Would that be comfortable to hold? Just what is its Use, boy?"

Medford stared at the floor. He knew what he'd done.

"Do not do that again," Boyce said. "This is serious, a banishing thing, Medford."

But of course he did do it again. And again. Sometimes it seemed every piece of wood had a shape inside, waiting for him to find it. He had almost run out of room under his bed at Boyce's before he moved out. In his own house, he had secret carvings hidden under the bed and up on the rafters.

All the more reason to carve something he could show someone. Right now.

He got up and hurried out through the kitchen. He paused on the porch, as he often did, to breathe the lively air and look at the sea, shining in the west. But he didn't stop for long. He hastened to the southern end of the porch, which was open for storage.

The carving stock was mixed in with the firewood. He spent several minutes sorting it all out. He had lots of Tanningbark, but where was that half log of Syrup Tree? He knew he had it because he could remember . . . Ah, there it—

Something snuffled near his left ear. He felt hot, close breath, which stank. A lot. Something cold and wet touched his cheek.

Medford yelped and hurled himself back on all fours. He crab-walked backward until his head and shoulders banged up against a corner of the house.

There by the porch opening stood a shaggy white Herding Creature with black patches around its eyes. Medford knew what it was because the Shepherds brought such creatures—they called them dogs—into Town now and then. *What is a dog doing here?*

The creature sat down and grinned at him, its tongue hanging out the side of its mouth. Seaweed and grimy feathers were in chunks all over its back.

Something blocked the sun. Medford looked up and saw a figure standing there, impossible to make out distinctly with the sun blazing behind it. The smell assaulting his nose was so complicated he almost forgot to gag. He identified salt, something horribly decayed, several kinds of wet animal, wet wool socks, wet hay. Then his brain gave up, overwhelmed.

"Sorry to sta-a-artle you," said a low, guttural voice, a cross between falling rocks in a quarry and the wind shushing through tall grass.

Medford struggled to his feet and steadied himself against the cabin wall. He blinked the sun out of his eyes, then got a good look at the figure before him.

The man's face was long and thin, with a scraggly gray beard and bushy eyebrows. His head was bald on top, the rest covered in tangled gray hair. He was wearing a purple robe with a dirty white sash draped across his chest from right shoulder to left hip. His droopy horns were a dull white, with tarnished brass-colored knobs on the ends.

His horns. Medford wished the ground under his feet would stop moving around.

The man had a tall staff in one hand. Leaning on it, he stepped forward and put a hand out as if he might touch Medford, although he didn't. The man's gait was funny, but Medford couldn't worry about that. He was having trouble catching his breath.

"So-o-orry—," the man began again.

"Don't hurt me," Medford said.

The wind picked up, cool and damp, right off the ocean. The man raised his hands in the air and tottered back a couple of steps.

Which was when Medford looked down and saw that the man had hooves.

Which was when Medford fainted.

CHAPTER SEVEN

❦

The Goatman's Wind

Remark not upon the Deformities of Others, nor any little blemishes of the Skin nor soil on a Garment. Avert thine eyes if thou must, and talk of Other Matters.

—*A Frugall Compendium of Home Arts and Farme Chores by Capability C. Craft (1680), as Amended and Annotated by the Island Council of Names (1718–1809)*

MEDFORD OPENED his eyes to a cloudless blue sky above. And that horrible, dense, complicated smell everywhere. He closed his eyes again.

If he kept his eyes closed long enough and didn't breathe much, he decided, the world would be back to normal when he opened them again.

He'd never fainted before, although he knew what fainting was. The Book said you should hold Spirits of Treesap under someone's nose when he fainted. He spent a pleasant minute or two wondering whether he still had any under the sink.

Then his brain returned, reluctantly, to the reason he'd

fainted. There was a man with horns. There were hooves where there shouldn't be. A Herding Creature, a dog.

He'd never been so close to a dog before. The Shepherds kept to themselves in Island's wild, lonely southeast highlands, and the creatures were of no Use to anyone else.

He'd had no idea they smelled so bad.

He'd never seen a man with horns and hooves. Were there Mainlanders who looked like that? The Trade drivers wore colorful shirts and trousers of a stiff blue material, but otherwise they looked just like Islanders. He'd never heard of one with horns.

The thought came to him like a bucket of pond ice dumped on his head. *Cordella Weaver. The man in her Unnameable Woven Object. His hat was really horns.*

Just like the horn he'd carved into Twig's trencher earlier today.

He wouldn't think about that.

Someone lapped his face. *Please let it be the dog,* he thought. He opened his eyes. The dog backed off a yard or so, sat down, and proudly stank.

The man sat a few feet away chewing on a blade of grass. His staff was on the ground, a handsome piece of Wheelwood with carving Medford wouldn't have minded seeing closer.

The man had his legs crossed, his robe hitched up. This gave Medford a chance to see that in addition to hooves his visitor had the skinniest, hairiest shins he'd ever seen.

The shins of a goat, in fact—a Lesser Horned Milk Creature if you felt Bookish.

He wondered how far up the goat parts went. What he could see of the man's upper body looked human.

Except for the horns.

The man took the blade of grass out of his mouth and flicked it away. "Do you feel be-e-etter?" he said. At least that's what it sounded like to Medford.

"Aye," Medford said. The man's speech, not to mention the horns and goat shins, made him queasy. But he had to admit the creature had done nothing to threaten him.

He'd never met a stranger before, even one *without* horns. He tried to decide what to say. "Who are you?" and "You talk funny" seemed rude. "Is that a hat?" was no better.

"What is that smell?" Medford said. He felt himself turn red.

But the man didn't seem to mind. "Sti-i-inky rolled in a dead bird," he said. "She likes to sme-e-ell like dead things. The smell fools the pre-e-ey."

The dog wasn't the only stinky one. In fact, the really complex smells belonged to the man. The wet wool socks smell, certainly, and the wet hay and another sort of gamy odor Medford couldn't identify. And something spicy and something rancid and—

"Makes the little cr-i-i-itters think, *Not to worry, only a dead bird walking along.* And then, surpri-i-ise! It turns out to be a dog and . . . disgusting things ha-a-a-appen."

"Why do you talk so strange?" Medford said.

"I do not," the man said. His bushy eyebrows twitched together. A gust of wind ruffled his hair, then subsided.

"Beg pardon," Medford said hastily. "Is . . . Stinky the name of your dog?"

The man threw back his head and made the most Unnameable sound Medford had ever heard. It sounded like "Bweh-eh-eh-eh-eh." It sounded even windier and grassier than the man's regular speech. "Her na-a-ame," the man said to the sky. "Heh."

"Her name is funny?"

The man beamed as if Medford had said something smart. His teeth were uneven yellow stumps. "I am on my ramble," he said, as if that explained everything.

"You're on . . . what?"

"You ask about the dog's na-a-ame. She has none."

"But . . . you called her—"

"She sti-i-inks," said the man. "Right now she sti-i-inks. Tomorrow I'll call her something else." He thought about that. "Mi-i-ight not, though."

The dog waggled the tip of her tail, wafting odor.

Medford's brain had rusted up. "So her name changes—"

"She has no na-a-ame," the man said patiently. "I have no na-a-ame. If you must call me something right away ca-a-all me the Goatman, since I am the only goatman here."

"You have no name," Medford said.

"Na-a-ames weigh us down," the Goatman said. "Tie us to a rock."

"No name," Medford said.

"Lock us in a cage. Hold us i-i-in a house."

No name. Horns.

Medford found that he was extremely calm. *Good news*, his brain said. *None of this is actually happening.* He discovered that he was on his feet and walking. He walked up the front steps, across the porch, and through the door to his cabin, shutting it behind him. He walked into his bedroom and shut that door, too.

Then, although it was only afternoon and he had neither eaten supper nor brushed his teeth, he went to bed. He fell asleep immediately with his clothes on.

He slept straight through the night, rolling over exactly twice. The next morning he awoke before sunrise and lay there, confused. It seemed he'd gone to bed unusually early, in his clothes, and with no food. Had he been sick? He couldn't remember.

And hadn't he had a strange dream? A vivid dream, scary. It had purple in it. Hooves. Cordella's Unnameable Woven Object.

As he did every morning, Medford sat up and wriggled down to the bottom of the bed to lean against the windowsill and watch the day begin. He tucked his blankets around him and looked out.

He knew every root and branch of the woods around his house, but at this hour they were as mysterious as Mainland, black tinged with dull green and bronze. As he watched, a wash of apple pink appeared in the sky behind the trees and the shadows lightened. Soon the world would be familiar again.

At the edge of the yard, beyond the vegetable garden, a white furry figure emerged from the woods. The white stood out against the murky trees, almost gleaming. The dog flopped onto her back, rolling and twisting, feet waggling in the air.

He heard a voice, slightly muffled. "Nightfa-a-arts," it seemed to be calling. "Where a-a-are you, Nightfarts?"

Medford thought he might like to blink but that didn't seem to be possible. The dog rolled to her feet and bounded out of sight. Then she bounced into view again, came to a dead stop, and sneezed with a great shake of her head and scattering of droplets. She trotted off in the direction of the voice.

There was something jaunty about her that made Medford smile. Then he remembered whom she was with.

It hadn't been a dream.

He shivered. He tried to imagine himself walking out onto the porch and . . . doing what? Saying what? It was too much. He buried his face in his pillow, inhaled the oily earthiness of the fleece inside. He pulled the covers over his head.

Someone knocked on the front door. He waited. Whoever it was knocked again.

Trouble doth not depart, the Book said. *Face it, thou.* Medford threw back the covers and swung his feet to the floor. He had shoes on, he discovered.

When he opened the door, the Goatman was leaning on his staff in the dim morning light, gazing out to sea. "Nice da-a-ay," he said when Medford stepped out onto the porch. "No wind."

Medford swallowed and freed up his voice. "I don't mind wind," he croaked. He swallowed again. "A breeze, anyways. I like the leaves to move."

"You do?" The Goatman turned around. Apparently Medford had said something smart again. "Can you make it do what you wa-a-ant?" He leaned forward on his staff, examining Medford's face.

"Make *what* do what I want?" Medford asked, backing up.

"The wi-i-ind," the Goatman said. His eyes were the most startling blue, even brighter than Prudy's. "The breeze. Can you make it do what you wa-a-ant?"

"Cry mercy, of course not," Medford said.

The Goatman sighed and turned back to the ocean. "Neither can I," he said.

Change the subject, Medford's brain said. "Wouldst thou take tea?"

"Everyone e-e-else can do it," the Goatman said. "Not me, though. Call it up, I can do tha-a-at. But then it does what it wa-a-ants. And I can't make it go awa-a-ay."

"Perhaps some bread and butter?" Medford said.

"I don't understa-a-and. I think all the right things, move my ha-a-ands right."

"With honey, perhaps."

"In the city they ha-a-ave gizmos for it. I looked in a window and a lady poked her finger at a thi-i-ing with blades and then she had wi-i-ind in her face."

Ah, Medford thought, *'tis a Mainland thing, like a motorwagon.* "So you poke something with a finger," he said.

"Almost," the Goatman said. "I do this." He faced the ocean, then stuck his forefinger in his mouth to wet it. He held the finger up, waggled it a little as if beckoning someone who was already paying attention.

Medford heard a distant *whup-whup-whup* coming from Mainland. He looked out at the water, which was smooth as varnished Sapwood at this early hour.

Except—Medford went to the porch rail and squinted—except for what looked like a little herd of whitecaps far out to sea. The disturbance was speeding toward Island, moving faster the nearer it got. The waves were unusually tall for being so far out, getting taller as they neared land. The Pitch Trees lining the field across the road began to dance.

"Uh-oh," the Goatman said.

Medford barely had time to say "What . . . ?" Then a blast of wind hurled him to the floor and back against the side of the cabin. He could hardly open his eyes, the wind was so strong. The Goatman was beside him, flung against the door, his robe up around his waist. It occurred to Medford that this would be a good chance to see how far up the goat parts went but he couldn't keep his eyes open long enough.

The dog yelped, sounding far away. Something crashed inside the cabin. Medford remembered that he'd gone to bed yesterday without closing up his workshop.

And then the wind was gone, just like that. Medford kept his eyes shut, afraid to move. The Goatman was muttering to himself. He rustled and creaked, getting up. "Like ye-e-esterday i-i-in that boat," Medford heard. *Creak-creak-rustle.* "Only a-a-all in one place."

Medford opened his eyes, focused on the porch rail. His head hurt where it had banged against the cabin wall and his shoulders felt bruised. A hand came into view, the palm grimy, the nails long and thick and yellow, with matted gray hair between the knuckles.

"He-e-ere," the Goatman said. "Let me help you."

The hand hovered there. If Medford touched it, the world would tilt.

The Goatman snorted. He threw down his staff, hauled Medford to his feet, and staggered back against the porch rail.

Medford's head throbbed. *Tea with Tonic Root,* he thought. There were fresh roots in the cupboard.

"My sta-a-aff." The man was scowling, clinging to the rail.

Medford started to hand him his staff. It was the goat head at the top that stopped him, one of four carved in such deep relief that the horns looked round. Below them, various swirls danced and curled and whirled down the staff.

The swirls are the wind, Medford thought. He frowned at himself and shook his head. Wind is invisible—how could something look like wind?

"Bweh-eh-eh-eh," the Goatman said.

"Oh, beg pardon." Medford handed the man his staff. A question, an important one, caught in his windpipe.

"My uncle ca-a-arved the goat heads," the Goatman said. "I did the wind swirls." The blue eyes were kind, although there was a tinge of . . . what was it, foreignness? Creature-ness? *Unnameableness,* Medford's brain suggested.

He ignored his brain. "Would you like a cup of tea?" he asked.

☙

CHAPTER EIGHT

Rambles and Tales

The Book says one should never turn a visitor away hungry. I say, Capability C. Craft never lived down the road from Martin Candlewright, who turns up at dinnertime regular as the tide.

—*Journal of Colby Tailor, 1966*

MEDFORD REGRETTED inviting the Goatman into his cabin. It would have been better to have thanked him for his visit, walked inside, and shut the door. The Goatman would have gone away and Medford would be working on a new bowl for Twig right now.

The Goatman stood in the middle of the kitchen, leaning on his staff and watching Medford the way you'd watch the first flea of summer. This made Medford so edgy he almost dropped the teapot, a Transition gift from Clarity. It didn't help that the sink pump wasn't working right—three pumps for one squirt of water. For some reason Medford found this embarrassing.

The dog kept nudging Medford's hand with her nose. He gingerly stroked her forehead, the only part of her that looked to be free of bird chunks. She sat down, closed her eyes, and sighed. While he made the tea she stayed where she was, gazing up at him.

Maybe she liked him.

He found he minded her smell a little less.

Not much less.

Medford poured the tea through a strainer into two mugs, then put the strainer down on the counter next to the sink. The Goatman grabbed it and lapped out the mass of soggy leaves. "Mmmm," he said. "Li-i-ike a pricker-bush."

Medford didn't often wash the tea strainer. He decided he would have to do that before the next pot of tea.

The Goatman peered into the mug Medford gave him as if the tea were alive and unpredictable. "What do I do with thi-i-is?" he asked.

"Drink it," Medford said. "'Tis good."

The Goatman sniffed the tea and stuck out his tongue to touch it. He twitched. "Ow. Hot," he said. He shot an accusing look at Medford.

"'Twill cool. Really," Medford said. "You'll like it. Sit down, if it please thee."

The Goatman set his tea mug on the floor and lowered himself awkwardly to sit next to it. He put down his staff and cupped his mug in both hands.

"Wouldn't you like a chair?" Medford pointed to the table and three chairs under the porch windows.

"Bweh-eh-eh," the Goatman said. He used his staff to haul himself up onto his hooves and inspected the chair facing the windows, brow furrowed. He lowered his hind-quarters onto the seat and perched on the edge, unable to sit all the way back.

Medford grated Tonic Root into his tea and opened the window before joining his guest at the table, hoping he wasn't being rude. The dog curled up at the Goatman's feet, so what had been separate smells became one united stench. Medford breathed through his mouth rather than his nose. That helped.

He wanted a closer look at that goat-headed staff, which was leaning against the table. "May I?" he asked, reaching for it.

"Of course," the Goatman said. He kept sniffing at his tea, poking it with a finger, sipping a little, sniffing at it again. "Hot colored wa-a-ater," he whispered.

The wind swirls on the staff were rough in places, Medford saw. He could see where the blade had slipped or gotten caught in the grain and gone wrong. The goat heads, though, emerged from the wood as if they'd grown there. They looked as if they had goat bodies hidden behind them in the staff. Medford could see individual strands of hair in their beards. How could anyone carve so delicately? With his thinnest blade and a lot of practice, perhaps he could—

Medford caught himself. *This*, he thought, *is how the Unnameable creeps up on you.* He could hear Deemer Learned's voice in his head, reading from the Book: "*Does it feed us? Warm us? Shelter us? Then is it good. If it does none of these things, turn away."*

The Goatman was watching him. "Do you ca-a-arve?"

"No," Medford said and felt his face turn hot. "I mean, aye. Well, not like this. This . . . isn't allowed." He'd never uttered such a broad, general lie before.

"Allowed," the Goatman said. "What's allowed? Who allowed? Allo-o-o-owed. Allowed-allowed-allowed." He made the word sound foreign, almost comic.

"The Book doesn't allow, doesn't let us . . . It says we can't do some things," Medford said. "It says some things are bad for us."

"Book—that's words. On . . . pa-a-aper. How does it know wha-a-at you're doing?"

"It doesn't. People, the Councilors, read the Book and tell us what to do."

"They think you'll cut yourself doing fa-a-ancy carving."

"That's not it." Medford felt his headache getting worse. He breathed in some Tonic Root fumes. "I carve. And I cut myself aplenty. I carve bowls and spoons and . . . 'Tis just . . . things have to be Useful. They have to have a Use."

"Useful." The Goatman ran his fingers over the wind swirls he'd made. "Heh. So it's true."

"What's true?"

"I heard about this Useful thing," the Goatman said.

"I di-i-idn't believe it. I thought it was an old tale. Heh. When I go home it'll be a ne-e-ew tale."

"Have goatpeople—"

"Goatfolk."

"Goatfolk, beg pardon. Have they been here before?"

The man nodded. "On rambles. Makes a good ta-a-ale, this Naming and Useful."

"What's a ramble?"

But the Goatman pushed himself up from the table and grabbed his staff, his eyebrows up in little peaks. "Wha-a-at's this?"

He clip-clopped into the workshop. Medford jumped up, annoyed. The Goatman might cut his finger on a blade. He shouldn't be barging into people's workshops.

The Goatman inspected the chisels and knives lining the wall, each in its own slot on a rack Medford had made. "You carve a lot, I see," he said. He picked up one of the bowls Medford had managed to finish for Twig. "Ni-i-ice work. Smooth."

Medford felt an almost irresistible urge to run into his bedroom and fetch a Useless carving. Nice work, indeed. The Goatman should see what he could really do.

Pride in the Useless be the road to the Unnameable, the Book said. Medford leaned against the doorjamb. His head still throbbed. He needed to work on Twig's bowl.

He noticed that his rack of mallets, which he kept by the window facing the sea, had blown over in the Goatman's wind. Nothing seemed to have broken. He picked it up, shut the window, and turned to find the Goatman stooping for a better look at the tiny wood chips on the floor, left over from the Pinky bowl.

"These didn't come from tha-a-at," he said, pointing at the bowl on the workbench. "Whe-e-ere's the carving that goes with these?"

"You must be hungry," Medford said. "Come eat oatmeal. Bread. Honey. Eggs."

"I don't eat the young," the Goatman said. He scuffed at the wood chips on the floor, eyebrows in peaks again, but allowed Medford to usher him out of the workshop. "Oats I li-i-ike—no need to cook them. Don't know about honey."

Medford spooned oats into a dish and cut thick slices off a loaf he'd bought in Town. It had cost three of the tokens he'd earned selling his spoons at Boyce's shop and usually would have lasted almost a week.

The Goatman tipped the dish up and poured the oats into his mouth. A lot of them scattered on the floor and the dog lapped them up. They made her sneeze.

The Goatman did know what honey was, it turned out. "Ah. Bee fodder," he said.

All three of them ate slices of bread. Medford put butter and honey on his. The dog wrinkled her nose at the honey but accepted bread with butter. To Medford's delight she took a slice neatly from his hand and chomped it up with barely a dropped crumb.

The Goatman poured honey on his bread until it

dripped down the sides, then shoved the soggy mass into his mouth. He had honey and oats and crumbs all over the front of his robe when breakfast was over.

Medford handed him a dish towel in case he wanted to mop up.

"My tha-a-anks to you," the Goatman said. He wiped the honey off his mouth with his white sash, then bit into a corner of the towel and ripped off a mouthful. He chewed it slowly, intent. "Mmm." He swallowed. "Tough, but ta-a-asty."

Medford opened his mouth but shut it again. He couldn't think of what to say, so he made more tea, which they took outside so the Goatman could sit on the grass while he finished off the towel. The dog trotted off into the woods.

"I li-i-ike your bread," the Goatman said. He looked for a clean spot on his sash and blew his nose on it. "Now, about those wood chips. Whe-e-ere is the other—"

"Where do you live?" Medford asked. He knew he should just say, "Those are bowl chips. There is no other carving." Why was that so hard?

"Right now, I live under your porch," the Goatman said.

Oh, the Book, Medford thought.

"Normally, I live over the-e-ere." The Goatman waved his hand toward Mainland. "A fla-a-atfoot gave me a . . . a . . . I thi-i-ink he called it a sailboat."

"Do you live in the City?"

"Whi-i-ich one?"

"There's more than one?"

The Goatman blinked. "They're a-a-all over the place. I don't live in any of them, though. I live in mountains."

Medford had never seen a map of Mainland. He realized with a jolt that he didn't know much about it, even though his chisels and tea came from there. Even though he was from there himself. He looked out at the sea, cold and deep and impossibly wide. The world must be vast. Far too vast to be captured in one conversation.

Best not to ask about it. Best not to think about it.

The Goatman looked pointedly at the workshop window. "Whe-e-ere is that—"

Better ask about something, though. "Uh . . . What's a ramble?"

The Goatman got a look on his face like New Prudy, but allowed himself to be distracted. "Well. Wi-i-inters are long. Once the goats are te-e-ended we have nothing to do. We sit in a she-e-elter and tell tales."

"Tales?" The word reeked of Dexter and Arvid. "Lies, you mean."

"Not lies. Lies deceive. A-a-and they're too much trouble."

"What's a tale, then?"

"Tales explain the world. Organize the sta-a-ars, introduce the ants. Heh. Make fun of my she-cousin, who thinks she's so sma-a-art. Some make their tales up—grasswatchers we ca-a-all them. Anyway, a ra-a-amble is what starts it all."

"But what's a ramble?"

"A journey, that's a-a-all. We just go."

"All of you at once?"

"No." The Goatman snorted, as if Medford weren't so smart after all. "We go alone. But e-e-everyone goes. Four seasons, five. My cousin, she was gone se-e-even, eight seasons. Found a city with shelters big as mountains. The ta-a-ales she brought back . . ."

Medford tried to imagine what it would be like to leave Island, but his mind just couldn't catch hold of the idea.

"Everyone said, 'Ooo, that she-cousin of yours, she's so bra-a-ave, going to tha-a-at bi-i-ig ci-i-ity,'" the Goatman said, his voice loud and piercingly goatish. "She had a place by the fi-i-ire the whole wi-i-inter she came ba-a-ack and I was by the door."

He sat up, jerking his robe angrily so Medford saw his hairy shins again. Medford tried not to look at them. The dog trotted out of the woods, the fur around her mouth stained dark. She wiped her muzzle on the grass.

"Ugh," the Goatman said. "He-e-ere comes Gory Mouth."

"That's three names she's had since yesterday," Medford said. "How do you get her to come when you summon her?"

"She hears my voice. If she wa-a-ants to be with me, she comes."

"But what about you?" Medford said. "You said you don't have a name, either."

"Of course not." The Goatman's eyebrows twitched. "No one summons me-e-e."

"What if there are two goatmen, and I want to tell someone something about you? How do I do that?"

"Say I'm the one wi-i-ith the purple robe."

"The other one has a purple robe, too," Medford said. "And a white sash," he added before the Goatman could speak. "He looks just like you."

"To you, maybe," the Goatman said. "A-a-anyway, you could point."

"The person I'm talking to isn't looking at me."

"Sa-a-ay, 'The one to the south.'"

"You can't keep saying 'the one to the south' and 'the one with the purple robe,'" Medford said, frustrated. "'Tis too . . . it takes too much time."

"Wha-a-at's your rush?" the Goatman said, showing his teeth. "Heh. This na-a-aming of everything. Always a good tale."

"Names are important," Medford said, setting his tea mug down so he could wave his hands around for emphasis. "They tell us who we are and what we do and what everyone else does and where we all belong." He stopped for breath.

"They tell you a-a-all that? What if your name is Abercrombie?"

"Abercrombie? And what, pray, does an abercrombie do?"

"I don't know," the Goatman said. "But it's a name I heard. A-a-and there's O'Neill and Rabinowitz and Thomas and Cha-a-ang and Rashid and—"

"None of those names mean anything. Nobody's named like that."

"Yes, they are," the Goatman said. "Those names are a-a-all over the mainland."

Medford had always figured the Mainland drivers he'd met had names like, well, Driver. But these other Mainland names were nonsense—they didn't tell you a thing. He felt sick.

"Wha-a-at is your name?" the Goatman said.

Medford felt sicker.

"My foster father's name is Carver," he said. "He taught me to carve. And there are Bakers who bake and Carpenters who build things and Potters who make teapots—"

"So your name is Ca-a-arver?"

Medford shook his head, dismayed to find that his eyes were stinging. He tried to force the feeling back to wherever such feelings came from. "My name is Runyuin," he said when he thought he could speak. "Medford Runyuin."

"Wha-a-at is a runyuin?"

Medford bent his head so the Goatman couldn't see. "There is no such thing as a runyuin. My name doesn't mean anything. I wasn't born here."

"Why not na-a-ame something after yourself? That tree, maybe."

"'Tisn't the way it works."

Medford heard rustling noises and grunting. The air got smellier. He looked up and was startled to see the Goatman's face inches from his own, his eyes blue and gentle.

"I want to see those ca-a-arvings," the Goatman said. "The real ones, this time."

❧

CHAPTER NINE

Grass Tunes

I made a song today to help us raise the gayble ends of
Mistr'ss Cook's house. 'Twas thus: Pull—pull, fellows—
pull—pull thy weight. 'Tisn't much, now that I see it writ.
But 'twas Useful, so that's what counts.

—*Journal of Rowan Carpenter, 1753*

A N HOUR LATER a dazed Medford Runyuin was
standing beside his kitchen table, which was covered
with Useless Carved Objects. More Useless Objects were
on the counter by the sink. He didn't bring out the seashell bowl with the horn in it. That seemed like too much
to deal with right now.

They started with a covered bowl. The handle on the
cover was a trio of Sap Tree cones. You took it off to find
a squirrel—a Red Furred Nutgatherer, if you were feeling
Bookish—curled up inside the bowl, asleep in a nest of Sap
Tree needles. Medford was proud of that squirrel. It looked
so real that sometimes he thought it was breathing.

Next was a seabird floating on a tiny ocean (also originally a bowl). Medford had kept a dead seabird in the woods for three days so that he could get the feathers right.

The Goatman hovered for a long time over a bird's view of Bog Island that had started out as a platter. Medford had carved a log bridge, an island of trees and Nameless brambles, even the box that held Cordella's Unnameable Woven Object. He'd worked his knife in under the sheltering branches without breaking off a twig.

The effort had made him sweat. When he'd finished, the carving was so perfect it seemed to him that someone else must have done all that. It couldn't have been him.

Medford giggled, embarrassed, as he unwrapped the next carving from last year's winter shirt. He hardly knew how this one had happened. It was a rolling pin whose handles had turned into human ears. Engraved eyes stared out from the middle of the pin, the eyebrows cocked in surprise.

The Goatman made a sound between a whimper and a whinny. "A gra-a-asswatcher you are," he whispered. The more carvings he saw the twitchier he became. The last two made him shudder as if he had a fever.

One was a bowl with Boyce's face staring out of it, the eyes closed as if in sleep. That had been scary to carve and was so lifelike Medford still wasn't comfortable looking at it. The other was no longer even faintly recognizable as anything Useful, a nice block of Sap Tree wood having turned into Prudy's head and shoulders. Her braids were coiled up at the nape of her neck, the way they'd been at Transition.

"Is that your love?" the Goatman asked, touching her cheek.

"No, no," Medford said. "No, no, no. We grew up together."

Leaning against the table was a collection of decorated walking sticks. One was carved with rocks and seaweed, better than the Goatman's wind swirls but not as detailed as the goat heads. A seabird took flight from the top.

When the Goatman saw that, he lost all control. He grabbed the seabird stick and held it up over his head so the wings almost touched the ceiling. "Bwee-eh-eh," he cried, teetering on his hooves and prancing. "Bweh-eh-eh, bweh, bweh-eh-eh-eh!"

He crooned like a broody Egg Fowl, squawked like a seabird, chattered like a Striped Nutgatherer. He bobbed the stick up and down, staggering all over the kitchen floor. The dog began to whine under the table.

Whup-whup-whup! Medford lunged forward, thinking he could grab the Goatman to make him stand still.

Too late. The cabin shuddered. The door flew open, slammed against the wall. A blast of west wind hurled itself through the windows like something solid. Medford flung himself to the floor, and the walking sticks fell over, rolled every which way.

The blast caught the Goatman in midprance and he toppled over with a cry Medford could barely hear over the tumult of the wind. The seabird stick flew out of his hands, crashed through one of the eastern windows. The southern windows rattled, then the ones on the north, then the west ones. Medford heard his mallet rack tip over again.

With a loud, final *Whup!* the cabin went silent. Panicky birds twittered in the woods. A piece of the broken window tipped onto the floor and shattered. Medford, facedown with his arms over his head, dared to look up.

The Goatman was on his back under the eastern windows. "Why?" he asked the rafters. "Why, why, why, why, why."

"Did you do that?" Medford whispered.

The Goatman sat up, aglitter with glass shards. "So-o-orry," he said.

"How did that happen? I thought you had to lick your finger and—"

"Tha-a-at's the way it's supposed to be."

"Did you mean it to start blowing like that?"

"No."

"Then why . . . ?"

"I don't know. I get exci-i-ited."

"Does it happen often?"

"Often enough."

"Does it happen to other . . . goatfolk?"

"No." The Goatman looked pathetic, slumped back against the wall, his finger toying with a chunk of broken glass on the floor beside him.

Medford had never felt sorry for anybody else before.

It wasn't a bad feeling. "Stay right there if you're comfort-able," he said. "And I'll make us more tea."

The Goatman pointed to the squirrel bowl. "May I see tha-a-at?"

Medford hesitated. The Goatman's eyebrows twitched. "I will be ca-a-areful."

Medford handed the bowl to him, then crunched around on glass shards to fill the kettle and stoke the stove. The Goatman held the bowl up close and stroked the squirrel with one finger, just what Medford would do.

Medford swept the glass off the floor, put flypaper on the broken window.

As they drank their tea, the Goatman had Medford explain why he'd carved each Useless Object. He asked to see the tools Medford had used, made him demonstrate how he held a knife, a chisel, a mallet. At first Medford found the questions hard to answer, because he usually tried not even to think about his secret carvings. His words trickled, then flowed, then rushed out like Mill Stream the time the dam burst.

Some things he couldn't explain very well. "'Twas there in the middle, the shape of a Nutgatherer," he said, as the Goatman poked at the squirrel bowl with a grimy finger. "Once I saw it I couldn't just leave it. 'Twas already there, you see."

The Goatman nodded as if he did see. Some kind of longing bubbled up inside Medford. People nodded like that when Boyce talked sometimes.

Medford didn't mention the buzz he felt when he carved such things (or the hum or the song or whatever it was)—that was too scary to put into words. But he talked about everything else that came to mind. He couldn't stop talking. He couldn't see how he would stay silent after this. Hunger was all that slowed him down, and only when it was well past time for the midday dinner.

He invited the Goatman to stay.

Medford had leftovers of Myrtle Cook's Egg Fowl Stew in the springhouse, a small stone building with a spring-fed stream running through it to keep the contents cold. The stew had to be eaten, but the Goatman wouldn't touch it. So Medford and the dog ate the stew and the Goatman ate beets and potatoes—Starch Root, to the Bookish—from Medford's garden.

They drank Millicent Brewer's bottled root beer, cold from the springhouse. The fizziness made the Goatman sneeze but he said he liked it anyway. The Goatman ate his linen napkin to finish off the meal. He didn't like it as much as the towel that morning, he said, looking sideways at another towel hanging by the sink.

Medford explained about cotton and linen cloth and how expensive it was. "For spe-e-ecial," the Goatman said, nodding.

"Why don't you eat your clothes?" Medford asked. "They're cloth."

"They are goat hair," the Goatman said in shocked tones.

Medford looked closer and saw fine fibers mashed together into a thick, stiff fabric. He had to admit the cloth
didn't look edible. But he'd never taken a bite out of a dish
towel, either.

The Goatman watched, agog, as Medford washed the
dishes. Medford was not surprised to learn that the Goatman had never encountered soapsuds. The Goatman blew
his nose on his sash and then used the sash to polish his
horns, with no apparent result.

They spent the rest of the afternoon outside. Lying on his back in the sun, the Goatman pressed a long
grass blade lengthwise between his thumbs, held it to his
mouth, and blew gently. The noise he made was almost
like one of the songs the Fishers used to keep everyone
together while hauling a net. But no human voice could
make such a sound. It lilted like birdsong, skipped like a
rock on a pond, darted like an insect in sunlight. Hearing it made Medford happy, although he couldn't have explained why.

"How is that used?" he asked when the Goatman
paused for breath.

"Used?" The Goatman sat up. "It ha-a-as no use that I
can think of."

Useless, Medford thought.

The Goatman handed him a blade of grass. "You try,"
he said.

Medford shook his head. *Useless*, he thought.

A cunning look flickered across the Goatman's face.

"We could use this to call goats. Because they don't have na-a-ames."

"I don't need to call goats."

"You ne-e-ever know."

No sound Medford made was anything like the Goatman's. But the more gruesome the noises the better he felt. They excited the dog, who kept romping over to lick Medford's face in a frenzy. Medford hadn't laughed like this since before Transition.

They worked on the sounds until the sun went down. The Goatman started calling Medford Goat Gas. *Almost like Nightfarts,* Medford thought.

They ate bread and beets for supper. They spent the evening by the fire. When the Goatman hitched up his robe, Medford found he could look at the hairy shins without shuddering and glancing away. "My secret Friend from afar." That's what Cordella had called her goatman. Had he called up the wind and broken a window, too?

Or perhaps he'd just admired her weavings, made her feel they were almost Useful.

"There's something else," he told the Goatman. He brought out the seashell bowl.

The Goatman didn't notice the horn right away, distracted by Pinky and its rosy stripes. But then he twitched. "Bweh-eh-eh. When did you ca-a-arve this?"

"Yesterday. Just before you came here."

"How di-i-id you know what my horns would look like?"

"I saw an Unnameable Woven Object." Medford told how he and Prudy had unearthed the box on Bog Island, about Cordella and the man on the cloth.

"Do your people come here often?" Medford asked.

"I don't think so. But I told you we have ta-a-ales about this place."

"What do the tales say?"

"That you name everything and everything has a use like the na-a-ame. And someti-i-imes . . ." His voice trailed off.

"Sometimes?"

"Sometimes you ma-a-ake people leave."

"I don't," Medford said.

"No. The ones like you are the ones they se-e-end . . ."

Again, he didn't finish his sentence. He didn't have to.

CHAPTER TEN

⚘

Once a Runyuin

Do not Yawn nor Spit when another is talking. Offer no criticism of thy companion's speech, nor moralize upon his life unless called upon to do so.

> —*A Frugall Compendium of Home Arts and Farme Chores by Capability C. Craft (1680), as Amended and Annotated by the Island Council of Names (1718–1809)*

NIGHTFA-A-ARTS. Where are you, Nightfarts?"

Medford opened his eyes. It took him a minute to remember why someone would be saying "Nightfarts" outside his bedroom window at daybreak. Apparently a goatman could call someone the same thing twice, almost like using a name. That was comforting.

Otherwise, comfort was scarce. The more Medford lay there thinking about it, the more certain he was that Prudy and Earnest would visit him today, as they often did midweek. And when they came they would find a horned man living under the porch.

A horned man with no name.

A horned man with no name who knew all about Medford's Useless carvings.

Perhaps I could tell him not to say anything about the carvings, he thought. But keeping the Goatman from talking would be like trying to control the wind, he suspected.

There was only one answer: The Goatman must be gone when Prudy and Earnest arrived. If he could be gone for good, so much the better. Full of resolve, Medford jumped out of bed. He stoked the stove and re-hid his carvings, Usefulness on two legs.

The Goatman was surprisingly easy to get rid of. "I must work today," Medford said after an exceptionally messy breakfast of honey and oats. "'Twould be best if—"

"I will go," the Goatman said. "I found the-e-ese"—he held out a handful of Pitch Tree cones—"and I will look for more. Nightfarts will hunt."

So the Goatman borrowed a potato sack and loped off into the woods with the dog beside him. Medford went into his workshop and did an excellent imitation of a fourteen-year-old boy working blamelessly on a blameless wooden trencher.

To his astonishment, reality caught up with the imitation and he actually did make progress on the trencher. It was well shaped and ready for sanding by the time Prudy knocked on the porch door in late morning, carrying a pie.

"Clayton Baker sends thee this," she said. "'Tis Red

Keeping Fruit. He thinketh he gave thee not enough for the spoons."

Earnest rolled his eyes. His respect for New Prudy's Book Talk hadn't grown any since the head-under-the-pump incident.

Prudy deposited the pie on the table and sniffed the air. "Hoo. What stinketh?"

"I . . . ," Medford said. He swallowed, thinking fast. "I forgot a chicken I had . . . 'twas in the cupboard. It went bad."

"Thou keptst Egg Fowl in the cupboard? Raw Egg Fowl?"

"Aye," Medford said. "Don't know what I was thinking."

"It must have been there awhile to make a smell this bad. Where wert thou?"

"Oh, I was here. I was . . . I was concentrating on my work."

New Prudy gave him the same look she'd given the Sap Tree cones at Transition.

"Why art thou so red?" she asked, exactly as she had then.

"The pump's dripping," Earnest said in a hopeful tone.

"Aye. And 'tis not pumping well," Medford said, realizing just too late that he should have kept his mouth shut.

"Oh, aye?" Earnest's face lit up. He advanced on the

sink, pulling a small wrench out of his pocket. Earnest had taken to wearing trousers instead of knee breeches because the pockets were so much bigger.

"Oh, no, Earnest," Medford said. "Don't—"

The first bolt hit the floor.

"Better go outside, Medford," Prudy said. "You won't want to watch this." She caught sight of the flypaper on the broken window. "What happened there, pray?"

"Oh. I . . . ah . . . my knife slipped." Medford tried to keep his face from moving, but he couldn't help wincing. He really wasn't good at this.

Prudy gave him a dour look that she must have learned from Deemer. She marched out the door, white-blond braids hanging straight against her stiff, straight back. He knew the look of that back. That was New Prudy—or even Old Prudy—spoiling for a fight. In this case, spoiling to find out what Medford was up to.

"Art thou coming?" she called from the porch.

"Aye," Medford said. He was tired and he was going to need his wits about him. Lying was turning out to be hard work. It was easier when you hid things under the bed and didn't have to talk about them.

"'Tis the leather diaphragm," Earnest muttered behind them. "Must be." Another bolt plonked onto the floor.

Medford sat down on the steps next to Prudy, who was sitting as if she had a rod for a spine, feet Firm and Even as the Book taught.

"Medford," she said. "What ails thee? Master Learned

says thou hast been acting strange ever since Transition. And I agree with him."

"I'm not acting strange," he said, trying to make his voice deeper the way Arvid had. "I'm just working hard."

"Pa says thou hast not finished his bowls."

"I'm on the third-to-last one."

"That's what thou saidst last week. Master Learned says industry be our best—"

"'Tis in there on the workbench, Prudy, if you'd like to see it." How dared she question him like this, with all her *thees* and *thous* and *arts* and *shalts*? "I have things to do other than carving, you know. I have this cabin and the garden to keep up and firewood to get in. You live at home, don't forget."

"Others live alone. Thy last spoons were two weeks ago. People say . . . They say—"

"They say what?"

She was the one turning red this time, but she didn't flinch. "They say once a Runyuin never a Carver."

"I wonder who could possibly have said that." Actually, he did wonder. It could have been Arvid or it could have been Deemer. He supposed it didn't matter which.

"Medford, you've always had more to prove than anyone else. That's nothing new. Why court trouble?" She'd dropped the Book Talk. Praise the Book.

"I don't court trouble," he said, adding under his breath, "'Tis courting me."

A goatman, a stinky dog, a bedroom full of Useless

Carved Objects, and now New Prudy in a scolding mood. What next?

At that exact moment, what was next bounded into view on four muddy feet. She had a dead squirrel in her mouth.

The dog shook her head furiously, squirrel tail flapping. She bowed and stretched, placed the corpse tenderly at Medford's feet. Then she sat, her long, wet tongue dangling out of her mouth. A drop of saliva rolled onto the ground. She waggled the tip of her tail.

"Hoo," Prudy said. "There's that smell."

"Another fla-a-atfoot!" a grassy and windy voice called from the woods. "Back off, Killer. Let the she-fla-a-atfoot breathe."

The dog gave a welcoming yelp, grabbed her squirrel, and pranced over to greet the Goatman as if she hadn't seen him in days.

Medford buried his face in his hands. He heard Prudy gasp and scrabble to her feet. By the time he lifted his head she'd made it to the road and was heading north, even though the road home was to the south.

"Prudy!" he yelled. "Come back! He . . . it . . . 'tis fine."

Because she was Prudy, her curiosity got the better of her and she turned to look. The Goatman was bouncing and bowing, waving his hand back and forth in what he clearly thought was a friendly and inviting fashion.

Medford heard a faint *whup-whup* from Mainland and

a louder *Whup!* from the north, where there was nothing but empty blueberry lands and open sea. He saw a little herd of whitecaps coming from Mainland, approaching fast.

He leaped to his feet. "No!"

The dog whimpered and ran over to him, squirrel dangling from her mouth.

The Goatman regarded his hand in horror. "I don't understa-a-and."

"Prudy!" Medford shouted. "Get down on the ground!" He flung himself onto the grass. The dog huddled next to him.

A deep moan rolled in from the north. Seabirds screeched to the west. Treetops hissed louder and louder, then louder still. The dog snuggled in closer to his side.

The wind hit from both directions at once, two gusts colliding right over Medford and the dog—he could hardly breathe, the air around him was moving so fast and in so many directions. He thought his cabin roof might come off but could hear nothing except the shrieking and moaning of the wind. It would kill him, this wind, kill them all, pick them up and hurl them into the sea, strip Island of its trees, its houses, its people. It would go on and on and on and on and—

The air went dead. The wind just stopped. The birds in the trees talked and twittered and protested. Everything else was silent.

In the side yard, the Goatman groaned and sat up. He looked around for his staff. The dog unburrowed herself, licked Medford's hand, shook herself from head to tail. She retrieved the squirrel from under Medford's arm.

"Medford," a faint voice said.

Medford ran over to where Prudy was just managing to sit up. She was coated in dust from the road and her braids were frayed. One of them had flipped over onto the wrong side of her head, leaving behind a long, frazzled strand of escaped hair wafting around beside her cheek. He hauled her to her feet.

"What in all the Names was that?" she said. "There was something like it yesterday. And who . . . what is that . . . that—"

"He came yesterday," Medford said, trying to sound as if horned men were both Useful and commonplace. "In a sailboat. No, that was the day before. He's on a ramble."

"'A ramble'?" Prudy said the word as if she'd never heard it before. "Oh, the Names, that's a hat on his head, isn't it? Medford—isn't it? We said it was a hat when we saw it . . . on Cordella's . . ."

Medford had never felt so miserable in his life. "'Tis not a hat. 'Tis horns. And he has hooves. There's a city with shelters like mountains."

Prudy looked at him as if he'd suggested she call herself Handkerchief or Pickle.

"Prudy, just come over and meet him," Medford said. "He

smells funny and he talks funny, but he's nice. Really. He's a nice man. You hardly notice the horns." The hooves were hard to ignore but he'd let her find that out for herself.

She shook her head, then nodded. Then she shook her head again.

Medford had never seen Prudy look so scared. He'd hardly ever seen her look scared at all.

Earnest was on the porch with his mouth open, holding his wrench up like a weapon, transfixed by the Goatman crawling around looking for his staff.

"Is he from Mainland?" Prudy whispered. "Do they have horns over there?"

Medford didn't answer. As he walked Prudy over to the porch steps, all he could think about was the Prudy head bundled up under his bed with the other carvings.

How would he keep the Goatman from talking about his Useless Objects?

Prudy sat down on the steps, hunched over and gnawing on a braid in a way that would have horrified Capability C. Craft. Earnest, wrench at the ready, finally managed to say something. It sounded like "*errff.*"

"I'll be right back." Medford hastened over to the Goatman, who was on his feet now. The dog waggled her tail at Medford as he approached, the squirrel at her feet with its head gone. Apparently she had decided to eat it herself.

"So-o-orry," the Goatman began.

"I know, I know," Medford said. "We'll talk about it later. I have to tell you . . . Those are my friends Prudy and Earnest over there and they can't know . . . Please don't say anything about my carvings."

"You wish me to te-e-ell them a lie?" the Goatman said.

"No," Medford said. "I wish you to say nothing."

"Too ba-a-ad," the Goatman said. He hobbled off in Prudy's direction.

"What happened?" Medford asked, catching up. "The wind, I mean. I thought you had to lick your finger or be greatly excited or—"

"Tha-a-at is what I thought, too," the Goatman said. "I have never seen it ha-a-appen like that. This pla-a-ace has unruly winds."

He stopped three feet shy of the steps and stared at Prudy, who was staring at his horns. "I am a goat-ma-a-an . . . ," he began.

"Do. You. Speak. Our. Language," Prudy said, louder than necessary.

"I just was," the Goatman said.

"What. Be. Thy. Name," Prudy said, even louder.

"Prudy," Medford said. "You don't have to—"

"Bweh-eh-eh," the Goatman said. "You ask an i-i-interesting question."

Medford moaned. Prudy flicked a glance at him.

"Prudy," Medford said. "Take a deep breath before he answers. He's fine. He's a nice man. 'Tis fine, just fine."

The Goatman waited politely for Medford to finish. "I have no na-a-ame," he said. He waited for Prudy to react. She didn't. "If you must call me something ca-a-all me the Goatman, since I am the only—"

"Tuh," said Earnest, lowering his wrench hand.

"La-a-ater you may want to address me in other ways. My friend here"—the Goatman started to gesture toward the dog but stopped, one eye on the treetops—"is called Ki-i-iller today, since she caught a small animal when I was standing ri-i-ight—"

"Huh," Prudy said. "No name at all. Huh."

She didn't look upset. In fact, the color was returning to her face.

"Prudy," Medford said. "Don't faint. 'Tis fine."

"Of course 'tis fine," Prudy said. "So he has no name, so what?"

Medford noticed that his mouth was hanging open.

"Oh, Medford," Prudy said, "surely you don't think all the world lives the way we do? That's why we are here and not there." She pointed toward Mainland. "Where some people have horns, I guess."

"You've never talked to that Trade driver with the black whiskers," Earnest told Medford, pocketing his wrench and sitting down next to Prudy. "His name is Humperdinck. 'Tis not much of a leap from that to no name at all."

Medford felt dazed. He would have expected Earnest to be calm in the face of novelty. But was this the same Prudy who had just said, "Once a Runyuin never a Carver"?

This wasn't New Prudy. It wasn't even Old Prudy. It was New Old Prudy.

The Goatman flopped down on the grass.

The dog did the same.

"So," the Goatman said. "What would you li-i-ike to know about me?"

CHAPTER ELEVEN

൭

Prudy's View of the World

For those who Trade, some contact with Mainlanders be unavoidable. But beware Useless conversation with foreigners, for the Unnameable hovers nearby.

—*A Frugall Compendium of Home Arts and Farme Chores by Capability C. Craft (1680), as Amended and Annotated by the Island Council of Names (1718–1809)*

SO THERE SHE WAS, Mistress Prudence Learned, braider of braids, crusher of shells, speaker of Book Talk, listening to a Nameless, smelly man with horns talk about mountains and goats and the exact dimensions of his last winter shelter.

She was sitting at Medford's kitchen table, having tightly rebraided her hair. She'd wanted to wash her face but the pump was in pieces all over the floor.

"'Tis the diaphragm," Earnest said, waving a leather disk. "The seal has to be good or there's no suction. 'Tis all dried up. I think John Piper has oil for it." He was happier than Medford had seen him since Essence left.

"Can you put it back together?" Medford was surprised a pump had so many parts.

"Don't know," Earnest said, pleased at such a novel and exciting question. "Nobody's let me near one before."

Medford sighed and sank into the chair by the workshop door. In the past forty-eight hours he had experienced joy, despair, fascination, annoyance, and terror—more Useless emotions than he'd known in his entire life. Except for the pump, everything seemed to be all right for the moment. He was exhausted.

While Medford and Prudy made dinner preparations, Earnest put the pump back together. To his delight, he found he had a gasket and three screws left over. He took the pump apart to figure out where they went. Then he assembled it again. "Won't be truly fixed till I get that oil," he said. "But I think 'twill be better than before, now that I've loosened up that leather thing."

Earnest stood back so everyone could see and pumped the handle three times. Nothing came out. He pumped it four more times. Nothing. He pumped it so many times Medford lost count, but not a drop of water appeared.

Earnest beamed. "I'll have to take it apart again," he said.

"Let's eat first," Prudy said.

They ate the last of Medford's bread, with butter and cheese from the springhouse, plus Clayton Baker's pie and beets cooked in water from the stream. Baked eggs for

Prudy, Earnest, and Medford made the meal into a reasonable midday dinner.

"No Egg Fowl in the cupboard?" Prudy asked as she sat down. Medford said nothing, just paid attention to his plate and felt himself go warm.

Prudy kept a fascinated eye on the Goatman as they ate. Although she once again was straight of back, feet Firm and Even, she didn't seem to mind when he coated his robe with a flurry of crumbs and a glaze of honey.

Medford did not give anyone a napkin.

"Hast thou been here before?" Prudy asked the Goatman. "Or . . . or thy people?" Medford knew she was thinking of Cordella Weaver's cloth man but didn't want to talk about it in front of Earnest.

"Others ha-a-ave come here," the Goatman said. "We have ta-a-ales of you."

"Then why have we no tales of you?" Prudy demanded. "I'm surprised Pa hath not heard of you from the radio voices." Because so many of his tools came from Mainland, Twig was one of a handful of Islanders trained to use the Trade radio in Town Hall.

The Goatman shrugged. "We do not show ourselves to many fla-a-atfoots."

"And another thing," Prudy said. "Those winds we've been having the past couple of days—what have they to do with thee?"

At first the Goatman acted as if he hadn't heard her,

picking at a glob of honey on his robe. "They're mi-i-ine," he said at last, barely audible. "I called them."

"Called the winds? That can't be."

The Goatman stuck his finger in his mouth. He looked at Medford. Medford shook his head. The Goatman took his finger out again and dried it on his sash.

"I saw him do it," Medford told Prudy. "He wet his finger and waggled it and the wind came and knocked us over. But then later it came when he got excited about . . . something. Today he just waved his hand in the air."

"Tuh," Prudy said. "Thou standst in a windy place and believ'st the wind obeyeth thy behest."

Medford could see that the Goatman had no idea what she'd just said, praise the Book. The last thing they wanted was the Goatman trying to prove himself.

"Pray tell us, Prudy," Earnest said, "when was the last time you saw winds like these, hey? Where do you think they came from?"

Prudy made a face at him, not persuaded.

"Not that there's any Use in them," Earnest added. "Do they ever help anyone?"

The Goatman sighed. "Not me. My uncle, my cousin . . . everyone else can call it up to bri-i-ing in the rain or blow the bugs away. The best can shape the clouds or da-a-ance the trees for our pleasure or make a soothing sound on a wa-a-arm night."

"Well, there's certainly some Use in bringing rain," Medford said. But the thought flitted across his brain—

here, then gone—that he would like to see someone shape the clouds and dance the trees.

"No one can call the wind," Prudy said, making up her mind.

Her brother snorted. "Seen many men with horns of late?"

The Goatman contemplated Prudy, who was looking uncommonly stubborn, and apparently decided to ingratiate himself. "You have ni-i-ice hair," he said. "I like it be-e-etter like this than bundled up behind your head that other way."

"Other way?" Prudy said. "What other way?"

Medford didn't know what the Goatman meant, either. Then his spine turned to ice.

The carving of Prudy. With her hair up for Transition.

He tried to think of something to say. He imagined his hair crinkling as frost crept up from the roots.

"The other way—the wa-a-ay you had it—oh." The Goatman looked at Medford, eyes round.

Prudy's eyes were slits, her back a rod of iron. "The way I had it at Transition," she said. "I thought he'd just arrived."

"He," Medford said. "Ah."

Prudy had that hard-eyed look he'd seen on Bog Island, when she was standing over Cordella Weaver's Unnameable Woven Object. She'd scared him then and she scared him now.

"He was here for Transition?" Prudy said quietly. "That was last spring."

"He wasn't," Medford said. "In truth."

"Then how did he know about my hair?"

Medford breathed in, out, in, out. He kept his eyes on Prudy, arranging his face. What did sincerity look like? "I told him," he said.

"Oh, aye? Then how did he know whether he liked it or not?"

"I said I like it better down."

"That's it," the Goatman said. "Fancy Carver Boy said he li-i-ikes it this way."

"Oh, aye? And exactly how did the topic of my hair . . . Fancy Carver Boy? Why dost thou call him that?"

Medford sat down. He had to think this through and there wasn't time.

This was Prudy. On the one hand, she was Deemer Learned's apprentice and had wanted to burn Cordella's Unnameable Woven Object. Had she told Deemer about that cloth man? Medford didn't even know.

On the other hand, she had no trouble settling down for a chat with a Nameless horned man. She even seemed to like him.

Her stare was so sharp it hurt him. She looked like Deemer, almost.

This was Prudy. He'd known her all his life.

"He has seen you with your hair up," he said. "I carved a . . . something Useless."

Prudy's eyes were blue granite under ice. "Let's see it," she said.

Medford went and rummaged around under his bed.

And then Prudy, braids down, stared back at Prudy, braids up.

Outside the kitchen door, the dog sat up in a hurry to scratch her ear with her hind foot. Her foot kept sliding off her ear and slapping onto the floor, *Scritch, scritch, scritch, whap—scritch, scritch, scritch, whap.*

The Goatman did not speak.

Medford did not breathe.

Earnest took one look at Prudy's face (the live one—he barely looked at the wooden version) and decided this would be a good time to crawl into the foundation and examine the sink piping from underneath.

A Honeybug buzzed in and settled on a piece of fruit in the bowl Medford kept on the counter beside the sink. It was the Sweetwood bowl, the first he'd ever made. He kept it polished but he kept it in use.

"This isn't the only one of these things thou has made, is it?" Prudy asked.

"'Tis not," Medford said.

"I want to see them."

The Goatman, apologetically silent, helped carry the other Useless Objects out from the bedroom. There were still more in bundles on the rafters but Medford didn't say anything about them. This would be quite enough Useless Objects for one afternoon.

Prudy had a white, closed-to-trading look on her face. She didn't touch any of the carvings, just peered at them and into them. Medford held his breath when she came to the unfinished seashell bowl, breathed again when she reached in to touch Pinky with a trembling forefinger. "My shells," she whispered.

She'd see, Medford knew it now. She'd see that he was thinking of her when he carved that bowl.

Then she noticed the horn. He could tell because somehow her braids got straighter. She whirled and confronted the Goatman. "What brings you here?" she demanded, forgetting Book Talk. "To Island, I mean. To Medford. There have been others before you, we know that. And other . . . objects like these."

The Goatman backed up a step. "This is where the wi-i-ind blew me."

"Did you make Medford do this?"

"I've been carving these things for years," Medford said, feeling oddly insulted. "That one's not even finished yet."

She gave him one agonized look and he knew he'd blundered. She walked out the door. When Medford followed she was pacing around on the grass as if walking off a cramp. The dog watched closely in case Prudy did something that involved food.

Medford sat down on the porch steps and waited. And waited.

Prudy walked the length of the front yard, walked it again. A couple of times she rubbed her hand across her cheek. If it had been someone else, Medford would have thought she was crying. She was not, however, chewing on a braid. She was upright, stiff. A Learned.

She turned abruptly and marched straight toward Medford. He stood up because it seemed safer. "How long hast thou been making those things?" she demanded.

"Years. Almost from the beginning."

"You . . . thou wast making them when we still went to Bog Island?" It was the first time either of them had said that name in almost a year. "All that talking we did and you said nothing?"

He didn't have to respond—she knew the answer. It had never occurred to him to burden her with the knowledge. He hadn't meant to keep secrets from her.

He wished she would cry. He wanted to stroke her cheek, tug on a braid—anything to get that hardness out of her eyes.

"Did Boyce teach thee?" she asked.

"I taught myself."

"Medford. How couldst thou teach yourself—thyself—to make such . . . such Unnameable—"

"You think I'm lying? And they aren't Unnameable. They're Nameless, aye—"

"Of course I think you're lying. Thou hast been lying to everyone for years. To Master Learned, to me."

"I never lied to Master Learned. And it wasn't so much lying as . . . just not saying."

"'Tis the same thing," Prudy snapped. "Secrets are

just like the Unnameable. Only . . . only secret. 'Tis bad enough that my own mother behaves so . . ." She stopped, gulped, then plowed ahead. "And as for these things being Unnameables—Medford, what else can they be? Master Learned says a Nameless thing is . . . is a thing no one bothers with, a weed or a seabird. They harm no one. But these things—"

"You think my carvings are harmful? Exactly who is harmed, Prudy?"

"You, for one. You . . . thou hast been working on those things when you should have been working on something Useful like my father's bowls. Just like Merit Learned said about . . . about Cordella."

"I told you, I'm almost finished with Twig's bowls. The third-to-last one is right—"

"That's not the point, Medford, and you know it." Prudy's hands were balled up into fists on her hips. Her back was straight. Her legs were straight. Medford couldn't see them, but he was sure her braids were two straight lines down her back.

"Well, then, what is the point?" he said. "Why all this fuss? You're perfectly happy talking to a Nameless man with horns."

"This is different and if it weren't, then you . . . *thou* wouldst not have lied about it," Prudy shot back. "My shells, of all things!"

"Your shells—so what? You think Master Learned will blame you? And you'll be gone like Essence, is that it?"

"'Tis not . . . It just can't . . ."

She's run out of answers, Medford thought.

But then she raised her hands like Councilor Learned quieting everyone down after the dinner break. She was pale enough to be Deemer, too, and her eyes made Medford shiver in all the heat of his anger.

"Enough," she said. "'Tis wrong, Medford, and thou knowst it. I am a Learned and my obligation is clear, Master Learned says. Thou hast made the Unnameable and it hath conquered thee. For thine own good—"

Prudy snapped her mouth shut. She turned and stalked back to the road.

"What are you going to do, Prudy?" Medford called after her.

She didn't answer. She didn't look back at him. She marched south toward Town.

CHAPTER TWELVE

ℜ

Nutcakes

Master Tanner and I disagree on a Useful name for the Oak Tree. I would call it after its Fruit, the Acorn. He wishes to call it Tanningbark after its Use in his tanning solution. I believe Master Carpenter supports Master Tanner, so there's an end on't.

—*Journal of Samuel Farmer, 1751*

WHEN MEDFORD returned to the kitchen the Goatman was sitting on the rug by the stove, the squirrel bowl in his lap, Earnest standing beside him. Earnest had his watch in his hand, a sign that he was uneasy, but he hadn't started to take the watch apart. Yet.

The cover was off the bowl and the Goatman was poking at the little creature curled up inside. "This is what Ki-i-iller ate. I would like my uncle to see this."

Earnest looked everywhere except where Medford was standing. "I'd best be going," he said to the stovepipe. "She sounded upset."

"Aye." Medford sat down in the chair by his workshop door. He surveyed the carvings cluttering the kitchen.

He'd better hide them again before . . . before what? What would Prudy do? Would she tell Deemer Learned? Boyce? And what would they do?

"I'd best be going," Earnest said again, this time to the sink. "I'll be back . . . sometime . . . with that oil for the pump."

The pump. On top of everything else, Medford couldn't get at his well water.

"Sorry about no water," Earnest told the door latch. He pocketed his watch.

"I can haul from the stream," Medford said.

"Aye." Earnest jiggled the door latch, which was a little loose. To Medford's relief, he did not reach for his screwdriver. "These carvings. They be . . . skillful."

"My thanks."

"Unnameable."

"If you say so."

"I wish thee luck."

"I thank thee."

It didn't sound as if Earnest would be back very soon. The porch creaked under his feet. The steps creaked. Then the world was silent.

There was little point in hiding the carvings, when you thought about it. If Boyce or Deemer Learned demanded to see them, Medford could hardly deny their existence. No one would think Prudy was making up such a tale. If she said there were Unnameables at Medford's, there were Unnameables at Medford's.

But what if Prudy didn't tell? Earnest would keep quiet unless someone asked him a direct question. What if Prudy thought about it on the way back to Town and decided to do the same? Then what?

He imagined hiding the carvings away again, life going on just as it had before.

Prudy would come by next week, probably with Earnest. She would look him in the eye and give him Old Prudy's mischievous smile.

Except that New Prudy would keep an even sharper eye on how much work he turned out. Every time he fell behind she would think—she would know—that he'd been working on something Useless. Something Unnameable, she'd say.

She wouldn't be able to stand it, this secret plus Cordella Weaver's cloth man. She would have to tell someone about something.

And then thou shalt be Gone.

His brain and pretty much every other part of his body were screaming, *Get up now and hide those objects! Better yet, burn them. Now, before 'tis too late.*

But somewhere, hidden deep, a voice said, *You'll just make more of them. If not tomorrow then next week. Time to face it. Time to stop hiding.*

Medford thought about Essence Learned sitting in the motorboat with her stern father. That could easily have been him and Boyce. He looked around his cabin. He realized that he loved the place, loved taking a cup of tea into the workshop early in the morning, a day of carving ahead of him. The smell of the sea on a summer day. The dancing light in the woods when he and Boyce were scouting trees. He couldn't live anyplace else. "I'm not going," he said.

"Good," the Goatman said. "Le-e-et's have tea."

The Goatman went outside on some mission. Before long, sharp banging sounds drifted in from the yard. Medford peeked out and saw the purple figure hunched over an outcropping of ledge near the woods. He was using a rock to whack at something.

Medford decided he didn't want to know what the Goatman was doing. He moved the teakettle to the hottest part of the stove, added a couple of small logs to the firebox. He left the door to the firebox open.

His carvings covered every inch of the kitchen table. He picked up the rolling pin with the ears and eyes. He squatted before the open fire, weighing the rolling pin in his hand, eyeing the flames.

He thrust the rolling pin into the firebox and shut the door. He stood up, feeling like someone else. He picked up the seashell bowl, which now would never be finished. He could make another fancy rolling pin, maybe, when it was safe. But his hand wouldn't hold the knife the same way, nor would it be that particular piece of wood with the shapes trapped inside it, alive as any creature.

The reality of it hit him like a blast of wind.

Medford dropped to his knees, grappled with the

firebox door, hauled the rolling pin out of the flames. The ears were a little dark, the rest of it hot but not yet singed. He dropped it on the table, shook the heat out of his hands, and burst into tears.

As he stood there snuffling, tears rolling down his cheeks, he knew that whatever anyone thought of them, these carvings were him. He wiped his eyes and shut the firebox.

He wished he could go back two days, to when he was secret and safe. When hooves belonged to Greater Brown Beef Creatures and horns to actual goats. On the other hand, the Goatman might be the only friend he had left.

The porch creaked. The Goatman teetered through the door, carrying something in the lap of his robe. He dumped it into the sink with a loud and rolling clatter. When Medford went over to look, the sink was full of every kind of nut he'd ever known: Tanningbark and Gum Tree Nuts, Sweetnuts, a few Roasting Nuts, all of them shelled.

"How did you find all those?" Medford asked. "You weren't gone that long."

"It's what I eat," the Goatman said. "I will ma-a-ake nutcakes."

Medford wasn't sure he wanted to eat anything cooked by a person who ate dish towels. And yet not hurting the Goatman's feelings was becoming important to him.

"I need . . ." The Goatman made a grinding gesture with his hands. "I need to turn them to dust. Powder. Flour, I gue-e-ess you'd say."

Medford got out his mortar and pestle and showed the Goatman how to use them. He made tea for them both. Then he cleared the table of his Unnameable carvings (even he was starting to think of them that way). He found spots for them on windowsills, shelves, and the tops of cupboards. He wasn't going to hide them under the bed anymore. The next day he might even bring down the ones hidden in the rafters.

He wouldn't hide anything anymore. *Trouble doth not depart. Face it, thou.*

"I. Need. Large. Wet. Leaves," the Goatman said, his words following the rhythm of the pestle. "I. Need. To wrap the cakes. And bake them in. The ashes."

Glad to improve the supper prospects, Medford showed him how to use the oven and his Mainland metal baking pans. The Goatman was skeptical. But because Medford showed no inclination to go out and gather leaves, he gave in.

"I need goatmi-i-ilk," the Goatman said.

"I have cow's milk," Medford said. "I mean, Greater Horned Milk Creature milk." If he couldn't act Bookish, at least he could talk that way.

Out at the springhouse, he surveyed his stock of butter, eggs, and milk, which was getting low. He was out of bread now, too. He'd have to go to Town for more.

If Town didn't come to him first.

He'd better finish Twig's bowl tonight. He'd work on it before supper.

Sanding—mindless work, taxing to the muscles and yielding immediate results—turned out to be a cure for inner turmoil. He stopped wondering what Prudy was saying to Deemer. He concentrated his whole being on each rough spot on the trencher. The chisel marks faded and the wood took on the creamy texture Medford loved.

On the other side of the closed door, the Goatman was rattling pans, stoking the stove. The Goatman's noises harmonized with his into something like a pulling song, and Medford hummed as he sanded. It was like the early days when Boyce was teaching Medford to carve and they let the sound of their chisels talk for them, back and forth in Boyce's sunny workshop.

While the nutcakes were baking the Goatman came in to watch what Medford was doing. He didn't stay long. "Boring a-a-as leafwork," he said.

"What's leafwork?"

"I'll show you la-a-ater." The Goatman left, shutting the door behind him.

Medford had finished sanding and was sweeping up sawdust when the Goatman opened the door again. "Food," the Goatman said, cleaning his hands with his sash.

He'd piled a dozen small cakes on a plate in the center of the table with a wooden bowl of beets next to it. He'd set out two plates, two cups of Millicent Brewer's root beer, two forks, and two folded napkins.

The Goatman looked as though he had taken a cup of nut flour and dumped it down the front of his robe. Another cup's worth, at least, was scattered over the kitchen floor by the sink. He rubbed the flour he'd spilled on himself into the fibers of his purple robe. The robe seemed to suck it all in, leaving only a hazy residue behind. Medford wondered what else that robe had absorbed and for how many years.

When he sat down at the table, though, he thought nutcakes might be worth any amount of spilled flour. They were round like fish cakes, about three inches across and an inch high, light brown and crusty. The Goatman had ground some of the nuts into flour but had simply chopped the rest, so the cakes crunched when you bit into them. They were sweet as nuts, of course, but there was an additional taste that Medford couldn't describe, a wild, fresh taste like the air at Hunter's Moon tinged with woodsmoke.

The Goatman, perched uncomfortably on the edge of his chair, watched Medford take his first bite. Then he grinned and reached for a cake himself. "Didn't think you'd li-i-ike them, did you?"

"Mmmph," Medford said.

"Be-e-etter eat some of these red things, too. And don't eat too many cakes. They fill you up fa-a-aster than you expect."

Medford dutifully ate beets, then returned to the nutcakes. He ate three and reached for a fourth. The Goatman moved the plate away.

"Be-e-etter wait," he said.

He was right. Medford went to the stream for water, and by the time the teakettle was on the stove he was feeling that he might never eat again. "These things feed us all winter," the Goatman said. "They are ma-a-ade to last."

The Goatman was chewing hard. Too late, Medford noticed that half of the Goatman's napkin was gone and the rest was in tatters. This had to stop.

Medford held up his own napkin. "Goatman. I'm sorry, but I must tell you something about these things."

"Nothing to be so-o-orry about. They're ve-e-ery good."

"Nay, that's not it. They aren't . . ."

"Yes, they are. I li-i-ike them very much."

"Goatman, they are not food. They are napkins. If you get food on your face, you use them to wipe it off." Medford wiped the corners of his mouth to demonstrate.

"And the-e-en you eat them."

"No. Then you wash them—what I did to the dishes, remember?—and put them away and use them the next time you eat."

The Goatman stared at Medford, then down at the ragged half napkin in his hands. He sniffed at it, then looked back at Medford.

"Wha-a-at a waste," he said. "Can I finish this one?"

CHAPTER THIRTEEN

❧

Cold Nutcakes

The Four Humours—Blood, Phlegm, Black Bile, Yellow Bile—govern the Health of the Body as well as the Temperament. . . . In case of an Anger caused by Overabundance of Yellow Bile, cold Food hath proved Efficacious.

—*A Frugall Compendium of Home Arts and Farme*
Chores by Capability C. Craft (1680), as Amended and
Annotated by the Island Council of Names (1718–1809)

AFTER SUPPER Medford lighted the oil lamps. For warmth, he put more flypaper on the window the Goatman had broken the day before. He, the Goatman, and the dog settled in front of the stove. All three were silent, basking in warmth and comfort.

It was then, however, that the horrors of the day began to close in on Medford. Had he really shown Prudy and Earnest his carvings? Had Prudy really stalked off to Town, leaving the word "Unnameable" to hover over him like a carrion bird?

Why, oh why, had he never burned all those carvings?

When Medford tried to think about what was going to happen next—a confrontation with Deemer Learned and the Council, the stunned expression on Boyce's face—he wanted to run out into the dark and hide in the woods.

What if they make me leave? And they will, he thought.

"You can come wi-i-ith us when we go," the Goatman said.

Medford hadn't realized he'd spoken out loud. He looked down at the Goatman, lying there on the rug with the dog curled up next to him. He looked at the horns, the hooves, the yellow fingernails. He smelled the various smells that chased one another through the heat around the stove.

He felt he'd been asleep all his life, safe in Boyce's house and in Prudy's friendship, numb to the dangers lurking just outside the door. Suddenly he was awake and seeing the world as it was. A place where friends betray you, where you go out the door and it locks behind you.

He would stay on this island if he could but he probably couldn't. He straightened his back, Prudy-like.

There was a line in the Book that had always stuck with him, and not for the reasons Capability C. Craft had intended. The lesson was about fishing, a warning against taking more than you need. *If ye need it not, toss it free to seek thy net another day.*

Free. That was the word that caught him. He hardly knew what it meant. But it might almost be what he was feeling at that moment, as though he was about to be tossed out to leap through the waves at will. Leaving everyone else behind.

It was a windswept feeling, but something in it was dark and cold, akin to anger but more . . . well, Useful. There was strength in it.

Perhaps Mainland is where I really belong, whispered a tiny voice in his brain. *Aye,* a larger voice replied, *but do you know what's over there? A beach and a road away from it, that's what you know. What makes you think they'll like you any better over there?*

What was it the Book said? *Run not from thy woes, for they will follow thee.*

"My thanks," Medford said to the Goatman. "I may go with thee when the time comes. But not right away."

Before he went to bed, he gave the Goatman a couple of blankets to cover himself and the dog. He could always burn the blankets later.

The next morning broke without a rosy hue. The sky simply lightened behind the trees, pewter deepening to blue. The air was chilly, a foretaste of winter.

Hunched up in blankets at the end of his bed, leaning on the windowsill, Medford watched the dog wander around the garden, sniffing things. The kitchen door opened and the Goatman dumped an armload of wood into the box beside the stove.

Medford hauled on his breeches and scuttled out to make sure it was firewood going into the stove and not carving stock. He rescued three poles intended for walking sticks and showed the Goatman how to start a fire for the kettle. The Goatman obligingly grabbed a bucket and went out to the stream for water.

It was cold in the kitchen. When winter came, Medford would learn to use the stove dampers to keep the fire going overnight. He scuttled back into his bedroom to put on his shirt and stockings. He'd wash his face when the kitchen warmed up a bit.

It was time to pick the last of the beans for drying. In a couple of weeks Medford would bring in the onions and pumpkins (*Savory Roots and Pie Gourds*, his brain supplied primly) for the root cellar under his workshop. Boyce let the carrots (*Orange Stew Roots*) sweeten in the cold ground before harvest and Medford thought he'd do the same.

He'd never been in charge of a root cellar before. As he tied up his shoes, he thought about where he would put everything. He had a barrel of Starch Root already and one waiting for Red Keeping Fruit. He had a box of moss to keep the carrots from softening, shelves for the pumpkins. He'd braid the onions and hang them.

Intent on his harvest plans, he bustled around the kitchen spooning loose tea into Clarity's teapot, putting the kettle on the stove, and getting mugs down from the cupboard. But then the cluster of decorated walking sticks caught his eye, leaning against the wall by his workshop door. Every shelf, every windowsill, had its Unnameable Object on display.

The horrors returned. He might not be here to fill up his root cellar—he'd have gone off to a strange land where people were called Abercrombie. Medford sat down in the chair by the workshop door and hunched over, hugging himself, tea forgotten.

The Goatman poked his head in the door. "Wa-a-ant to see leafwork?"

Well, it was better than sitting there fretting.

At the bottom of the porch steps, the Goatman stuck the very tip of a finger into his mouth to wet it—"I'll be ca-a-areful," he said, seeing the look on Medford's face—and just barely beckoned to a red leaf lying on the ground. Medford tightened his grip on the porch railing. A thin breeze came up—he could feel it on his face. It was fresh from the sea, sweetened by the trees, and his heart lifted as if Book Learning had just ended. But his hair prickled at the same time. There was danger in a breeze—controlled for that moment but not forever.

The leaf rose into the air and twirled in a loop, following the Goatman's finger. "See?" the Goatman said. "Thi-i-is is how it's—"

Whup! Medford was flat on his back, birds screaming in the woods. He hardly knew what had hit him, the wind had come and gone so fast.

"I ha-a-ate my uncle," the Goatman remarked, splayed on the grass.

"Why was that your uncle's fault?" Medford felt the back of his head for lumps.

"Leafwork is hi-i-is idea. He says it trains the mi-i-ind."

"Doesn't it?"

"Bweh-eh-eh," the Goatman said, getting up. "Ti-i-ime for cold nutcakes."

The thought of eating anything made Medford's stomach curl up. But he followed the Goatman inside, made the tea, and sat down, cupping his mug in his hands. Part of him wanted to think about what he'd just seen but most of him was too tired.

"So," the Goatman said from the hearth rug, feeding the dog half a nutcake, "what happens toda-a-ay?"

Medford shrugged. He had to put a few coats of oil on Twig's bowl. He had to pick beans. He had to plan his life. None of it seemed important. The best thing would be to sit here and drink tea all day. All night. All week.

"Something's mi-i-issing."

Startled, Medford saw that the Goatman was narrowing his eyes at the Prudy head. He looked at it, too. Nose, chin, tucked-up braids—everything seemed to be there.

"When you stand back i-i-it doesn't really look like her."

Nose, chin, tucked-up braids. "'Tis her," Medford said. "The nose is perfect. So is the chin." Who was the Goatman to criticize, anyway?

"It ha-a-as all her parts but it is not . . . alive." The Goatman contemplated the Prudy head, chewing. "You should see my uncle sha-a-ape a cloud. It is there for just a blink but it lives."

"I don't see you shaping any clouds," Medford said, annoyance breaking through numbness. "You're finding fault with my carving because your leaf blew away."

"Leafwork i-i-is stupid."

"Even if it works?"

"It never works."

"Nothing does at first. You have to practice and then keep at it. Prudy's nose is perfect because I—" What was he saying? He was making the Unnameable sound like something Useful.

"Ma-a-aybe you should stop practicing and just do it."

This was so unfair it took Medford's breath away.

"Bweh-eh-eh. 'I ca-a-an't do it, i-i-it's not allowed,'" the Goatman continued, chanting in a high, whiny voice. Was that supposed to be Medford? "'I don't have a good na-a-ame. I don't fit i-i-in.'" The Goatman leaned forward. "Stop whi-i-impering, Fancy Carver Boy. Just do it."

Fancy Carver Boy. Stop *whimpering?*

"Tuh," Medford said, in an attempt at a scornful laugh. "Whimpering, am I?" Even his hair felt hot. "Why would that be, I wonder? Everyone finding out that I've been making Unnameable Objects since I was ten, could that be it? Or a goatman stinking up my cabin and eating up my towels and blowing me over in the wind, telling Prudy everything she's not supposed to know so she'll run back and tell Deemer Learned."

The Goatman was frozen on the rug, staring at Medford, eyes round.

Medford heard his own voice turn all windy and

grassy. "Sha-a-aping the clouds! Ca-a-alling the wonderful wi-i-ind! As if anyone could shape the clouds, especially him with his bweh-eh-eh and his arms waving around and his she-cousin who's so much better than he is. And lucky, lucky me, maybe when I'm thrown off Island because of him I could spend the rest of my life with a whole herd of smelly, lying goatmen—"

Medford ran out of breath.

In one fluid motion, impressive for a man with hooves, the Goatman hauled himself up, spun around, and hurled his mug at the window he'd broken the day before. The mug bounced off the flypaper and hit the floor, where the handle broke off.

The fact that no glass had broken seemed to infuriate the Goatman. "Bweh-eh-eh-eh," he cried to the rafters, trembling, his hands in the air. "Bweh-eh-eh-eh!" He punched out to the east, jabbed to the west, made rock-throwing motions to north and south. Various members of the wind family, sleeping among the Mainland hills and grasslands and far out to sea, jolted awake.

Whup-whup-whup. Whup! Whup! Medford slid off his chair. He huddled on the floor under the table, hands over his head. The dog rushed over and flopped down beside him. She snuggled her damp body against his side.

He'd closed all the windows the night before. There were no trees near the cabin. It would be fine.

But the world outside was screaming. Somebody huge

was stomping on the roof. There was a ripping sound as shingles lost their grip. The cabin walls shook.

Over Medford's head the two porch windows rattled, paused, exploded into the room with a shriek, glass raining on the floor, pelting the cookstove. The dog whimpered in short gasps, tried to burrow under Medford. The walking sticks fell over yet again, the shelves behind the cookstove crashed down, Unnameable Objects rollicked across the floor.

Medford grabbed the rolling pin with the eyes and held on as if it could save him.

Smoke belched into the room, blown backward down the chimney. Medford couldn't breathe, couldn't see, couldn't possibly survive, couldn't—

Whup! Silence. As it had before, the wind died, leaving behind not even a whisper. The dog's whining was the only sound.

Medford was just unfurling himself when a tremendous thud shook the ground outside. The shelf under the far windows gave way and crashed to the floor. The seashell bowl hit the floor squarely, upside down. And all was quiet again.

Medford waited on all fours for what would happen next. Nothing. He crawled out from under the table, still clutching the rolling pin.

The kitchen was a wreck. Objects, Unnameable and Useful alike, littered the floor. All the cabinet doors were open and a sack of flour had fallen over, coating the counter, the floor, and sundry objects in dusty white.

Medford sank into his chair by the window, then leaped up because of the glass shards all over it. He used his sleeve to wipe it clear and sat down again. The dog sat on his foot, possibly for companionship but more likely to avoid broken glass.

"Uh-h-h. Ow." The Goatman emerged from the other side of the cookstove, hauling himself up on his staff. He limped to the center of the room, surveying the mess.

He stared at Medford. Medford stared back. The dog waggled the tip of her tail at the Goatman but stayed on Medford's foot.

"So-o-orry."

"Me, too," Medford said without thinking.

But he wasn't sorry. He was stunned.

CHAPTER FOURTEEN

ᕯ

The Constables

Folks have been restless after them big winds, especially Cordella Weaver. Martha Shepherd volunteers to keep the peace. We think to rename her Constable.

—*Journal of Samuel Carter, 1814*

THE GOATMAN pawed at the spilled flour with a hoof. "I have a te-e-emper."

"I can see that."

"You said I sme-e-ell."

"I know. I'm sorry about that."

"I didn't know I smell."

"You probably don't notice."

"Some of it might be my robe. I spi-i-ill things on it."

"Aye."

"You said something about the . . . the na-a-appers."

"Napkins."

"You said you wa-a-ash them. We could wash my robe."

Medford considered his choices. He could stand up,

open the kitchen door, and demand that the Goatman leave Island immediately, taking the dog with him.

Well, maybe he could leave the dog.

But what would the Goatman do if Medford told him to leave? Whip up the wind until every tree was flat and Island underwater? And what would Medford do, left alone to face scandal and exile without a . . . Could you call someone a *friend* if he blew your house half into splinters?

Medford didn't have the brainpower to sort all that out at the moment. He decided to bide his time. "Aye, we could wash your robe. First let's clean up this mess."

Most of the Unnameable Objects were unharmed, although the seagull at the top of the walking stick was missing its beak and a wing tip. They found both on the floor. Medford assured the distraught Goatman that they could be glued back on.

The Book knew, he didn't want the Goatman to become agitated again.

They swept up the glass and flour. Medford nailed the shelves back up and replaced the objects on them. He decided not to paper over this batch of broken windows, at least not until nightfall. Life was bleak enough without covering up more windows.

By midday the cabin was almost back to normal. Medford, who hadn't had breakfast, was feeling hollow by then. So he and the Goatman ate nutcakes and cheese and pie, with the last of the root beer. They drank tea in silence while Medford considered whether he dared go to Town for supplies.

"Woof!"

Medford almost dropped his mug, the noise was so sharp and so loud and so startling. The dog ran to the door, which was open to let in the noontime warmth. She wagged her tail and woofed over and over, louder and louder.

"Ah," the Goatman said. "Vi-i-isitors."

Medford's stomach clenched like a fist. The Goatman went to the door to see what was going on outside. Medford didn't move. Couldn't move, to be honest.

"Woof! Woof! Woof!"

The dog kept looking up at the Goatman, wondering why he didn't do something to greet or fight off the visitors. So the Goatman did something—he stepped through the door. Encouraged, the dog bounded out, woofing, tail wagging.

"No!" Medford heard Prudy shout. "No! She's friendly!"

The dog yelped, whimpered. Then she yelped again.

"Bweh-eh-eh-eh!" the Goatman shouted.

Medford unrooted himself and rushed to the door.

The Goatman was flat on his back in the yard, struggling, Ward Constable and his brother, Bailey, holding him down. The dog cowered as Deemer Learned bore down on her, dressed as usual in his black Council robes and tricorn.

Prudy was clinging to Deemer's arm. "Let. Go," Deemer said to her. "It. Attacked." He kicked the dog in the belly so hard her paws left the ground.

"Bweh-eh-eh-eh!" the Goatman yelled at the sky.

Afterward, Medford couldn't exactly remember jumping down from the porch and rushing over to the dog. He did remember that she cringed when he went to touch her, as if she were afraid of him.

Deemer's face scared him, towering above him by half a foot, pewter eyes wide-open and furious, thin nostrils flared, skin white as birch bark, stretched so tight in places that it shone. The Councilor had his leg back, ready to kick again.

Medford balled up a fist and hit straight up, catching Deemer under his bony chin.

Pain. Pain, pain, pain, pain. Medford doubled up over his fist, gasping. It had never occurred to him that hitting someone would hurt this much or at all. He thought his hand might be broken.

Deemer staggered backward, more out of surprise than from the force of Medford's blow. Prudy, still attached to Deemer's arm, tried to hold him up but he was too tall for her and she ended up tripping him by mistake. His tricorn fell off. He squashed it when he landed flat on his back.

"Oh, Medford!" Prudy wailed, squatting down to help Deemer. "Oh no. Oh no."

The dog was gone. Medford caught sight of her white tail as it disappeared into the gloom under the trees.

A hand clapped his shoulder and he spun around to see Boyce's unhappy face.

Although Boyce seldom looked cheerful, Medford had never seen him look so pale and tired and sad. "Calm down, boy," Boyce said, giving Medford's shoulder a gentle shake. "It's over now. Better come quietly."

The Goatman was on his hooves, a terrified Constable brother on each side pinning his arms behind his back. With a firm grip, they marched him to Dexter Tanner's delivery wagon, which was waiting in the road. Dexter was on the driver's seat, avidly watching the goings-on but not rushing to participate.

"Goatman!" Medford shouted. "Hey, let him go!" He started to push past Boyce, but his foster father grabbed his arm.

"Leave them be," Boyce said.

"What are they doing?" Medford nursed his hand and watched the Constables boost the Goatman into the back of the wagon. Just hours before he had wanted the Goatman to disappear forever, but now he couldn't remember why.

"They're taking him to Town," Boyce said. "Figure out what he is and what to do with him."

"But—"

"Medford, that creature ain't *human*," Boyce said, his voice shaking. "He's got horns, by all the Names."

"He's from Mainland, Boyce," Medford said in a small voice.

"Mainland or no, he's part creature and he's got to be gone. This wind . . . half the shingles in Town are in the street. Look over there." A huge Pitch Tree had fallen across the road to the north. That must have been the thud Medford had felt after the wind died.

"Trees down all over the place between here and Town," Boyce said. "Boats washed up on the shore."

Medford tried to think of something to say.

"That fellow with the horns," Boyce said. "Deemer said he . . . calls the wind somehow."

Medford looked up at his roof. A whole section of shingles was missing.

"They're taking you to Town, too," Boyce said softly.

Medford tried to figure out how many shingles he'd need. Seven, eight maybe.

"Deemer said you've been making . . . Useless things."

He could get by with seven shingles if he spaced them out enough.

"Unnameable things, Deemer said." Boyce sounded hoarse.

Medford's gaze met Boyce's. Boyce looked down at his feet. Oddly, seeing him withdraw like that settled Medford's nerves. He felt, suddenly, that he'd been waiting all his life for trouble to come and for Boyce not to be there for him when it did. It was almost a relief not to be waiting anymore: tossed from the net. Set free.

"I'll get the Goatman's staff," Medford said. "Then I'll come."

Boyce stepped aside to let him pass.

Deemer Learned sat up, moaning, Prudy at his side. He looked up as Medford passed. His eyes were chilly and hard, as they had been the day Essence left. Prudy was as white-faced as Deemer. She didn't look at Medford as he passed.

The Goatman was sitting on the floor of the wagon, a nervous Constable on either side. The Constables were trying to stay close enough to keep the Goatman's arms immobile—Deemer must have told them how the wind got started—yet far enough away to keep his horns from whacking them in the neck. They had to keep their heads tilted to one side. *They'll have stiff necks tomorrow,* Medford thought.

The Constables were wrinkling their noses. "*Garghk,*" said Bailey, the older brother.

As Medford climbed aboard, the Goatman murmured, "He-e-ey, Fancy Fist. You have a te-e-emper, too."

Boyce climbed in to sit opposite Medford and the Constables. He avoided looking at the Goatman—especially the goat shins, Medford suspected. He dimly remembered feeling the same way about goat shins. *Was it only two days ago?*

When Deemer Learned appeared at the tailgate, his arms full of carvings, the whites showed all the way around his eyes. Unlike Boyce, he couldn't seem to look anywhere except at the Goatman.

Deemer handed the Prudy head to Boyce, who set it

down in the middle of a coil of rope. Boyce didn't hold on to the carving any longer than he had to. The Councilor handed off the seabird bowl, the rolling pin with the eyes, then the squirrel bowl. Boyce found safe spots for each of them, too.

"The Constables will come back for the rest," Deemer said. "No wonder you like to watch seabirds, Master Runyuin." He gave Medford an ill-meaning smile, then turned away. "Come, Mistress Learned."

Prudy had her hand on the tailgate, as if she would climb into the back of the wagon. But now she hesitated. Deemer climbed up onto the driver's seat next to Master Tanner. Prudy gave Boyce a wan smile—avoiding Medford's eye—and followed.

As Dexter turned the wagon toward Town, Prudy and Deemer sat up straight and stared ahead. The Councilor's black robe had a seam that ran right down the middle of his back, as unwavering as if it were nailed to a flat wall. Next to him, Prudy's braids followed the same unyielding line down her back.

The future, Medford thought, was not bright. And his hand was throbbing. He stole a glance at the Goatman. To his surprise, the Goatman appeared to be asleep, his head drooping on his chest and swinging from side to side with the motion of the wagon.

Ward and Bailey could straighten their necks but took turns being punched lightly in the chest by horn and globe. As Medford watched, Bailey gingerly touched his forefinger to the globe near him and pushed at it, trying to ease the Goatman's head toward his slightly smaller and much rounder brother.

Medford grinned. He glanced across at Boyce, thinking he'd share the joke. Boyce, however, was transfixed by the eyes on the rolling pin. He kept turning the pin in his hands as if hoping the eyes would disappear forever when they rolled out of sight.

But the eyes just kept rolling back up into view.

Boyce must have sensed that Medford was looking at him, because he put the rolling pin down next to the Prudy head, folded his hands in his lap, and examined them as if they were new to him.

Not wanting to make Boyce feel uncomfortable, Medford shifted around to face the back tailgate. Something caught his eye, off to the left. A flash of white in the trees, there for an instant, then gone.

Medford glanced around the wagon. No one else seemed to have noticed that the dog was following them.

But, amazingly, Boyce had taken the squirrel bowl onto his lap. He had the cover off and was examining the little creature curled up inside. He reached in with a long forefinger and barely touched the head, pulled his finger back as if it had bitten him. Then he just held the bowl and gazed deep like a child hunting frogs in a pond.

The trip down Main Street to Town Hall was short

but intense. Someone in a house cried out in fear; a scream echoed from a shop across the road. All the doorways were open, Islanders standing in them or just outside. Angry faces peered out of upstairs windows. Passersby stopped dead on the wooden sidewalks to gape, stony-faced. Every other roof had shingles missing and someone up on it, holding a hammer but not hammering, gawking instead at Dexter's wagon and its occupants.

Medford fought an impulse to lie down on the floorboards and hide.

"Ma!" yelled a tiny voice from a porch. "There's a man with horns!"

"Get back in here, Vernon. That's the windy man."

To Medford's surprise, the Goatman grinned. "Windy Man," he said, as if it were a compliment. If he were free to do so, the Goatman probably would be on his hooves, waving to everyone in the crowd.

Who then would be knocked over by the gale.

When the wagon stopped in front of Town Hall, Medford was the first to jump down into the road. The Constables half lowered, half assisted the Goatman until his hooves hit the dirt. Ward had to grab the Goatman by the shins at one point, his face puckered up in such an expression of fear and revulsion that Medford almost laughed.

They'd forgotten his staff. Medford retrieved it again.

As the Constables and the Goatman headed for the

Town Hall steps, the onlookers on the sidewalk backed away to make a path. A little girl wailed and hid behind her father, clinging to his legs.

Deemer Learned raised a hand as if declaiming from the Book. His jaw was purple where Medford had hit him.

"Master Runyuin's fate," he announced, "will be decided on the morrow. The Council will convene a Town Meeting, I believe. In any case, Master Runyuin and . . . and his creature shall spend the night below Town Hall."

"In the jail?" Boyce exclaimed.

"Where else, pray?" Deemer replied.

"Nowhere," Boyce said. He looked at Prudy, who looked away.

She'd had to turn him in, Medford knew that. But why wouldn't she look at him? Why wasn't she making sure he knew how sorry she was?

Maybe she wasn't sorry. How could she be, when you thought about it? She was Deemer's apprentice now. She thought what Deemer thought: that Medford didn't belong here. Boyce probably thought the same.

Medford was an inconvenience to them. Maybe even a danger now.

"Raggedy Runyuin," someone on the sidewalk said. Laughter rippled across the crowd, quickly silenced.

The Constables and the Goatman disappeared into Town Hall. Deemer followed them. Prudy turned without a word and stepped out into the road to avoid the crowd on the sidewalk. She walked away, toward her parents' house.

"Prudy!" Medford called after her. "Don't go." But he got no response, only the sight of two blond braids hanging straight as she marched away.

"Let her be, boy," Boyce said. He handed Medford the squirrel bowl. "You might as well keep this with you."

At the sight of the squirrel bowl, the Islanders in the crowd gasped and murmured and shifted their weight from foot to foot.

"Useless," Sarah Candlewright hissed.

"Unnameable," Martin Forester said, correcting her.

Medford hugged the bowl to his chest, feeling as small as when Boyce had made him start Book Learning. "It'll make an Islander of you," Boyce had said then. But he'd been wrong, hadn't he?

"Boyce," Medford said, "I'm sorry I caused trouble."

He waited for Boyce to say he was sorry Medford was going to jail. But Boyce had his head down so Medford couldn't see his eyes. He was gripping the rolling pin tight enough to leave dents in the wood.

The crowd staring, his ears burning, Medford started up the long flight of steps to the front door.

"Medford." Boyce was hoarse again. The crowd hushed.

Medford turned, five steps up. "Aye, Boyce."

"Medford." Boyce raised his head, looked Medford in

the eye. "Did I . . . ?" He gave the attentive crowd a side-long look and turned red.

"Did you what, Boyce?"

Boyce shook his head at the ground. He turned away and followed Prudy's path down the road, holding the rolling pin so his hand covered the eyes.

CHAPTER FIFTEEN

ॐ

Jail

We've got a Council to tell us what to do, and Constables to make sure we do it. Now we've got bars on the Trade storeroom in case somebody wants to take his own road. My Grandma would've had a thing or two to say about that.

—*Journal of Tansy Carver, 1824*

*I*F MEDFORD HADN'T known where the jail was he could have followed the sound.

He had just shut Town Hall's front door behind him when a series of bleats, thumps, bangs, crashes, and grunts echoed up the white-plastered stairwell.

He ran down the stairs to the cellar, the Goatman's staff in one hand and the squirrel bowl under an arm. Ward Constable was at the bottom, about to burst into tears.

"He hates it, Ragged . . . Master Runyuin," Ward said as the two of them hastened down the narrow hallway. "He struggled. Tried to bite me. Seemed like a nice enough fellow before that."

"Is he waving his arms around?" Medford stopped and listened for wind.

"Nay, Bailey has him pinned down. I said we'd tie him if he didn't calm himself."

"*Tie* him?" Medford got moving again.

"Didn't impress him much, I have to say. Canst thou control him?" Ward looked so hopeful Medford didn't have the heart to answer.

The hallway was crowded with barrels and crates and piles of baskets, Island goods destined for the next Mainland Trade. A door at the end opened onto a ramp up to Harbor Lane, which led to the Trade Wharf. Trade goods typically were stored in the jail cell, but the Constables must have cleared it out.

Harmony Weaver's baskets were scattered all over the floor.

"See?" Ward picked up a basket. "His hooves were everywhere. He tried to walk up the wall." He set the basket on a crate marked TOWN RECORDS—NOT FOR TRADE and gave the crate an angry kick.

The jail cell was three-quarters the size of Medford's kitchen. It was in a back corner of the cellar, and had a barred window in each of the two outside walls. The windows were open to let in the breeze off the harbor. The cell walls were whitewashed, the floor swept. Wooden benches lined the walls. The room was almost pleasant.

Or would have been, if there hadn't been a writhing,

bawling heap of Constable and Goatman in the middle of the floor. Bailey had his beefy arms around the Goatman, who was trying to butt him in the head, bite him on the wrist, and kick him in the shins.

"Bweh-eh-eh-eh!" the Goatman kept bleating.

Medford squatted in front of the squirming figure. "Goatman," he said. "Goatman. Stop. Hark to me. Goatman. Listen. Goatman."

"Bw-ee-eee," the Goatman said, arching his back and straining against Bailey's arms. "I will not sta-a-ay in a hole."

"This isn't a hole. 'Tis a room, just like my kitchen."

"They will"—the Goatman writhed and kicked—"lock me i-i-in."

"I'll be here, too. We can look out the window."

"Looking . . . is . . . not . . . be-e-eing."

"'Twon't be long. By tomorrow night we'll either be free or—"

Unexpectedly, the Goatman went limp. "I wa-a-ant this flatfoot to unha-a-and me," he said in a low voice.

"You have to calm yourself," Medford said. "You have to promise not to do anything . . . windy."

The Goatman grinned. "Windy Man," he said.

"Aye. But not now."

The Goatman looked Medford in the eye. "One day," the Goatman said. "I will sta-a-ay one day and then . . . I don't know wha-a-at."

"We'll take it," Bailey said. He dropped his arms.

"I need my sta-a-aff," the Goatman said, stretching his arms and flexing his fingers. Medford handed it to him. The Goatman got up and dusted himself off as if the floor were dirtier than his robe.

Bailey got to his feet. "Well," he said. "That was something."

"Thankee, Raggedy," Ward said.

"We'll leave ye now, young fella," Bailey said. "We'll be right upstairs today and down there at the end of the hallway tonight. And we'll bring supper from Cook's."

"No meat for him," Medford said. "No eggs. He eats cheese and vegetables and bread and honey, so far."

Bailey nodded with the air of a man used to surprises, his square, ruddy face expressionless. "You eat flesh, though," he said to Medford.

"Aye. I eat everything."

"C'mon, Ward," Bailey said. "Ward . . . hey, what ye doin' there?"

Ward was on the bench, the cover of the squirrel bowl in his hand. He peered into the bowl, poking the sleeping squirrel to see if he could make it move.

"Ward," Bailey said. "Leave that be. Let's go."

Ward looked up at Medford, eyes like an owl's. "'Tis real?"

"No," Medford said. "I carved it."

"By the Book, young fella," Ward said, "that's some carving."

"Ward," Bailey said. "*Now.*"

Ward patted Medford's arm on his way to the door. "That's some carving, young fella," he whispered. He stared in at Medford as Bailey clanged the barred door shut.

Up to this point Medford had been calm . . . numb, really. But watching Bailey lock the door, he suddenly understood why the Goatman had writhed so.

"Bailey," he croaked. "Master Constable, I mean. We'll stay right here, I promise. Does the door have to be locked?"

"We never put Clayton Baker in jail that time, Bailey," Ward said.

Bailey made a show of arranging the keys on their ring. "Aye," he said, not looking up. "But you saw that crowd, Ward. 'Tis safer this way."

Ward nodded and, with a final wink at Medford, followed Bailey down the hall.

The Goatman lowered himself onto the floor in the corner. "I don't li-i-ike this."

"It talks!" screamed a voice from the window.

"Bweh-eh-eh!" the Goatman cried, cowering.

Medford stumbled backward and fell onto a hard wooden bench.

The windows were dark with faces peering in: Arvid and Fordy, Hazel Forester and her aunt, Irma Cobbler. *That's who screamed*, Medford thought.

"Make it talk again, Raggedy," said Martin Forester, wedging his face between Arvid and Fordy.

"No-o-o," Irma moaned. "I can't stand to hear it." Her face disappeared and Medford heard her shout, "Come 'ere, Violet! The thing talks!"

Murmuring arose outside, as if a large crowd were gathering. People took turns squatting down to peer in— except for Arvid, who clung to the bars like a Merchant to a Trade token. "Run-you-in," he said, leering, "mayhap we'll run you out now. Pa says thou almost killed Master Learned. And the horned man butted Ward till he bled."

"Bweh-eh-eh," the Goatman protested, and everybody screamed.

"And lookit that wooden thing there," Irma Cobbler said, pointing at the squirrel bowl. "Did you ever see anything so Unnameable?"

"Why wait for Town Meeting?" Martin said. "Let's send Medford away now."

"I ain't taking nobody out on the water at this hour," Violet Waterman said.

"Who needs a boat?" said a pair of feet. "Let 'em swim for it."

"All right, folks, all right," a new voice said. "Go home now."

"That boy blew down my grandpa's Tanningbark Tree," a pair of feet protested.

"Don't care what he did. 'Tain't right, worrying at a prisoner like this," Bailey said. "Go home and come back tomorrow, see if there's a meeting."

"There'll be a meeting," Hazel said. "Won't there, Auntie Irma?"

"Get going now, folks," Ward said. "Enough is enough."

Arvid's face disappeared, and the others. Soon all the feet were gone.

"Sorry about that, boy!" Bailey called through the window. "They're gone now. We'll keep an eye out so they don't come back."

"Thanks, Bailey," Medford called back. Ward's face appeared in the window. "Thanks, Ward."

"Nothing to it," Ward said. "You rest up now, young Raggedy." He disappeared.

"Bweh-eh-eh," the Goatman said. "That was scary."

"Aye." Medford sank down on the wooden bench. "'Twas."

"Who sa-a-ays I butted tha-a-at fla-a-atfoot until he bled?" When he was nervous, Medford noticed, the Goatman got a lot more goatish.

"Dexter Tanner said it, I guess. The man who drove the wagon. He tells . . . tales."

"Lies, you mean. So he's na-a-amed for what he does? Is a ta-a-anner a lie?"

Medford snorted. "No. But maybe it should be." He decided not to tell the Goatman about tanned hides and where they came from.

"Heh. You could sit around the fi-i-ire and te-e-ell each

other tanners." The Goatman took off his sash and began to polish his horns with it. "Bweh-eh. Wha-a-at will ha-a-appen now?"

Medford tried to get his thoughts unraveled. It was hard to think past those faces at the bars, those harsh voices. "Well, I guess we'll be in here overnight and tomorrow there will be a Town Meeting. And everyone will talk about my carvings and your . . . your winds. And then they'll probably send us away to Mainland, forever."

The Goatman stiffened in midpolish. "Who's the-e-ey? Those fla-a-atfoots in the window?"

"No, the Council of Names. There be five Councilors."

"Councilors."

"Aye. They read the Book and tell us what's in it. And they listen to what people think about things and then decide what to do."

"Why do the-e-ey get to do tha-a-at?"

"We vote for them. And then they're Councilors until they get tired or die."

"They will ma-a-ake me leave?"

"Aye, I think so. Why do you care? 'Tis not your home." Medford's throat tightened. "'Tis mine."

"I ca-a-annot go home ye-e-et," the Goatman said. "Even if I wa-a-ant to."

"Why can't you go home?"

"I ha-a-ave not learned enough. I cannot control the wi-i-ind."

Medford thought he understood. "All that story about being on a ramble . . . They sent you away because of your wind troubles, didn't they?"

The Goatman gave Medford a very goatish look. "This i-i-is my ramble. But they didn't let me choose where to go. My uncle said I should come to thi-i-is place because you are . . . unwindy."

"Unwindy?"

"Locked up, controlling everything. I would do better if I learned some of tha-a-at, he said." The Goatman sighed. "It ha-a-as helped before, the Old Goats say. But the wi-i-inds here are so strong, I can't work them."

"Perhaps if you calmed down. The Book says to take deep breaths."

The Goatman's eyebrows went up in peaks again.

"No, no, 'tis easy," Medford said. "See . . . breathe in, hold it, let it go. That's right. Think of something you like. Nutcakes, grass tunes."

The Goatman put his head back and breathed loud. He sounded like a collapsing pile of rocks. "*A-a-ah-hhhh*"—pause—"*hoo-oo-oo. A-a-ah-hhh . . . hoo-oo-oo.*"

A hand grasped a bar in the cell door. "Is that his language?" Earnest asked. "I never heard him talk like that."

"He's calming himself," Medford said. "Hullo, Earnest. Did you see that crowd?"

"Aye. I saw it." Earnest pressed his cheek against the bars as if he could bend them to get his head into the cell. "Hullo-o-o!" he called to the Goatman, in a voice the Fishers probably could hear. "How fare ye?"

The Goatman blinked up at him. "How fa-a-are . . . ?"

"Just say, 'Well. I fare well,'" Medford said.

The Goatman hauled himself up onto his hooves and bowed. "I fa-a-are well."

Earnest turned to Medford. "How fare ye?" he asked.

"I'm well enough now. I thank thee, Earnest."

Silence fell. Earnest stood there holding on to the bars, staring in at the Goatman's horns as if seeing them for the first time. "Prudy is upset," he said at last.

"So I should hope," Medford said.

"She told Pa about your carvings last night, and he told her not to say anything. She went to see Deemer Learned this morning. She didn't tell Pa she was going."

Twig let Prudy become a Learned, and then he wanted her to keep an Unnameable secret? *How strange*, Medford thought.

"I don't think she slept," Earnest said. "I heard her pacing her room at midnight."

"What did Twig say to her?"

"Who's Twi-i-ig? Who's Pa-a-a?"

"They're both Prudy's father," Medford said.

"Two na-a-ames? He has *two* na-a-ames?"

"Twig is his name," Medford said. "Pa is what . . . what someone calls his father."

"I see," the Goatman said, brow furrowed.

"What did Twig tell Prudy?" Medford asked Earnest again.

"She wouldn't say. They were closeted for more than an hour. He got loud once, said, 'Life is not so simple, Prudy.'"

"Did she say what Master Learned told her?"

"Nay, just that he was angry. He scared her, his eyes were so . . . bright, she said, and he made her feel cold."

Earnest stopped to ponder, then continued: "That big wind came just as she arrived at his house, and it knocked her over. Shingles everywhere, and she heard a tree fall. Councilor Learned came out and she told him about the Goatman. She hadn't meant to."

"So she believes after all," Medford said. "About the Goatman calling the wind."

"Aye, guess she does now. And she said Master Learned went all white and had to sit down. 'Horned man,' he kept saying. 'Horned man.' She stayed with him awhile for fear he might fall into a fit. But when she left him he was talking of the Constables."

Medford stared at his feet. He'd known Prudy had told on him, but hearing it confirmed was unexpectedly depressing.

Earnest dragged the TOWN RECORDS crate next to the door and sat down on it. "Wisht you weren't in there, Medford. Nothing in the Archives prepared me for this—I don't remember anything about carving small beasts." He contemplated the squirrel bowl as if he could take it apart. "Course, Master Learned was careful what he let me read."

"Wha-a-at's archives?"

"Books," Earnest said. "There's a record of every Council meeting. And there are shelves and shelves of journals, starting with the Originals but going right through the centuries. Some were written by people who just died a little while ago."

"What di-i-id they write about?"

"Oh, the weather, the tides. Same as my pa does now. What they did that day. 'Tisn't that interesting." He contemplated the door frame, seeking inspiration. "Essence got to read things I didn't. I heard her laughing once. Master Learned didn't like it."

Earnest poked at the plaster in the door frame, wearing the stony look he got when he or anyone else mentioned Essence. A chunk of plaster fell to the floor.

"Why do you think she was banished?" Medford asked quietly. He'd never dared discuss this with Earnest.

Earnest pulled his finger away and watched a second chunk of plaster hit the floor. "No one would tell me anything," he said, as if the plaster were all that mattered. "Pa said he tried to find out but . . . Well, I guess he gave up."

He brushed his finger against his trouser leg to get the plaster dust off. "Anyways, I always figured it was because of something she saw in the Archives."

CHAPTER SIXTEEN

☙

Stinky Returns

'Tis a Parent's duty to foster Healthy Growth in a child, providing Example and Instruction in How to Benefit Society.

> —*A Frugall Compendium of Home Arts and Farme Chores by Capability C. Craft (1680), as Amended and Annotated by the Island Council of Names (1718–1809)*

Medford felt his brain was expanding too fast. He and Prudy had been so busy wondering what Essence had done, it had never occurred to them that the problem might have been what she knew.

What could Essence have seen that was serious enough to banish her? How could anything surprise a Learned? Hadn't they been steeped in the Archives from childhood?

Could there be other journals like Cordella Weaver's?

"What do you think she read up there, Earnest?"

Earnest managed to pluck out a chunk of plaster, which he examined with interest. "Not enough horsehair," he said, holding it out to Medford. "See how it—"

"Earnest."

"Oh, I don't know what she read, Medford. More than sunsets and tides, anyways. Somebody wrote something her pa doesn't want us to know, that's all."

"Good notion, son," said a voice down the hall. "Mind you keep it to yourself."

"Aye, Pa," Earnest said. "Same as always." He held out the chunk of plaster as Twig sauntered into view, hands in the pockets of his knee breeches. "See this?"

Twig took the chunk and examined it at nose-length. "Not enough horsehair," he said. He crumbled the plaster in his fingers, then noticed the dust and plaster bits on the floor around the crate Earnest was sitting on. "Planning a jailbreak?" he asked his son. "Hullo in there, Medford. How fare ye?"

"Well enough, Twig, thanks. What's a jailbreak?"

"Did I say *jailbreak*?" Twig winced. "I meant . . . Oh, the Book, Medford, 'tis just a Mainland word I heard on the radio one time. Fellow got away from a prison, that's all. Kind of a Useless word for us . . . well, Useless in normal times."

He shook the door to see if it really was locked. It was. His head twitched as if he were bothered by an insect. Then he caught sight of the Goatman huddled in the corner and stood there with his hand still wrapped around the bar, lost for words.

The Goatman grabbed his staff and pulled himself

to his hooves, got his balance, and bowed. "I am a goat-ma-a-an . . . ," he began.

Twig held up his hand to stop him. "I know what thou art. How . . . how fare ye?"

"I fa-a-are well," the Goatman said, beaming.

"Pa," Earnest said, "why don't you ever let me say what I think about Essence?"

Twig leaned his shoulder against the door frame, got out his pocketknife, and became interested in working a wood splinter out of his thumb. He gave no sign that he'd heard Earnest, but Medford knew he had.

In the silence, dockside chatter floated through the cell windows. "Tie 'er up good 'n' tight," Medford heard. "Case we get another of them big blows."

Twig worked the splinter out and flicked it away. He closed up his knife and stowed it in his pocket.

"Pa," Earnest said.

Medford sat down on the bench next to the squirrel bowl. The Goatman lowered himself back down to the floor.

"I heard you, son," Twig said. "And I don't have an answer for you."

"But—"

"I keep telling you, boy—I don't know what happened to Essence. Deemer said he was following the Book and that's all he'll say. If a person was to have a hunch he'd keep it to himself for the time being, especially around anybody named Learned."

Anybody like Prudy, Medford thought.

"That's what you always say," Earnest said. "You always say to keep things to myself. And 'tis always for the time being."

Twig grabbed a bar in the door and leaned back, straightening his arm to let the bar take his weight. Swinging a little, he regarded his son. "No sense starting a hurlyburly unless thou hast an end in view, boy. Bide thy time now, that's all I can tell thee."

He let go of the bar and did a controlled totter backward to get his balance. Then he bent over to peer at the large square lock on the door. "Mmm. Must be one of them big iron keys in the Constables' room. Surprised it hasn't rusted up."

He looked his son in the eye. "We'll know soon enough what Essence saw, boy. Someone's certain to find out sooner or later. Need anything, Medford? Food? Drink?"

"The Constables will bring something, thankee, Twig." Medford felt let down—he'd been hoping Twig would say something about Prudy and how she'd betrayed him.

Maybe Twig didn't know she had.

Twig gave his son's shoulder a friendly slap and nodded to the Goatman. "Pleased to make your acquaintance," he said. "Fare well."

"I fa-a-are well," the Goatman said.

Earnest watched his father walk down the hallway. They heard Twig mount the stairs. "So," Earnest said, "we need a jailbreak."

"What?"

"You heard him. A jailbreak."

"He didn't mean—"

"Aye, that's exactly what he meant. You know Pa. He doesn't tell you what to do—wisht he would sometimes, but that's Pa. He just says a few things and walks away."

"But what did he say? I didn't hear him say anything."

"He said people break out of jail sometimes and where the key is. And that he thinks Essence saw something upstairs that made Deemer send her away. And he said someone—that's us—will find out what it was."

"Your father would never send us to do that. If he wanted it done, he'd do it."

Earnest just looked at Medford, a half smile on his face.

"Anyways," Medford said, feeling desperate, "how will that help me?"

"Don't know. Don't think Pa knows. Guess we'll find out."

"Earnest." Medford got up and grabbed two bars in the door, thrusting his nose between them. "You want to steal the key, let us out, and go up to the Archives? When is all this going to happen?"

"Tonight. Got to—Town Meeting tomorrow."

"Earnest. How are we going to get the key? The Constables will be right there."

Earnest pondered. Then he got up and flipped open the lock on the door to Harbor Lane. He worked the door back and forth until it stopped creaking. "I'll be back," he said. He stepped outside.

"Earnest, wait." Medford thrust his hand through the bars in a hapless attempt to stop his friend. Earnest ignored him and pulled the door shut.

He was gone. To do . . . who knew what?

Medford sat down, hugged the squirrel bowl to his chest. It was good to have his hands on something familiar, something that remembered his workshop and the sparkling sea out the window.

"You all ri-i-ight, Fretting Boy?"

"This is Uselessness," Medford said. "This is insanity."

"I don't understa-a-and about the Archives yet. But your friends are sma-a-art."

"There are so many things that can go wrong." Medford set the bowl down so he could count on his fingers. "One, we have to get the key out from under the Constables' noses. Two, everything has to happen in the dark and there's no moon tonight. So three, we need a lamp. Four, Deemer lives behind Town Hall and all he has to do is look out his window and he'll see that there's a light in the Archives. Five . . ."

"What's a la-a-amp?"

Oh, the Book. "You saw lamps at my house. At night, after supper, I lighted them when we sat by the stove to talk. You said they smelled funny." *Look who's talking,* Medford had thought at the time.

"Oh, those things. Very pretty, but I don't under-sta-a-and why you need them. All they do is smell bad and make it bla-a-ack outside."

"They don't make it black outside. It gets black all by itself and you light them so you can . . ." *Wait a minute.* "What do your people use to light up the dark?"

"What's da-a-ark?"

"Dark. When the sun goes down. The world gets . . . black."

"No, it doesn't." The Goatman was patient, instructing a child. "Well, it does in the ci-i-ity and at your house because you light . . . la-a-amps, and they make your eyes squint. I've seen it at home when we have a fi-i-ire. It looks black near the walls of the shelter when the fire's bla-a-az-ing, but not when it burns down."

"You can see in the dark," Medford said. "Like a night creature."

"I can see at night. Not in the da-a-ark, but it only gets da-a-ark when you light—"

"You can see at night." Medford chewed his lower lip, thinking. "This helps."

"You will ha-a-ave to show me how."

"We cannot see at night. That's why we light lamps. The night is . . . black for us without them."

"That's just a ta-a-ale."

"Nay, 'tis true. If there be no moon to guide us, we need a light."

"Ah," the Goatman said. "I wi-i-ill be the moon."

"Aye," Medford said, feeling ceremonial. "Thou wilt be the moon."

For some reason, this minor bit of good news lightened Medford's heart. There was still the problem of how to get the key, plus the fact that they didn't know what they were looking for and had only one night to find it.

But he'd leave all that to the stars. Or to Earnest.

The sun was dropping toward the sea when the Constables returned. The covered basket Ward was carrying smelled so enticing that Medford, who had thought he'd never enjoy anything ever again, found himself looking forward to whatever was in it.

Bailey unlocked the cell door. As Twig had guessed, the key was made of iron and was huge, about six inches long. The lock was squeaky. The cell door screeched halfway open.

Supper proved to be one of Myrtle Cook's Beef Creature pies, with rolls by her husband, Clayton Baker, plus late green beans and a flask of root beer. The Constables brought in blankets and an oil lamp.

The Goatman saw the lamp and smirked at Medford.

"Ye can bed down on the floor," Bailey said, setting the

lamp on a bench. "Floor's clean, I think." He bent over and scrutinized it. "Aye. 'Tis fine."

He shut the windows. "I brought extra blankets, because there ain't much heat. We got a stove down in our room and we'll stoke it up and leave the door open, but I guess nobody ever thought about someone sleeping in the cell in cold weather."

Or didn't care if the prisoners were cold, Medford thought.

"Thankee, Bailey," he said. "We'll be comfortable, I'm sure. My thanks, Ward." He tried not to mind when Bailey locked the cell door again.

Comfortable wasn't quite the word for their situation. But they made nests for themselves out of the blankets and they ate every scrap of the food. The Goatman ate the napkins. Medford caught himself saving some of the pie for the dog, then remembered that she wasn't around. So he ate it.

"Don't worry about her," the Goatman told Medford. "She wa-a-as on her own when I met her. She'll be fi-i-ine."

"I hope she wasn't hurt," Medford said. "And she isn't afraid of us now."

"She's smarter than tha-a-at," the Goatman said.

"I think I saw her running through the woods as we came to Town."

"I sa-a-aw her, too."

"You were asleep."

"I was thinking. And trying to hit those me-e-en with my horns."

"What were you thinking about?"

"How to escape. If I wa-a-anted to."

"You didn't even try."

"I wanted to see what would ha-a-appen. I was sorry when they put me in here but then it was too la-a-ate."

"This will make quite a tale."

"Bweh-eh-eh. My cousin never got put in . . . what is this ca-a-alled?"

"Jail."

"Jail. My cousin ne-e-ever was in jail."

Medford watched the Goatman pummel his blankets into a shape he liked. The question was out of his mouth before his brain knew anything about it. "What is it like, calling the wind?"

"How would I know?" the Goatman said. "I don't do it ri-i-ight."

"You call it and it comes. What is that like?"

The Goatman closed his eyes. "I feel it—the ca-a-all-ing—and it gets strong and it fetches the wind so fast I can't tell it what to do."

"But what does it feel like, this . . . calling?"

"A whoosh. A zoom," the Goatman said. "A whiz. A fweeee."

"You don't have a word for it?"

"You mean a na-a-ame?"

"A word doesn't have to be a name. You have words for *shelter* and *dog* and . . ." It occurred to Medford that he didn't have a word for that buzz or hum he felt when he saw shapes in the wood. He wouldn't think about that. "So you need to slow it down and . . . and command it, this . . . this whoosh."

"Te-e-ell me something I don't know," the Goatman said, giving the blankets another punch.

"'Tis a matter of practice and discipline, I'll be bound. Work on it a little each day . . ." He sounded like New Prudy. "And . . . and take deep breaths."

"*Aaahhhh-hoooo,*" the Goatman said.

"Maybe not right now," Medford said.

The windows darkened. The Constables came back for the basket and said their good nights. Medford could hear them rustling and thumping at the other end of the hall. Then all was silent. Medford turned the lamp down low so the Goatman's eyes would have an easier time adjusting to the dark when Earnest came back. *If* Earnest came back.

Medford had almost dozed off when he heard a creak out in the hallway. Then a whisper, saying something he couldn't catch. Something white scuttled past the cell, having slipped through the door from the harbor. It headed toward the Constables' room.

Medford caught a whiff of something. Something indescribably terrible, more terrible than anything he'd ever smelled before. Something dead, perhaps.

Something dead quite a long time. Dead in chunks. With a hint of seaweed.

Medford breathed through his mouth, afraid he'd gag. The ramp door was open a crack—he could hear water lapping against the docks outside, feel cold air seeping into the cell.

Then down the hallway came the sound of two large Constables surprised by a smell and retching as one. "*Gargh,*" Medford heard. "*Ohgg,* Bailey, what . . ."

"There, Ward! See, it's white, there . . . no, there . . . Oh, the Book, it's up the stairs."

Heavy feet pounded on the stairs. Four paws' worth of toenails skittered down the hallway overhead. He ran to the cell door. The harbor door banged open and Earnest pelted down the hall. He was back in an instant, hands full of keys.

"That one," Medford said, pointing.

Earnest unlocked the door, not worrying about the creak from the lock. Then he dashed back down the hallway to return the keys. Judging by the diminishing noises overhead, Medford thought the dog had led the Constables up another flight to the auditorium.

Freed from its latch, the cell door swung open. Medford stepped into the hall, uncertain what to do. "Earnest," he hissed.

From behind, someone shoved a strip of leather into his hand. "Lock the harbor door after us and tie the cell door shut," Prudy whispered.

Earnest was back, panting. Brother and sister hustled out the door. "Prudy," Medford whispered. "The Goatman can see in the dark. That'll help, won't—"

"Sssshhh. We'll be back."

And Prudy and Earnest were gone.

CHAPTER SEVENTEEN

❧

Up to the Archives

Funny to think that, thanks to the Learneds and their Archives, future generations may read this journal. Future generations of Learneds, I suppose. What's the Use of anybody else reading about dead people?

—*Journal of Honey Cook, 1905*

T HE CONSTABLES never did catch the dog. They had to content themselves with opening Town Hall's front door and driving her outside, shutting the door behind her with a bang.

In the jail cell, Medford and the Goatman huddled under their blankets. When Bailey came down the hall to check on them, Medford snored a couple of times. Bailey pulled at the harbor door, said, "Hunh," and tested the door into the cell. Everything held. The leather thong was invisible in the dim light, tucked under the latch in the cell door.

"Don't know how that Herding Creature got in here," Medford heard Bailey say, back down the hall. "Door's locked. Cell's locked. Medford didn't even wake up. Everything all right in here?"

"'Cept for the stink."

"Open the window a minute. Then I'm going to sleep. Tomorrow's a big day."

Medford lay there for what seemed like an hour while the Constables creaked around. Finally he heard the thumps and squeaks of two large men snuggling down on wooden cots that weren't quite strong enough. The Constables began to snore like summer thunder.

Medford turned the lamp off completely.

The Goatman might have been asleep, too. He didn't exactly snore, but every breath had a distinct life cycle. The rhythm of his breathing, combined with the snores from down the hall, began to get on Medford's nerves as the night darkened.

He wanted to doze off but his mind kept gnawing on one thought: *Prudy*. At daybreak she was telling Deemer Learned about Medford's carvings. At midday she was accompanying Medford to Town with two straight braids down her back. At nightfall she was helping him escape from jail.

Summoning the wind would be easier than figuring this out.

Was Prudy his friend again? Maybe. Would she remain his friend? Maybe not. He couldn't trust her; he had to keep reminding himself of that. She was a Learned. So why had Earnest gotten her involved? And why had she agreed to join them?

Maybe she just wanted to know what they were up to so she could tell Deemer.

Medford was overcome by longing for Old Prudy chewing on a braid, collecting shells. For simpler days, when he knew who hated him and thought he knew who didn't.

But he was feeling something else, he realized, something almost like hope. He didn't know what was in the Archives or how it would help him, but at least he wasn't just sitting there waiting for his boat to Mainland.

What in all the Names does Prudy think she's doing?

The fretting and puzzling finally exhausted him. He was almost asleep when he didn't quite hear—just sensed, in a jangled-nerve kind of way—that someone was outside one of the cell windows. A fingernail tapped against the glass.

Medford eased to the window, freezing every time a floorboard creaked, listening for any change in snoring volume. The only light was from the stars, faint and gray.

He opened the window an inch. Earnest's whisper floated in, barely audible. "Prudy says let us in the front door."

"Wha-a-at . . . ," the Goatman said.

"Hissshhh," Medford said. He eased his way to the cell door, stumbling over blankets, felt for the leather knot, and picked at it, wishing he hadn't pulled it so tight. The hand he'd used to punch Deemer was stiff, although it no longer ached.

He heard a light *clip, creak, clip.*

"Let me-e-e," the Goatman whispered.

Undoing the knot probably was easier if you could see it and had long yellow nails. Sure enough, the leather strip fell to the ground and the cell door swung inward. Medford stopped it with his hand before it could squeak. "Give me your sash," he breathed.

He bunched up their blankets as best he could, hoping they'd look like sleeping bodies if one of the Constables came by to check. He arranged the Goatman's sash to look as if it had flopped out from under the covers.

He eased back to the Goatman. "Go slow," he whispered. "Watch for squeaky floorboards. I'll hang on to you."

He grabbed a handful of robe. The cloth felt thick and stiff, yet oddly soft on the surface. When they were in the hallway, Medford tied the door closed with the leather strip. They inched down the hall past the piles of Trade goods. Medford leaned by mistake into a stack of baskets, felt it sway. He steadied the pile and breathed again.

When they neared the Constables' room, the Goatman slowed their pace even more. Not that they needed to worry. The Constables snored together, not missing a beat: *SNO-O-ORE-snork SNO-O-ORE-snork SNO-O-*

ORE-snork. On the stairs Medford and the Goatman matched their gait to the snores, taking a step when they were louder, waiting through the softer noise, moving when the noise got loud again.

Medford flipped the front door lock on a loud snore so Prudy and Earnest could slip in. "The Goatman leads," Medford whispered. "We hang on to one another in a line."

"Medford," Prudy whispered.

"Shhh," Medford said, and turned away. Let her face an unfriendly back for a change. He took a handful of purple robe, felt Prudy grab the back of his sweater. The hooved leading the blind, they inched toward the staircase to the second floor.

It was a slow, tortured climb up that flight of stairs, down the hallway outside the auditorium, up another flight. Finally they were on the third floor, the Archives door to their right at the head of the stairs. They huddled there, staring at what they could see of the doorknob, a Mainland metal import gleaming dully in the starlight from the stairwell window.

"Is it locked?" Medford whispered.

"Aye," Prudy said. "But there's a key." She swished her hand down the doorjamb. "Oh, the Book. There's a nail to hang the key on, but 'tis empty." She rattled the doorknob but it wouldn't budge.

"I'll have to take it apart," Earnest whispered.

"In the dark?" Medford asked.

"Aye." Earnest sounded as if he'd been waiting all day just for this chance.

"Oh, the Book," Prudy said again. But they didn't have much choice. Medford, Prudy, and the Goatman stood there trying not to creak, hardly breathing. They heard Earnest fumbling around in his pocket, the *tick-tick-chink* of a miniature screwdriver on metal, the *gnarl-gnarl-gnarl* of screws being unscrewed. Earnest kept handing things to Medford and Prudy—screws, faceplates, lock innards— and they tried to place all of them in a neat pile in the corner. Who knew, maybe they'd want to put the lock back together.

At last it was all over. Earnest pushed the door open with just a tiny squeak of the hinges and they stepped inside the Archives. There were holes in the door where the lock used to be.

Medford was conscious first of a deadness in the air. His hearing seemed to have dulled, as if something were soaking up the sound. He knew, suddenly, that he was in the presence of paper, a great deal of paper. More paper than he'd ever experienced in his life. He smelled dust, dry mold, time. Faint, gray light came from three windows, one just inside the door and two at the far end of the room.

And then he had a terrible thought, a thought so startling that he almost cried out. *The Goatman can see in the dark, aye. But can he read?* How could he have been so stupid? Why hadn't he thought about this? What, oh what, would New Prudy say?

But maybe she'd known this would happen. Maybe she had her hand over her mouth even then, stifling her laughter at Medford's incompetence. *Show not thy Mirth.*

The starlight . . . wobbled or something. A human shape showed briefly against the gray rectangle of window nearest him. Another shape appeared in one of the windows at the other end of the room. He couldn't make out what the shapes were doing. The rectangles disappeared. A dark human shape appeared at the second window on the far wall. That rectangle vanished, too.

Medford was giddy, floating in the dark. He concentrated on the floor under his feet, not sure he could keep his balance with nothing to look at. He held his hand up before his nose and could see no glimmer of flesh.

A match snapped. Earnest appeared, golden and flickering. He was lighting a large oil lamp.

By lamplight Medford saw that the room's three windows had heavy brown blankets covering them.

"No sense trying to read in the dark," Prudy said briskly, her voice low.

She kept her wits about her, he had to give her that.

They were in a large attic room with sloped ceilings. It was lined with bookshelves, not one of them completely full. Additional freestanding shelves dotted the room, but

Medford couldn't see why they were necessary—all of them had large gaps, too.

The books on the shelves were thin, a foot tall, bound in brown leather or pasteboard. They looked like Boyce's journal. And Cordella Weaver's. Did Prudy think about Cordella when she was up here in this musty room all day, reading, reading, reading?

A long table stretched down the center of the room, lined with oil lamps, ink bottles, reams of soft and yellowish paper, and trays full of dipping pens. Straight-backed chairs were arranged along the table, four to a side.

In a far corner was a comparatively cozy nook, furnished with a desk, a lamp, and a wooden armchair. Whoever had put up the bookshelves had left space for a wall clock and its pendulum. The clock's ticking was barely audible, muffled like every other sound in that room.

"Now," Prudy said briskly, "these shelves here against the wall are the 1900s. The 1800s are over there, but I haven't read any of them yet. Those are the 1700s at the back of the room. Earnest, what color were the books Essence read, mostly?"

"What color?"

"Aye." Prudy smiled in a superior way. She was enjoying this. "Red or brown?"

Earnest screwed his face up like a Pickler tasting brine. "Red, I think."

"These here." Prudy bustled over to the corner where the desk was. The books on those shelves did seem to be red. "These are the very oldest. Light this lamp, Earnest."

"Thi-i-is book looks good," the Goatman said. He picked up a journal and ripped a page from it, stuffed it into his mouth.

"No!" Medford and Prudy yelled, then clapped their hands over their mouths.

"Books aren't to eat, Goatman," Prudy said, taking the journal away from him.

"They're words on paper," Medford said. "I thought you knew all about them."

"Not a-a-all about them," the Goatman said, sounding grumpy. "I don't know why you don't eat them. Or why you put the words on pa-a-aper in the first place."

"The people who wrote these books are dead, but we can still read what they wanted to tell us," Prudy said.

The Goatman looked slightly impressed. "Wha-a-at did they want to tell you?"

"We don't know," Medford said. "That's why we came up here to read."

"I can read," the Goatman said. "*Walk.* And *Yield.* I don't li-i-ike that one." He paused for thought. "*No Left Turn.*"

Medford didn't know what any of that meant. But it occurred to him that the only thing worse than reading in a hurry would be reading in a hurry with a bored

Goatman trying to sneak a bite. "Would you keep watch outside the door?" he asked the Goatman.

The Goatman picked up a stack of paper from the table. "Ma-a-ay I take this?"

"Of course," Prudy said. "Wouldst thou take a pen? Ink?"

"I don't know." The Goatman bit into the paper, chewed it thoughtfully. "Is it be-e-etter with ink?"

CHAPTER EIGHTEEN

Jeremiah Comstock

My heart aches for my Dear Son, who hates to Weave. I
try to interest him with Colours, but must not waste Time
gathering Berries when Common Stuff will do.
—*Journal of Hester (Comstock) Weaver, 1723*

WITH THE GOATMAN comfortably set up at the
head of the stairs, Medford returned to find Earnest studying the red journals in the corner by the desk.
He was shaking his head. "Where are they all?" he asked
Prudy.

"What dost thou mean?"

"These shelves were full when I was up here," he said,
sticking a hand into an empty space as if to make sure it
was really empty. "Half of the books are missing now."

"'Tis the way it's been since I've been coming up here,"
Prudy said.

Earnest surveyed the room. "There are journals missing everywhere."

"Where are they?" Medford asked, squatting down to
look under the long table.

Earnest snorted. "You won't find them under there. He's taken them away."

"He would not do such a thing, Earnest," Prudy said, fists on hips, braids straight. "These journals are precious, Master Learned says. This is Island's history."

"Oh, very precious," Earnest said. "Like *Rose afore dawn, planted peas?*"

"Aye, every single word." Prudy's voice rose. "How darest thou suggest that Master Learned—"

"Shhh," Medford said.

"'Tis just as I thought, Prudy," Earnest whispered furiously. "'Tis plain as Baker's bread—Essence read something he doesn't want anyone else to see. So he got rid of what she read and then he got rid of her."

Prudy looked like she might cry. "But I'm the only one who ever comes up here. He would trust me."

"Oh, aye? Have you read about anything other than planting and harvesting? Ah, beg pardon, I forgot . . . sweaters, you've read about sweaters. And motorboats."

"Master Learned says I have to work my way backward. Of course the recent journals aren't very interesting, but—"

"Prudy, I'd say about a fifth of these journals are missing. Look at the gaps, look here." He strode over to a half-empty shelf. "Here . . . Oh, look, his own mother, Constance Learned, 1945, 1946, all the way to 1955 and then nothing. She lived until the 1990s. Think Constance just stopped writing journals the last half of her life?

Something happened, something she wrote about, and Old Prune Face doesn't want anyone to know."

Prudy slumped into the chair behind the desk. Medford forgot, for the moment, that she was Mistress Learned. She was Prudy, trying not to cry. And succeeding, as usual. He cleared his throat. Prudy didn't look at him but Earnest turned around.

"Should we even bother with the journals that are left?" Medford asked. There had to be seventy-five or eighty red books up there on the shelves. Just looking at them made him tired. "I mean, if the important ones be gone . . ."

"Tuh," Prudy said. "So Earnest wants to believe."

"What about the desk?" Earnest asked her, as if there were no disagreement. "Think he keeps anything in there?"

Prudy tugged listlessly at a drawer. "'Tis locked."

"Oh dear," Earnest said, hauling out his screwdriver. "Whatever shall we do?"

He heaved Prudy out of the chair, sat down, and started prodding, rattling, and jiggling Deemer's bottom desk drawer. He was making entirely too much noise but Medford couldn't think of what to do about that. To distract himself, he grabbed one of the red journals, sat down at the end of the long table, and opened it up to read.

Prudy sat down opposite him. She had a red journal, too. "Master Learned never lets me sit in this chair," Prudy said.

"'Tis where Essence sat," Earnest said.

Prudy sniffed and opened her journal.

Medford could barely read his book, the ink was so faded. The handwriting didn't help—the letters were tiny and jammed together, probably to conserve paper. "Earnest," he whispered. "What are we looking for?"

"I don't know," Earnest said, rattling something. "Just read."

Even if they found the missing journals, how could they possibly read enough in a few hours—a few months even—to do Medford any good? Especially when they had no idea what could possibly help. The hope born at sunset began to fade. He'd be on a boat for Mainland before the sun went down again.

Benefit Weaver, His Booke, he saw at the top of the first page, and under that, *1780. Third Day of the Growing Moon.*

Warm, Benefit Weaver had written. *Light breeze from Southwest. Planted late pole Beans. Linen Thread from Mstr's Spinner, gave her a bolt of Common Stuff in Trade. Picked young greens for supper, ate last of chicken.*

Medford forced himself to skim that page, then the next. Then the one after that. He could see why Earnest had told the Book Learning class, "They planted beets."

"There's nothing to unscrew on this thing," Earnest said softly. "Guess I'll have to . . ." He grunted. There was a bang and a snap. "Ah. That helps."

"Did you break it?" Prudy whispered, horrified.

"Might as well be banished for a sheep as a lamb," Earnest said, head down, screwdriver scrabbling at something Medford couldn't see.

"Fleece Creature," Prudy muttered. "Newborn Fleece Creature."

Medford went back to his book.

Benefit Weaver had had an ordinary life, not much different from Boyce's except that he was a Weaver instead of a Carver and said "chicken" instead of "Egg Fowl." Boyce, too, recorded the weather and what he'd sent to the Trade. Did Boyce ever write anything interesting in his journal? Medford doubted it.

Medford imagined himself writing down everything he'd done in a day. He'd write, *Started another Unnameable Object, hid it under the bed. Met a goatman. Betrayed by best friend. Taken to jail.*

His life, he realized with a start, already made more interesting reading than Benefit Weaver's. On the other hand, Benefit probably never faced exile to Mainland.

Medford suddenly wasn't sure which life he'd prefer. The idea that it might be all right to be uncomfortable and miserable, rather than just plodding along planting and weaving, surprised him so much that he stopped reading to think about it.

He imagined waking up every day and carving just what he was supposed to carve. One spoon after another, followed by plain bowls and walking sticks. He would take pleasure in smoothness, in Usefulness, in beautiful wood well shaped and sanded. There was comfort in the thought of all those virtuous, Useful days. But would it content him? He couldn't decide.

"Here we are," Earnest said, depositing a handful of metal parts and wood splinters on the desktop. He hauled the drawer open and took out a stack of about twenty red journals. "Not many, but 'tis a start. You two read. I'll work on the other drawers."

He disappeared from view and started rattling things again.

Prudy was blinking fast. *Were those tears? Couldn't be.* "Why would Councilor Learned hide them from me?" she whispered. Medford wanted to tug on a braid, take her out to run, anything to make her feel better.

He grabbed a journal off the top of the stack. It was by someone named Jeremiah Comstock. "What's a Comstock?" he whispered to Prudy.

Prudy shrugged.

"Comstock, Comstock," Medford mused, tantalizingly. "What could that mean?"

Prudy heaved a deep sigh and straightened her back. "Thou art forgetting thy Book Learning," she said in a tone so annoying that Earnest snorted from under the desk. "They all had different names, meaningless names, when they got here. This Comstock must have been writing before they renamed themselves." She took a journal from the stack, too.

Medford opened Jeremiah's journal. He read:

Fifteenth day of the Codfish Moon, 1718. Today I be fifteen years of age, and Pa hath giv'n me this Booke to keep as journal of my days. Bright today, hot, winde from the southwest. I made a round potte on the wheel, of local claye. Pa put it in the kilne & baked it and it came out faire.

Medford darted from page to page. He found nothing of interest until he reached the twenty-third day of the Snow Moon, 1719:

A bright daye, cold, winde from the northwest. Studied Grammar with Grandfather. He recalled Days of his Youthe in the Olde Colony and why they come here to escape the Evils of Rank and Prejudice. I asked why they chose the Compendium Booke to bring with them. He said 'twas the beste they cld finde as they prepared to depart, not all of them knowing what was needed to survive.

It seems a good Booke for the most part, since we have survived by its precepts. I still have my Warte, though, and Ma believes my sore throat would have cured on its own without my stocking wrapt round it like the Booke says.

And then, a page later:

Twenty-eighth day, Snow Moon—Cloudy, warmer thanne before. Samuel Baker says there be not enuff

*Werke for another Potter. More Weavers be needed,
as stuffe be easy to trade on Mainland. Pa said I must
be a Weaver and do as is best for this Island & the
Trade.*

Medford heard an odd noise outside the door. It
sounded like *"Aaaahhh-hooooo."* He turned the page and
read about Jeremiah's grandfather's recipe for mussel
stew. Jeremiah was just warming up on the subject of bad
mussels and stomach cramps when—*whup!*—one blast
of wind slammed into the building behind Earnest, who
dived under Deemer's desk in a downpour of red books.

The door opened. "So-o-orry," the Goatman said, trying but failing to whisper. He was beaming. "I slowed it
down."

"Goatman," Medford whispered. "Not now."

"You said I mu-u-ust practice."

"I know. But not right now."

"Bweh-eh-eh." The Goatman shut the door again.

"Practice?" Prudy said in a horror-struck tone.

Medford couldn't imagine how the Constables would
have slept through all that. But he went out to check and
was sure he heard snores rising from the basement.

Jeremiah continued:

*Twelfth day, Ice Moon. Cold and Damp all the day.
I like not to Weave and cannot conceive why we must
divide up like this. I say I could make potts some, too.
But Pa says a man gets good at only one thing.*

Ma taught me to dye Linen thread with maple bark. She's got an old blue cloth I like, but she says 'tis Indigo and must be brought over the sea. What we got right here will give us Brown enough to hide the Dirt she says.

And, on the next page:

Eighteenth day, Ice Moon—The ponde so cold it crack'd. Samuel Baker and Resolve Mitchell propose a Meeting to decide on names for everyone, matching what they do. They want to write our new Names in front of the Compendium Booke. They said 'tis time to break with the Old Ways and Names be as quick a route as any. Grandfather ain't so sure, nor Pa neither. They say Comstock's a fine name and proud. Grandfather don't like Samuel telling me what to do for my Living.

Medford skimmed ahead several more pages:

Twenty-first day of the Worm Moon—Warming nicely. Samuel Baker here again. He said there should be Order, with so many of us on Island now, and some Things should be written down as new Texte at the end of the Compendium Booke. "Thou art thy Name" be one.

Pa yelled. He said Samuel desireth to rule like a King and thatt's what we meant to leave behind. Pa said Capability C. Craft be naught but a fake. Some of his advice works same as anything Pa's gramma would have done, just like common sense. But others be just

> *Fibs, like moleskin to cure the Cancer or saltwater on*
> *a Wart.*
>
> *Pa said all knew there was no Person named*
> *Capability C. Craft . . .*

Medford gasped. Nobody heard him because Earnest was rattling things again. Just as well—Medford didn't want to stop reading.

> *Pa said all knew there was no Person named Capability*
> *C. Craft, that 'twas a compendium of items stole from*
> *a Mistress Wolley and a Master Murrel and Old*
> *Wives and such, published by an unscrupulous Printer*
> *for Gain and naught else. Samuel said Pa should shut*
> *his Mouth for the good of this Island and its People.*

Medford couldn't read any more. All his life, Capability C. Craft had been Island's hero, answerer of questions, settler of arguments. Now he was Wolley and Murrel (more senseless names) and "an unscrupulous Printer," whatever that was.

He read the words again—*no Person named Capability C. Craft*—and tried to make them mean something else. But there was nothing else they could mean.

What else did the Book lie about? Would the shellfish fritter recipe really feed fifteen people? Was there a floor beneath his feet? The room felt cold, the world outside dark and lonely and dangerous.

Was this what had made Essence laugh? Had she

teased her father about it and made him angry? Threatened to tell other Islanders, maybe?

The next entry in the journal was routine, all about planting and weaving. So were the next one and the two after that. But then:

Twenty-eighth day of the Sowing Moon. I be Jeremiah
Weaver now, and my Name in the Booke as such.
Pa is still Comstock, as he says he ever will be. Ma is
Weaver. They ain't speaking.

"There's something strange here," Prudy said.

"Here, too," Medford said.

"This isn't in a journal. 'Tis in the table. Something scratched into the wood."

"Aye," Medford said. "But what I've got here—"

"You have to see this. Now."

Reluctantly, Medford marked his place with some of the yellow paper and joined Earnest to peer over Prudy's shoulder. Scratched into the wood was a little . . . Medford didn't know what to call it, but it was like a little man with very skinny arms and legs, something square in one of his hands. He seemed to have a coat on and a hat on his head.

"A tricorn hat like Master Learned's," Prudy said. "And a Councilor's robe."

"'Tis nothing," Earnest said, sounding disappointed. "A joke of Essence's, making fun of her father."

"Who would do such a thing in the open like this?"

Prudy shuddered. "'Tis Unnameable, just like Medford's—"

"But what's this?" Medford used his finger to trace another scratch, a double line that ran from the little man over the edge of the table. He squatted to follow the scratch under the tabletop all the way to the beam down the center of the table. And there, in the crack between the beam and the tabletop, was a folded scrap of Archives paper.

"Keeps the table from wobbling," Earnest said, squatting beside him.

Prudy dropped to her knees and joined them.

"I don't know about that," Medford said. He pulled the scrap out and unfolded it. He couldn't read the four hastily scribbled lines in the darkness under the table. But at the bottom, scrawled black and large, was a signature anyone could read anywhere.

From Essence, it read. *Soon to be gone.*

CHAPTER NINETEEN

ℭ

The Map in the Dark

We must lock the Archives. These accounts of past lives do
breed rumor and unrest. But anyone may read them as long
as I or Brother be there to advise.

—*Journal of Haywood Learned, 1856*

T HE ARCHIVES door opened.

"Bweh-eh-eh. Where a-a-are you?"

Earnest snatched Essence's note from Medford's hand,
backed out from under the table, and tried to stand too
soon, soundly whacking his head on the tabletop.

By the time Medford had extracted himself, Earnest
and Prudy were hunched over the scrap of paper, Earnest
rubbing the back of his head.

The Goatman shut the door behind him. "Why were
you under the ta-a-able?"

"We found a note from Essence Learned," Medford
said. "Deemer's daughter, who was sent away from here."

"Wha-a-at's a note?"

"More words on paper."

"I thought those we-e-ere by dead people. Is she dead?"

"No, but she's gone. She left a note behind to tell us something."

"Bweh-eh-eh." The Goatman grabbed paper and an inkwell. He dribbled ink on the paper and spread it around with a pen.

Prudy and Earnest paid no attention, just squinted at the note in the flickering lantern light. "Usually her handwriting's quite neat," Earnest muttered. "She was in a hurry."

"This first sentence . . . ," Prudy said. "Let's see . . . that's *Medford*, dost thou agree?"

"Aye," Earnest said. "*Medford's parents*, I'd say."

"My parents?" Medford tried to push Prudy aside but she wouldn't budge. She moved the note so he could see it. There, in the middle of the first sentence, was something that did look like "*Medford's parents*." The sentence said, 1. *Oily hose, stralit lim, Medford's parents (sonth eud) Enst to TH.*

"*Oily hose, Medford's parents?*" Prudy said, sounding offended. "What does that mean? And then what's this underneath? 2. *Bott drawer.*"

The Goatman looked up, chewing. "She didn't write a ve-e-ery good note."

"'Twould slow her father's understanding, in case he found it," Earnest said.

"So now she's slowed *our* understanding." Prudy muttered.

"*Bott drawer,*" Earnest mused. "She means Deemer's bottom drawer, the one we just opened. She's telling us what he did with the journals he took from the shelves."

"It could be any bottom drawer," Prudy said. "She might not even be talking about the journals."

"What else would she be thinking about, sitting up here?" Earnest said.

Prudy ignored him. "And what about this first item? *Medford's parents.* What would they have to do with our journals?"

"I thought you said she wasn't talking about the journals."

"I didn't say she wasn't. I said she *might* not be."

Medford let them bicker. Why was Essence writing a note about his parents? He tried to think but his brain wouldn't work.

"Enough, Earnest," Prudy said. "We need to concentrate. *Oily hose, stralit lim, Medford's parents Enst (sonth eud) to TH.* She can't really mean *oily hose,* can she? And what does she mean by *Enst?*"

Medford had a brainstorm. "Short for Earnest!"

Even in the lamplight, they could see Earnest turn red. "Why would she be writing about me?"

"Something to do with Medford's parents," Prudy said. "What hast thou to do with Medford's parents?"

"Nothing," Earnest said. *"Something something, something something, Medford's parents something something Earnest to TH.* Maybe she was telling me to go to Town Hall?"

"But the note is *in* Town Hall," Prudy said. "If she wanted thee to come here she would have put the note someplace else."

"I think *TH* is Town Hall, though," Earnest said. *"Something something, something something, Medford's parents something something Earnest to Town Hall.* Essence, what in the Names are you telling me?"

"South end," Medford said. "That thing in the brackets. That's south end."

"Aye. South end," Prudy said. "Maybe *Enst* isn't Earnest after all." She held the note closer to the lamp and squinted at it. "Enst . . . Enst . . . that's definitely an *E* but that *n* really could be any letter in the alphabet. *A, B, C, D* . . ."

"Could it be an *a*?" Medford asked. *"Medford's parents (south end) East to Town Hall?"*

Something was nagging at him. He went over what he knew, or thought he knew. When had Essence written this note? *Soon to be gone.* Probably after that last Book Learning class, when Deemer had made her sit far away from her New Learners.

In his mind's eye, Medford saw her sitting there, sitting there, sitting there, staring off into space. But wait . . . she wasn't staring at nothing, was she? She was staring at that huge map on the wall, *Island and Surrounding Waters.*

"Deadman's Shoal," he said. "In that last Book Learning class, she was staring at Deadman's Shoal." Prudy and Earnest looked up. "Where my parents died. Let me look at that note again."

He held it close to the lantern the way Prudy had, concentrated on the words that looked like *Oily hose.*

"*Oily hose,*" he said. "*Oily hose, oily hose, oily hose . . .*"

Earnest peered over Medford's shoulder. "Only house."

"*Stralit lim, stralit lim,*" Prudy said, scribbling the words on a piece of paper. "Starlight limb. No. Stra-a-a . . . straight! Straight . . . line. Straight line."

Only house, straight line, Medford's parents (south end) East to Town Hall. That was it. Had to be.

"But there are three or four houses between Town Hall and the south end of Deadman's Shoal," Earnest said.

"Only the oldest houses are on the map," Prudy said.

"And maybe only one is on a straight line between the south end of the shoal and Town Hall," Medford said. "We have to go down there and see."

"Wha-a-at's a map? Who is dead? Wha-a-at's a shoal?"

"And we have to do it in the dark," Prudy said. "We don't have enough blankets for all the windows in the auditorium."

They all looked at the Goatman. "I wi-i-ill be the moon," he said.

They didn't bother cleaning up after themselves. Repairing Deemer's desk and replacing the lock would take too much time and Earnest wasn't sure he could fix either of them, anyway. They did take the red journals they'd found in the desk drawer.

Medford made sure he took Jeremiah's journal. He didn't want to distract everyone with the news about Capability C. Craft. He'd tell them later.

Closing the Archives door as best they could, they made their way slowly, quietly down the stairs behind the Goatman. The Constables weren't making as much noise as before, but every now and then one of them would let out a loud, reassuring *snork*. Otherwise, Town Hall was silent as a Dairyman at dinner.

As they crept down the stairs and across the landing to the auditorium door, Medford had time to think about *Island and Surrounding Waters*. He'd stared at that map every day of Book Learning, especially at Deadman's Shoal. He could see it in his mind's eye as if it were right in front of him. He thought he had a pretty good idea which house was on a straight line between the shoal's south end and Town Hall.

He wouldn't say yet, though. No point in upsetting Prudy until he had to. Not that she hadn't figured it out for herself, most likely. Earnest, too.

The auditorium's eight windows let in more starlight than the three in the Archives. Medford could just see where the desks and chairs were, but no matter how he squinted he couldn't tell what was what on the map.

"We'll move the Council table over to the wall so we can stand on it," Earnest whispered. "And we can use Deemer's ruler to draw a straight line between the shoal and Town Hall."

"I'll get it," Prudy said.

Medford and Earnest moved the table over to the wall and stood there, contemplating how to get the Goatman up on it.

"I could run a-a-and jump," the Goatman said. "I'm good at running and jumping. I don't even need my staff if I'm moving fa-a-ast enough."

Medford wondered if the Goatman was as good at running and jumping as he was at windwork. "May we lift you instead?" he asked.

"Bweh-eh-eh," the Goatman said.

"Is that aye or nay?" Prudy whispered to Medford.

"Aye," Medford said, hoping he was right. "Prudy, you get on the table and hold on to him when Earnest and I get him up there."

"Will it hold all of us?" Prudy said.

"Grandpa built it," Earnest said. "Of course 'twill."

Sure enough, the table didn't even creak when Prudy clambered up on it, nor when the Goatman, Medford, and Earnest joined her.

Even up close, Medford couldn't see much on the map. "Goatman," he said. "The first thing you have to find is the beach on the shore to your left and . . ." Did the

Goatman know left from right? Medford seemed to remember him saying he could read "No Left Turn," whatever that meant.

"Prudy," Earnest whispered. "What in the Names are you doing?"

Prudy seemed to be tapping. The sound was familiar but Medford couldn't place it.

"Here," Prudy said, handing the Goatman something. Medford reached out and felt what it was . . . a chalkboard from the Book Learning class. "I wrote down the two names we're looking for. This top one is 'Deadman's Shoal'—try to match it first. 'Twill be right where thou art standing."

"Prudy," Medford said, trying to stuff fourteen years of friendship and admiration into one word. For the moment, he didn't care how much of a Learned she was.

"Thou art annoying," Earnest said, "but thou art not stupid."

The Goatman found the right word sooner than anyone could have hoped. "He-e-ere's that half-moon shape in the front"—*that's the* D *in* Deadman's, Medford thought—"the-e-en some smaller shapes then a bi-i-ig snake shape." *That has to be* Shoal.

"Put the end of the ruler under that word and Medford will hold it straight," Prudy said. "Then move this way"—she eased him to the right—"and find this other word, with this big . . . um . . . table shape in front."

The Goatman found "Town Hall," too, and put the other end of the ruler under it.

"Now," Prudy said, "tell us what you see in between, just above the ruler."

The Goatman was silent only for a minute. "You mean li-i-ike this little round thing here? It has a word beside it."

"Tell us what the word looks like," Prudy said.

"A big shape I know from before I ca-a-ame here, then some little shapes." He pondered, then announced proudly, "It says *Left Turn.*"

Prudy scribbled on the chalkboard. "Is it this?"

"Ye-e-es," the Goatman said. "Tha-a-at's it."

"I knew it," Prudy whispered fiercely. "I just knew it."

"What did you write?" Medford asked.

Silence.

"Prudy?"

"I wrote *Learned,*" she said, sounding as if her throat were sore. "'Tis Deemer's house. He must have moved the journals to his house when I took over for Essence. He doesn't trust me."

"He told you a ta-a-anner," the Goatman said.

"Told me a what?" Prudy said.

"I'll explain later," Medford said.

"We have to go over there." Earnest jumped down from the table.

"And do what?" Medford asked.

"I don't know. Something."

Medford sat down on the table, buried his head in his hands. This night just kept getting longer and longer. Prudy sat down and leaned against him, smelling like grass.

"Come on, you two," Earnest said, helping the Goatman down from the table.

"Aye," said Old Prudy. "Come on, Medford. Let's see what Prune Face is up to."

They crept outside, rounded the corner of the building . . . and had a shock. A light shone through one of the windows on Town Hall's first floor.

"That's the radio room," Earnest whispered.

"Was somebody in there all this time?" Medford whispered.

"They would have heard us," Earnest said. "Someone probably just left a lantern burning."

"That's not very safe," Prudy said. "All our history is upstairs in the Archives. Imagine if those journals burnt up. It would be like burning the people themselves."

"No, it wouldn't," Earnest whispered. Medford could almost hear him rolling his eyes. "People are people. Paper is just paper."

"How canst thou say such a thing, Earnest?" Prudy said. "Those journals live, they breathe—"

"Bweh-eh-eh."

"Can we talk about this later?" Medford said, eyeing the lighted window uneasily.

"Hmph," Prudy said.

The world was fast asleep, not a breath stirring. *It has to be past midnight,* Medford thought. The starlight was brighter outside than it had been in Town Hall, but they still hung on to the Goatman and one another. Life just seemed safer that way.

ODDLY, A LIGHT was burning at Deemer's house, too.

"Now, I *know* Master Learned didn't just leave a lantern going," Prudy said. "He's always telling me never to leave a room without blowing everything out."

Sure enough, the Councilor's dark shape crossed in front of the window.

"What now?" Medford whispered as they stood just outside the pool of light from the window, clutching their stacks of red journals. The window was too high to see in from close up.

Earnest set his journals down on the ground and dropped to his hands and knees under the window. "Climb on, Medford," he whispered.

"Bweh-eh-eh," the Goatman said softly.

The Goatman was right. This was a terrible idea. What if Deemer looked up and saw a scared, white face at the window? "Might as well be banished for a Fleece Creature as a Newborn Fleece Creature," Medford muttered.

Balancing on someone's back turned out to be harder than he'd expected. Earnest kept shifting his weight around to make himself more comfortable. Medford tried to grab the window frame without bumping into anything or rattling the glass. Nothing kept him from teetering back and forth like a Waterman ashore.

"Uhhhh," Earnest groaned softly.

"Shhhh," Prudy whispered. "Stay still, Earnest. He can't be that heavy."

"So you say."

Through the thick window glass, Medford saw a wavy-looking Deemer Learned kneeling in front of his parlor stove, stoking the fire. The logs were flat and odd looking. Was Deemer burning shingles?

The Councilor reached into a crate next to him and grabbed another . . . shingle?

And at that moment Medford knew exactly what was going into the stove. He gasped and instinctively stepped backward in surprise.

"What are you doing?" Earnest whispered desperately.

Medford teetered, tried to keep hold of the window frame, scrabbling at it with his hands. He lost his grip and windmilled his arms in a last-ditch effort to stay upright.

Don't yell, he told himself. *Don't yell. Don't yell. Don't . . .*

He hit the ground. He didn't yell. Neither did Earnest.

They didn't have to. "Bweh-eh-eh-eh!" the Goatman said. He sort of whispered it, but he sort of didn't.

"Up against the house!" Earnest hissed. All four of them flung themselves into the darkness under the window and huddled there.

The window opened. "Who's out there?" Deemer said. He went silent, listening. The window rattled shut. They heard quick footsteps fading toward the front of the house.

"Back porch!" Prudy whispered.

They scrambled around the corner and into the darkness under Deemer's back stoop. Medford had to rush back and retrieve his stack of journals, and while he felt around for them on the ground he heard the front door open. He scuttled around the corner and under the stoop as Deemer's feet pounded down the front steps.

Silence. A twig snapped.

"Where art thou?" Deemer said. Another twig snapped. "I see thee there."

But Medford didn't think Deemer really saw them. His voice was too far away. Several minutes passed in silence. Then another twig snapped, so close Medford almost cried out. Deemer mounted the steps over their heads.

"I see thee out there in the woods," Deemer said, above them. A bird twittered and some small beast chattered back. Dry leaves rattled in a sudden breeze.

They heard the door open and close.

"He tells a lot of ta-a-anners," the Goatman whispered.

"What if he goes to Town Hall?" Prudy breathed. "What if he sees you're gone?"

"He won't," Medford said. "He'll hide what he's doing before he goes out again."

Because those weren't shingles Deemer was burning. They were red journals.

CHAPTER TWENTY

The Last of Alma

I am going to knit sweaters. I am going to invent a new stitch that will fight the wind. And I am going to make Boyce Carver laugh if it is the last thing I do.

—*Journal of Alma Weaver, 1970*

H E WOULD NEVER," Prudy said.

"He is right now," Medford said.

They had crept into the woods near Deemer's house so Medford could tell Prudy and Earnest what he'd seen.

"That's our history he's got in there," Prudy said.

"Not for long," Earnest said.

"Words on pa-a-aper. What a bad idea," the Goatman said. "Nobody can burn a tale you te-e-ell out loud."

"We have to make him stop," Earnest said.

"Oh, aye," Medford said. "We'll just march in and tell him to stop it right now. I'm sure he'll do exactly what we say."

"He'll call the Constables and hide the journals," Prudy said bitterly. "He'll say Medford stole them and nobody will believe what Medford saw him doing. Medford will be gone by noon tomorrow."

He would be gone anyway, no matter what they did. Medford leaned back against a tree and stared up through the leaves at the starry sky. It would be the same sky on Mainland, the same stars. They couldn't take that away from him, at least.

And then he came to a decision that astonished him. "I'm going to be gone anyways," he said. "We might as well try to save those journals."

"Medford," Prudy said. "We won't let you go." *No Book Talk. Praise the Book.*

"We may not be able to stop it," Earnest said. "I think Medford's right. We should save what we can."

"But how? We can't just rush in there."

"Why not? There are three of us."

"Four," the Goatman said.

"Four of us, beg pardon," Earnest said. "We could grab the journals and run."

"But we won't have time to read them, or even to hide them," Medford said. "Deemer will have the Constables on us as soon as we're out the door."

"Bweh-eh-eh. Better if you lure him awa-a-ay first."

"Lure him away?" Medford said. "What do you mean?"

"Whe-e-en you want to milk a goat, you wave fodder at her, lure her to you. Except you lure this Prune Fa-a-ace away from you instead. Then he won't see who took the words on paper."

Earnest snorted. Prudy shushed him. "But what do we have for . . . for fodder?"

"You ha-a-ave me."

Huh, Medford thought. *It could work.* "You'll lure him out the front, we'll go in the back. Is that what you mean?"

"Bweh-eh-eh. And then I'll run awa-a-ay."

"How can you run when you can barely walk?" Earnest asked. Medford had been wondering the same thing.

"I fa-a-all forward," the Goatman said. "But I don't hi-i-it the ground."

Medford tried to imagine what that would be like. "How do you stop running?" he asked.

"I hit the ground."

We'll just have to trust him. "And we'll take the journals to . . . to where?" Medford asked. "Someplace nearby would be best. Your parents' house, Prudy? Your ma will be up." He could see her stiffen, silhouetted against the starlight. "Sorry, but she will be."

"They won't be any help anyways," Earnest said. "They don't have any backbone."

"How canst thou say such a thing, Earnest?" Prudy said. "They be thy parents."

"Oh and you don't think exactly the same as me? Look how they—"

"If you two don't hush up we won't be taking anything anywhere," Medford said. "Well, I guess there's always Boyce."

As best he could in the pitch black under the trees, Medford drew a map in the dirt so the Goatman could meet them at Boyce's. And so he'd know how to lead Deemer in the opposite direction.

The Goatman stumped off to the front of Deemer's house, leaving Medford, Prudy, and Earnest huddled in the woods. It was chilly, the ground damp under them. Something rustled in the fallen leaves. Rigging clanged on a boat in the harbor.

"Bweh-eh-eh-eh!" The silence shattered. The Goatman must have been standing in Harbor Lane. "Bweh-eh-eh! Bweh! Bweh!"

"This is it," Medford whispered. "Get ready."

Deemer's front door banged open. "I see thee, thou creature!" Deemer yelled, pounding down his front steps. "Get thee back here! Constables! Constables!"

Medford hoped the Goatman didn't hit the ground too soon. He hugged his armload of journals so hard the bindings bit into his arm. He heard Deemer pounding down the wooden sidewalk, heard a faint "Bweh-eh-eh" from beyond the Town Hall.

"Now!" Medford whispered. "Now!"

Crouching down—for no good reason except that it felt safer—the three of them ran to Deemer's back door, tumbled inside. In his sitting room were two crates of red and brown journals, one of them half empty. A stack of red journals sat beside the stove. Prudy whipped off her jacket and piled those journals into it as if it were a bag.

"Give me your books from Deemer's desk," she whispered. "I'll carry them. Earnest, you're strongest. You take the full crate. Medford, you take the other crate."

Earnest hoisted the full box. "Oof," he said. "How did Prune Face carry this?"

Medford couldn't imagine. The half-full crate was heavy enough.

"Hurry!" Prudy said.

They hustled out Deemer's front door and headed for Boyce's house, three blocks north and east. In the distance, well south of Town Hall, they heard a "Bweh-eh-eh-eh." Medford hoped Deemer hadn't given up on pursuing the Goatman.

They scuttled across Harbor Lane to the footpath that led to the junction of the Waterman and Harborside roads. The Waterman houses were silent and dark. Medford wondered what time it was, how long before dawn. How long before Deemer caught up with them.

How long before Earnest's wheezing woke everyone up.

"Canst thou run quieter, Earnest?" Prudy panted.

Earnest took the excuse to halt for a minute. "You

try . . . carrying . . . a full crate of . . . books . . . and see how quiet you are."

Medford had a stitch in his side but didn't want to admit it, since he had only half a crate. They took a brief rest and then hurried down Harborside Road toward Boyce's. They crossed the Wharf Road, saw the house up ahead.

"Wait." Medford panted. "Stop. Something's not right."

Boyce's house was lighted up as if it were suppertime. First that light in Town Hall, then Deemer's sitting room, now this. What was going on around here?

Could Deemer already have figured out what they'd done? Had he awakened Boyce? Was he waiting there now, hoping they'd turn up?

"You two stay here," Medford said. "No point getting you banished, too. I'll see what's happening." He slipped his crate in among Boyce's Hardy Leaf Crops while Earnest and Prudy leaned against a tree and caught their breath.

He heard a voice as he crept up Boyce's back stoop, avoiding the creaky second step. But it wasn't Deemer talking, it was Boyce. Medford leaned out over the railing so he could see in Boyce's double kitchen windows. Sure enough, Boyce was sitting at the table under the windows, a tea mug at his elbow. Something was on the table in front of him, something Medford couldn't make sense of at first.

Boyce seemed to be talking to it.

It was large, wooden. For one horrible moment, Medford thought it was one of the older Unnameable carvings that he kept on the rafters of his cabin. The carving was about two feet tall, looked like a figure sitting in a chair. He couldn't remember carving anything like that.

Boyce reached out and gently touched the carving with one finger, stroked it. Medford leaned closer, almost tipping himself over the railing, trying to figure out what he was looking at.

It was a woman, he could see that now. She was sitting in a rocking chair. She was dressed in knee breeches, leaning so far back her chair might fall over, her eyes on the sky and her mouth open in huge, lung-filling laughter. She had knitting needles in her hands, a sweater half made. But her hands were in her lap, forgotten in glee.

The truth struck him so hard he gasped out loud. That wasn't any carving of his. It was a carving of Boyce's.

Medford was exhausted. He was scared. He was hungry and thirsty.

But right now, more than anything, he was angry.

He crashed through the kitchen door. Boyce had to grab the table to keep from falling out of his chair, he was so startled.

"You!" Medford yelled. It felt good to yell. "You let them take me to jail, let them send me away, and all the time you're carving *that?*"

He kicked over a chair, kicked it again so it slammed into the cookstove. He grabbed Boyce's mug, hurled it against the sink where it broke into bits. Before he knew what he was doing, he grabbed one end of the kitchen table, heaved it up and overturned it. The wooden woman flew through the air, still laughing, and crashed against the cabinet under the sink. Boyce jumped up just in time to avoid getting the table in his lap.

Prudy and Earnest burst through the door and stopped dead, gaping at the shambles and at Medford, standing there trembling and glaring at Boyce.

"Medford!" Prudy gasped. "What's gotten into thee?"

Boyce retrieved his carving, cradled it in his arms. "This got into him," he said.

He laid the carving gently down on the counter next to the sink. The ends of the rockers had broken off. The woman's chin was gone, the uproarious mouth dented. She'd lost her fingers and the knitting needles were in shards on the floor.

"I made dozens of fancy carvings, years ago. This is the one I didn't burn." Boyce reached out to touch the crater that used to be the woman's chin. "'Tis Alma." He half turned toward Medford, not quite enough to look at him. "Sorry, boy. Guess I taught you everything I know."

"That's Alma?" Medford said. He moved closer.

He remembered her, in a way. She was somewhere inside him, so deep it was hard to reach her. Not a person so much as a feeling of safety, a hum in the rhythm of a loom, the squeak of her rockers on the kitchen floor.

"Her rocking chair used to be right here," Medford said, pointing to a spot near the cookstove.

"Aye," Boyce said.

Medford took another step closer.

The damage to the carving couldn't disguise the liveliness of it. There were places where Boyce's blade had gone wrong: an ear cocked funny, one leg too short. But the way Alma was sitting, her chair barely able to hold her, the way her head was thrown back in joy . . . the wood had been speaking to Boyce in a way it had only occasionally spoken to Medford. He wished Boyce really *had* taught him all he knew.

"She hated that I carved these things," Boyce said. "Made me burn them. I told her I burned this one but I couldn't somehow." He squatted and started picking up shards of knitting needles and rockers, piling them in his hand as if they were Useful.

Medford realized he was standing on part of a chair rocker. He moved his foot, throat aching from everything he suddenly wanted to say to Boyce.

"This is the only one you have left?" he whispered.

"Aye."

"You can fix it."

"Maybe."

"You can make another."

"No."

Boyce tipped the wood shards out of his hand onto the counter beside the damaged carving, all he had left of his late wife. Medford's anger was gone as if it had never existed, leaving behind an emptiness too painful for tears.

Silence.

Except for heavy breathing from Prudy.

Finally, she exploded. "Fix it, thou sayst? Make another? Medford, Boyce, hast thou lost thy senses? This thing be—"

"Unnameable. I know." Boyce turned his back on Alma and contemplated Prudy as if she were a decaying log of Platewood. "Which brings up the question of how Medford got out of jail. And what all three of you are doing out of bed at two o'clock in the morning."

Wham! A blast of wind slammed into the house, rattling the windows. Everyone grabbed for something to hold on to. But nothing else happened.

"All four of us," Earnest said.

"Let's make tea," Boyce said.

While the tea was brewing, Medford, Prudy, and Earnest retrieved the journals from Boyce's garden. Then they sat down with their tea and told Boyce everything that had happened that night. Medford told them all about Jeremiah Comstock, about Capability C. Craft being "a fake."

About there being no Capability C. Craft in the first place.

Boyce sat expressionless until they reached the part about Deemer burning red journals in his sitting room stove. Then he got up and took a turn around the room, still expressionless. He drained the last of his tea and set the mug down as if he were squashing something under it.

"Let's read them journals," he said.

CHAPTER TWENTY-ONE

ᚴ

The Naming

We shall have done with Elites and the Tyranny of Ancestors. Each shall be Named for a Useful purpose and rewarded for today's Industry. 'Tis a New World.

—*Journal of Samuel Carpenter, 1722*

ANOTHER MUG of tea by his side, the fire built up in Boyce's sitting room stove, Medford picked up where Jeremiah Comstock had left off.

Twenty-eighth day of the Sowing Moon, Jeremiah wrote. *I be Jeremiah Weaver now, and my Name in the Booke as such. Pa is still Comstock, as he says he ever will be. Ma is Weaver. They ain't speaking.*

How did their names get changed? They must have held a Town Meeting the way Samuel Baker had wanted.

Sure enough, in the very next paragraph:

We had walked to the Meeting Hall early in the forenoon, more than 150 Souls. Resolve Mitchell put the Compendium Book on a new stand made by Horace Clarke. Samuel Baker recalled to us how

Mainland explorers found this Island—difficult to approach but uninhabited and Sweet. How a group of them, growing to some 35 men and women, agreed to leave the Colony for a new life here, without rank and with women having their say. They brought people of all necessary crafts, among them farming, physick, pottery, weaving, carpentry.

"I got somebody here telling about when they all changed their names," Boyce said.

"Me, too," Earnest said.

"What's wrong with us knowing about that?" Prudy asked.

Nobody had an answer.

Medford went back to Jeremiah.

Up to now, Samuel said, we have needed few Rules to guide us, just advice from the Compendium Book about Cookery and Tonics and Farming. But we have learnt new things which we should write in the Booke ourselves, and we must protect ourselves from Disorder which could be the Death of us all.

Samuel made his Naming proposal. Said he would be Samuel Carpenter and Resolve would be Resolve Farmer. He said there should be Carvers and Weavers, Potters, Tanners, Bakers and such. Tailors, too. Pa asked what if there be too many Tanners and everyone laughed for Elmore Watson hath eight children, and he the Tanner.

"They were afraid we'd have too many Tanners," Medford said.

"Dexter by himself's too many for me," Boyce said.

Samuel's mouth got small and he said he was not to be made Mock of. But Pa said 'twas a serious Question and Resolve said someone should choose who was Tanner and the rest would be something else. Pa asked who chooseth, and all muttered about that.

Samuel said there should be a Council formed to decide and rules made. And children would take the name of which Craft they chose to follow, any new craft and name to be decided by the Council.

No one argued 'gainst that. They voted 92 in favor, 51 against, 6 not voting.

"The vote to change the names was ninety-two in favor, fifty-one against," Medford said.

"That's part of the trouble, I'm guessing," Earnest said. "Deemer doesn't want us to know some of the Originals didn't like the Naming."

Ma voted against like Pa did, but when the time came to write the Names in the Book she went up and bade me do so too. When Pa upbraided her she said a Vote's a vote and 'tis done now. Pa and several others kept their old Names, but as we left for home Elmore Tanner (who had been Watson) called out to Pa, Good night to ye, Jacob Potter, whether or nay.

"Someone's out there," said Prudy, who was sitting by a window.

They all stood up, not sure what to do. Was it Deemer? The Constables?

"Bweh-eh-eh!"

"Goatman!" Medford yelled, rushing for the door. "In here!"

The Goatman's robe was torn on one side and he had dead leaves all over him. He was soaking wet, which made him even stinkier than usual.

And the dog was with him.

"Hoo," Boyce said when the two of them were in the kitchen and the smell had time to register. "Ain't that something."

"I fa-a-are well," the Goatman said.

"Glad to hear it," Boyce said.

"He likes tea," Medford said. "Goatman, what was that bit of wind before?"

"I hi-i-it the ground but it was water."

"Where's Master Learned?" Prudy asked.

"Meaning Prune Face," Earnest said.

"He hit the water, too," the Goatman said. "More tha-a-an I did because he couldn't see."

"But where . . . ?"

The Goatman shrugged. "In the woods. Over the-e-ere somewhere." He waved his hand toward Peat Bog.

"He's in the bog? A . . . a wet place, marshy, with . . ."

Medford gestured to indicate a mound of peat and marsh grass.

"Ah. The wallow, you mean. We were the-e-ere but he was out the last time I saw him. I don't know now. The two bi-i-ig flatfoots are looking for him."

"The Constables? How did they get involved?" Boyce asked, shoveling tea into his teapot in such a frenzy Medford wondered if there would be any room for the hot water.

"They heard him ye-e-elling, I think. The-e-ey were looking for him when I left."

Medford reached out to brush the dead leaves off the Goatman's back. Boyce made kind of a gurgling sound— did he think the Goatman would bite? "We thank thee, Goatman," Medford said. "Thou hast done us great service."

The Goatman beamed. "Bweh-eh-eh." He gave a tremendous shiver.

"He has to get that wet robe off," Prudy said. "Get him a blanket, Boyce."

Boyce looked at her as if she'd asked him to lend the Goatman his skin.

"Boyce," Prudy said. "He's freezing. He'll get sick."

"I don't ge-e-et sick," the Goatman said. He sneezed, spraying droplets everywhere, and reached for his sash. But it was back in the jail, so he blew his nose on his sleeve.

"I'll get a blanket," Boyce said.

The Goatman retreated into the sitting room to get

out of his robe and wrap himself in the blanket. The rest of them huddled around the cookstove watching Boyce pour hot water into the teapot.

When the Goatman reappeared swathed in a woolen blanket (dyed dark brown to hide the dirt), Boyce poured tea for everyone. The Goatman grabbed the tea strainer before Medford could stop him and lapped it out with appreciative grunts.

"I tha-a-ank thee," the Goatman said to Boyce, handing back the strainer.

"Don't mention it," Boyce said faintly. He dumped the strainer into the dishpan.

The tea was so strong Medford could feel his teeth rotting as he drank it. The Goatman drank his right up and held his cup out for more. "Be-e-est yet," he said.

Medford gave the dog some water and they returned to their chairs.

"Bweh-eh-eh," the Goatman said when he saw the journals scattered all over the room. "These are what Prune Fa-a-ace was burning? Wha-a-at's in them?"

Medford told him about Jeremiah and the Naming vote.

"So these flatfoots ma-a-ade up all your names long, long ago?"

"Not mine," Medford said. "Unless I become a Carver, which will never happen now."

"Who sa-a-ays?"

"Can we get reading?" Prudy asked.

"Bweh-eh-eh," the Goatman said, but then he caught the look on Prudy's face. He and the dog settled down on the floor in front of the sitting room stove. The Goatman stared at the flames behind the stove's Mainland glass door, then closed his eyes.

Everyone else was reading with renewed haste, flipping through journals, skimming pages. The clock on Boyce's mantelpiece read half past three o'clock. Medford was surprised to find that he wasn't sleepy. He was so keyed up he might never sleep again.

Boyce wasn't concentrating. Every time Medford turned a page, he caught Boyce staring at the Goatman with the owl-eyed look of someone who'd just woken up. The air around the stove was pungent from the drying robe, the drying Goatman, and the drying dog. It all did take some getting used to, Medford had to admit. Smells didn't seem to bother him so much now. Maybe his nose was dying.

On one page turn, Medford found that Boyce was staring at him instead of the Goatman. Boldly, Medford looked Boyce in the eye.

Boyce shifted his gaze to the flames dancing in the stove. "We don't know each other real well, do we, boy?" he said softly.

Know each other? What did that even mean? "Guess not," Medford said, but only because he couldn't think of what else to say.

Prudy kept her eyes on the page in front of her but

Medford could tell she was listening. Earnest was oblivi-
ous, intent on his reading.

"What's poems?" he burst out at last.

"Poems?" they all repeated. They'd never heard the
word before.

"Durward Constable," Earnest said, "1830. Lessee . . ."
He flipped back a couple of pages. "*I be all of a dither today,*" he read. "One of the Learneds—Merit Learned, it
says here—made this Durward Constable arrest someone
named . . . oh, here it is, Cordella Weaver. *She hath created
the Unnameable, I know not in what form,* Durward says."

Cordella Weaver, about to be banished. Medford kept
his face as bland as Myrtle Cook's Sickbed Custard but he
could feel Boyce looking at him.

"I guess Cordella was weaving in colors, sometimes
stitching by hand to make the cloth look like a tree or a
flower—I can't imagine what that would be like, can you?
Anyways, they had a Town Meeting about it because she
wasted time gathering berries for dye and wasn't making
anything Useful."

"And they sent her away," Prudy breathed.

"Aye," Earnest said, "but old Durward, he wasn't sure
her weavings were so terrible. Listen to what he says here:
*To my shame, I could not stop looking at them. I said 'twas
disbelief that drew my gaze. But as I sit here tonight I admit
they did give me pleasure of an odd sort, a calmness of heart
and joy like a westerly breeze.*"

"And then, listen to this." Earnest flipped pages. "After they sailed her to Mainland, Durward says, *They burnt her weavings. I must burn my poems.*"

"Poems," Prudy mused. "Obviously something Unnameable."

"I'd give a lot to see one of them weavings," Earnest said.

Medford didn't look at Prudy. He suspected she wasn't looking at him, either.

The Goatman chose that moment to open his eyes. "Bweh-eh-eh. Stay-Awake-All-Night Boy has seen a cloth wi-i-ith a goatman on it."

Medford bent his head over Jeremiah's journal as if it contained vital information. He was aware of a smothering silence around him.

"Really," Boyce said. "Perhaps Stay-Awake-All-Night Boy would like to tell us about this cloth."

"A worthy thought, Master Carver. But if thou meanest Master Runyuin, I warn thee not to believe a word he doth tell thee."

Deemer Learned stood in the doorway, Bailey and Ward Constable towering behind him. All three were soaking wet. The Councilor was hatless, and Ward and Bailey hadn't dared tell him that a frond of some Nameless bog plant had draped itself across his head.

"At least Medford doesn't burn our Island's history," Prudy said.

"Burn history?" Deemer said. "Whatever dost thou

mean, Mistress Learned? Thou hast taken a fever, perhaps, which explains why thou art in present company. I
need hardly say how disappointed I am to see thee here,
and thy brother."

"Medford saw thee burning red journals," Prudy said.

"A Councilor of this Island, a Learned, settled by
his home fire to read his ancestors' words," Deemer said.
"Having no understanding of this, no ancestry of his own,
Master Runyuin mistook what he saw, peeping in my
window like a Nameless creature of the night. Burning
journals indeed. The very idea shocks me beyond words."

"You seem to me to have words to spare, Councilor,"
Boyce said.

"And a-a-all tanners," the Goatman said.

Deemer ignored them both. "Gather up these journals, Constables. They must be returned to safety. Then
take Master Runyuin and his creature back to the jail.
They will be gone from this Island at first light."

"These journals be safe enough here," Boyce said.
"Medford stays here, too. And no one will be gone until the
Town Meeting gathers to advise the Council. I fear thou
hast forgotten how our Island runs, Master Learned."

"These journals be Island treasures and the province of
the Learneds," Deemer snapped. "They be not for Carvers
and Carpenters. And the danger is too great to wait for
a Town Meeting. See how easily the boy and his creature
escaped this night? 'Tis a miracle we be not blown away
by the wind."

He stepped aside so Bailey and Ward had a clear path to Medford. "Boy and creature first, Constables, then come back for the journals." He looked down his nose at Boyce, the Nameless bog frond swaying next to his cheek. "And the journals shall be packed in readiness or Master Runyuin will have companions on the boat to Mainland."

Oddly, Bailey and Ward didn't move.

CHAPTER TWENTY-TWO

☙

Morning at Cook's

Bolt not thy food, nor converse when Breaking Fast. Let business await thy digestion.

> *A Frugall Compendium of Home Arts and Farme Chores by Capability C. Craft (1680), as Amended and Annotated by the Island Council of Names (1718–1809)*

W HAT'S WRONG with Carvers reading journals?" Earnest asked. "Or Carpenters." He fixed his gaze on Bailey, who hadn't moved from the doorway. "Or Constables."

Bailey stared back at Earnest, expressionless. Ward sidled into the room—with surprising delicacy for such a big person—and took Jeremiah's journal from Medford.

"Ward," Prudy said, "did you know that there never was a Capability C. Craft? That some of the Originals wanted to keep their old, Useless names?"

"That I'm not the first to get banished for Unnameable Objects?" Medford added.

"That . . ." Prudy paused and swallowed hard. "That this is not the first goat—"

239

"*Silence!*" Deemer thundered. He snatched Jeremiah's journal out of Ward's grasp and threw it into the crate beside Prudy. "Constables, I have given orders."

"Aye," Bailey said. "You have." But he still didn't move.

To Medford's astonishment, Ward retrieved Jeremiah's journal and opened it again.

"Ward," Bailey said, "you're dripping on that book."

"Oh. Beg pardon," Ward said to Jeremiah's journal. He waved it around to get the water off. A blurry brown streak ran down the middle of a page. Medford restrained himself from grabbing the journal away from Ward.

"Put it down till you're dry, Ward," Bailey said. Ward laid the journal tenderly on the table beside Boyce's chair, moving Boyce's teacup so it couldn't spill on Jeremiah.

"Constables," Deemer said.

"Hey, Bailey." Ward lit up with a sudden thought. "If young Raggedy wasn't in jail, where in the Names would he run to? If he chose to run away, I mean."

"That thought occurred to me, too, Ward," Bailey said. "This being an island. If he hid someplace, he knows we'd find him sooner or later. Same with that creature there."

"The creature could have run away tonight, Bailey, but he didn't," Ward pointed out.

"Aye, Ward, that's true. Young Raggedy did a terrible thing, making them carvings, but 'tisn't up to us to decide what happens to him, is it? 'Tis the Council's job,

as a group, after a Town Meeting. That's what Pa said—
'No one person runs the Council, Bailey,' he said. 'Town
Meeting runs the Council.'"

"Essence didn't get a Town—," Earnest began.

"Shhh," Prudy said, hitting him on the shoulder.

But Ward and Bailey were too intent on their own
thoughts to be distracted.

"Why do you suppose Councilor Learned had us take
those crates from the Archives to his house, Bailey?" Ward
asked. "Never did that before, did we?"

"No, Ward, we didn't. Can't remember the last time we
cleared the Trade goods out of the jail like that, neither."

"We didn't put Clayton Baker in jail when *he* was 'fore
the Council, Bailey. I think I mentioned that before."

"That's true, Ward," Bailey said. "Course, Clayton
didn't have a horned creature with him at the time."

"Seems like a perfectly nice horned creature once he
calms down," Ward said.

"That's true, Ward."

"Constables." Deemer's hands were clenching and un-
clenching like Pick-'em-out Shellfish headed for the pot.
"'Tis not the province of Constables to decide—"

"Aye, Councilor," Bailey said. "'Tis the Council's province. I believe we can leave Master Runyuin and the
horned creature here with Boyce. Mistress Head will call
a Town Meeting for tomorrow and then we'll see what's
what."

Deemer stood there a minute, adjusting to new circumstances. Had Ward and Bailey ever refused an order before? Medford doubted it.

"Mistress Head will call a Council session and Town Meeting for eight of the clock," Deemer said at last. "I will see to that. I expect all of you there at that time. Failure to attend shall result in immediate banishment." He stalked out. They heard the kitchen door slam behind him.

"That's true about Mistress Essence Learned," Ward said. "She didn't get a Town Meeting before she left. 'Twasn't right, neither." So he had heard Earnest after all.

"Not much time left before eight o'clock," Boyce said. "I'd suggest we sleep for an hour or so. Bailey, Ward, will you stay here?"

"We'll go home and dry off, thankee, Boyce," Bailey said. "C'mon, Ward."

"Bailey, Ward," Medford said. "I thank you."

Ward slapped Medford's shoulder on his way to the door.

"No thanks required, boy," Bailey said. "What's right is right."

Prudy went up to Medford's old room while Medford, Earnest, and the Goatman made beds for themselves on the sitting room floor. The Goatman's robe had dried enough to put on, so Boyce didn't have to give him a second blanket to sleep under. Medford could see that Boyce was relieved about that.

"Try to sleep, boy," Boyce said before heading up to his own bed. "We made strides tonight. 'Twill be fine in daylight."

But Medford couldn't sleep. Outside the sitting room windows, the darkness was lightening to gray. He had just over three hours before the Council convened. Who would be there? Would it just be Boyce and he, Prudy and her family, the Goatman, the Constables? How could Boyce think they'd made strides? Wouldn't the Council just do what Deemer said?

He pondered Bailey and Ward. Medford doubted they'd ever thought twice about the Archives, probably only went up there to fetch and carry for Deemer. But the minute Deemer announced that journals were only for Learneds, there was Ward, opening Jeremiah Comstock's journal and dripping all over it.

Too bad there aren't more Wards and Baileys, Medford thought, beginning to doze. He let his mind drift . . . the Constables and Jeremiah Comstock, Jeremiah and his pots . . . the Goatman's hooves and how far up the goat parts went . . . Ward calling the Goatman a creature but saying he was nice . . . Bailey . . . too bad there weren't more. . . .

The thought hit him like a Smith's hammer. He sat up. "There be more," he said.

"Mmmph," Earnest said, and slept on. The Goatman let out a gentle snore.

Medford could see the sky getting brighter outside the window, almost as he watched. What did he have to lose?

He grabbed Jeremiah's journal and Durward Constable's. He left a note on the kitchen table, *Gone to Cook's. Back soon.* Then he let himself out the kitchen door, tiptoed down the steps into the pale dawn, and hurried to Main Street up the alley next to Boyce's shop.

A lamp was burning in Clayton Baker's oven house. Medford's nose told him, whatever time it was, Clayton had taken the first bread out of the oven. His stomach gurgled.

The lanterns were burning at Cook's, too, and smoke was coming out of the chimney. The windows were fogged up. The door opened; voices and laughter tumbled out into the gray air. Violet Waterman emerged, smiling, coffee mug in one hand, steaming biscuit in the other.

Her smile faded when she saw Medford. She passed him by without a word. But once she'd passed he heard her say, "Trade voyage today, boy. Thou'lt be on it, I'm guessing."

He stood outside Cook's door for a minute, searching for courage. He never found it. But he opened the door, anyway.

The morning hubbub ceased as everyone saw who it was. In the silence, he set the two journals down on the wooden counter, met Myrtle Cook's eye. "Tea . . . ," he started to say, but the word caught in his throat and came out "toggh." He swallowed and tried again. "Tea, if it please thee, Mistress Cook. And a biscuit with ham."

Behind him, someone coughed. Someone else made a slurping sound, which made a third someone chuckle softly.

"I'll need to be paid for this past month's tally afore ye . . . if ye be leaving," Myrtle said, not moving to get him his tea.

"I won't be leaving," Medford said. "If I do I'll make arrangements through Boyce."

"Aye," said a booming voice from the end of the room. "Boyce be good for it. This boy be good for it, too, come to that. Get him his tea, Mistress Cook."

Chandler Fisher, Medford thought. Chandler could make himself heard in a northeast gale or a Town Meeting, and it didn't matter to him which was which.

"I don't see how thou knowst that, Master Fisher," said another voice, a polite, pleasing voice that savored bad news. Dexter Tanner, in his usual place by the window where he could keep an eye on the street. "I never heard of Master Runyuin trading for fish."

"I know good from ill, Master Tanner," Chandler boomed. "And truth from lies. A Useful skill in present company, I might add."

"Thought thou wast in jail, Raggedy," Arvid said, joining Medford at the counter. "Thou and thy creature."

"He was," Dexter said. "I drove him there myself. Quite a fight he put up, too, him and that horned creature. Biting, butting, kicking—"

More tanners, Medford thought. He almost smiled.

"Did they let you out to pack up?" Arvid asked.

"No, we let ourselves out last night," Medford said. "Then we went up to the Archives to read with Prudy and Earnest." The room made a sound that wasn't a sound, as if everyone had sucked in breath all at once. "Earnest noticed some of the older journals missing. So we went to Deemer Learned's and . . . and found . . ." Maybe leave the burning until later. "Well, we found the journals and took them to Boyce's and read some more, until Deemer Learned came and told us nobody but Learneds can read journals."

He stopped for a rest. Myrtle had put a mug of tea and a ham biscuit down for him, placing them gently so they wouldn't make a noise and interrupt him.

The room was silent, digesting. Chandler chewed on his lower lip, his beard bobbing up and down. Cooper Waterman took a noisy slurp of coffee but no one chuckled. Arvid had a wary look in his eye, as if he were waiting to see what happened next.

"Well, that's as it should be," Dexter said. "'Tis a Learned's province to read in the Archives. Nobody else would know what they was reading."

Medford slapped open Jeremiah's journal, getting everyone's attention. He read out the passage about there being no Capability C. Craft. Clayton Baker came in with a basket of bread and started to say something. His wife waved her apron at him and everyone else said, "Shhhhh."

Nobody said anything when Medford finished with Jeremiah, so he switched to Durward Constable. He read the whole section about Cordella Weaver's banishment, right down to Durward's comment about burning his poems.

"What's poems?" asked Amalia Fisher.

"Shhhhh," everybody else said.

"Got any more books there, boy?" Chandler asked.

"The rest be at Boyce's," Medford said. "But Master Learned says we can't read them."

"That's right," Dexter said. "We wouldn't know what to make of them."

"Speak for thyself, Tanner," Chandler said. "I know what to make of 'em just fine. What I can't figure out is why I don't remember any of this stuff from Book Learning."

"So what's poems, Chandler, if you be so smart?" Amalia persisted. "And I never heard you hankering after the Archives before. Why should you care who reads what?"

"Dunno what poems be and I'm no reader. But I'd like to know more about this Capability C. Craft being nobody at all. What else does that Jeremiah write, Raggedy?"

Medford told them about Jeremiah being forced to weave when he wanted to make pots, and about Samuel Baker suggesting the Naming. Twig came into the shop, along with Jeb Pickler and several others, as Medford was describing the Town Meeting in which fifty-one Islanders voted against the name change but were outvoted.

"Majority rules," Dexter said. "Always has, always will."

"Aye, that's true," Chandler said. "Why can't we know these things, though?"

Twig leaned in to Medford. "Tell them about today yet?" Medford shook his head. Twig tipped his head back for better volume. "And what will happen to thee next, Master Runyuin?" he called to the ceiling.

Everyone looked at Medford and his brain froze up. "Town Meeting," Twig muttered into his tea mug.

Ah. "There's to be a Town Meeting," Medford said. "Eight o'clock this morning. The Council will decide then whether . . . whether I'm to be gone." His voice dried up.

"I suppose they may take some action against my Prudy and my Earnest, too," Twig said, as if he were discussing the weather. "Maybe Boyce."

Chandler frowned. "I never heard about any Town Meeting."

"Mistress Essence Learned left without any Town Meeting at all," Cooper Waterman said. "I saw her go."

"Never did think that was right," Jeb Pickler said. "I told you that, didn't I, Cooper? Aye, I did. I said, 'That ain't right, just sending her away like that.'"

Everybody started talking to everybody else. Nobody was listening. Medford took advantage of the confusion to choke down his ham biscuit and sip a little tea, trying to remember how to breathe.

"Good notion to bring them journals here, boy," Twig said under the chatter. "I was just at Boyce's and everybody's up. Thought I'd join you, see if you needed help."

"I thank thee, Twig. What do we do now?"

"Don't need to do much, just wait for it to brew up. Best get Dexter moving, though."

"What do you mean, get Dexter moving? Wait, Twig, what do you . . . ?"

Twig put his arm around Medford's shoulders and steered him toward Dexter's table, leaving both their teas behind. Arvid had rejoined his father and the two had their heads together, talking close. Twig sat down opposite Dexter and rapped his knuckles on the table.

"Eh?" Dexter looked annoyed. "What dost thou mean by that, Master Carpenter?"

"I wish to ask thee a favor, Master Tanner," Twig said. "Now I think on it, I don't believe Master Learned has authorized anybody to talk about this Town Meeting. He'll be most annoyed if he learns Medford told you all. I beg thee not to spread the news any further."

Dexter and Arvid looked at each other.

Twig squinted out the window. "Day's moving on," he said. "Merchant's store'll be open now. Wouldn't do to tell the crowd there, nor at Smith's Forge. I beg thee to be discreet, Master Tanner. And thee, young Master Sawyer."

Dexter got to his feet. "I'll ponder thy request, Master Carpenter. Meanwhile, my boy and I must be about our business."

"And everyone else's, I'll be bound," Twig said, watching Dexter and Arvid make their way to the door. "Aye, there they go, one to the store and the other to the forge."

If he weren't so worried and worn-out, Medford would have felt like laughing. It was a twisty way to go about things, but he supposed it would work. What was it Earnest had said, just the day before? "*You know Pa. He doesn't tell you what to do—wisht he would sometimes, but that's Pa. He just says a few things and walks away.*"

Chandler's voice rose above the crowd noise. "Anybody know what 'tis o'clock?"

Myrtle stuck her head out of her kitchen. "Clock in here says half past seven, Chandler."

"I believe I'll go to that Town Meeting," Chandler said. "Invited or no. Anybody with me?"

Nobody answered but almost everyone stood up. There was a great scraping of chairs and creaking of floorboards.

Twig raised his voice, too. "'Twould be good," he called out, "if the Town Meeting could last until ten of the clock."

Chandler halted with his hand on the door latch. "Why wouldst thou want a *longer* meeting, by the Book?"

"Let's just say I want all the truth," Twig said. Medford didn't think that was the real answer and he could see Chandler didn't, either.

But Chandler nodded and opened the door. "Well, we'll follow thy advice, Twig. They do say—when a Carpenter's got a hammer, 'tis best not to look too much like a nail."

He left. Cook's emptied out after him.

CHAPTER TWENTY-THREE

꙰

The Council

There shall be a Council of five to assign Names and
tend the community's Health, Safety, and Ethics. But all
such matters shall be studied first by the Town Meeting.

—*A Frugall Compendium of Home Arts and Farme*
Chores by Capability C. Craft (1680), as Amended and
Annotated by the Island Council of Names (1718–1809)

MEDFORD HAD figured they'd all go to Town Hall
together, but outside of Cook's the crowd melted
away like ice in springtime.

"I'm going down to the wharf to get Violet," Cooper
Waterman said.

"I'll be right along," Jeb Pickler said. "Got to check the
new brine first."

Everyone seemed to have something to do at home or
in the shop before they made their way to Town Hall.
Before Medford knew what was happening, he and Twig
were alone on the sidewalk.

"Will they really come, Twig?" Medford asked as they
headed off to Town Hall.

"Oh, aye," Twig said. "'Twill be fine, boy."

Merchant's store was crowded to the doorway with murmuring Islanders. As Medford and Twig went by, they heard Dexter's voice rising above the crowd noise. "Don't go telling anybody I told you this," he was saying.

"So why *does* Master Learned want everything to be a secret?" Medford asked. "Why can't we know what's in those journals?"

"Deemer likes to know things the rest of us don't," Twig said. "Makes him feel important. His ma was the same. Maybe all Learneds are like that." He went silent, and Medford knew he was thinking of Prudy.

"Prudy's no Learned, then," Medford said. "She likes to know things but she hates to keep them to herself."

Twig smiled. "You're a fine boy, Medford," he said.

Upstairs in Town Hall, the auditorium seemed vast and chilly. The students' desks had been moved to the back of the room and a row of folding wooden chairs had been arranged in the front of the room, facing the Council table. Prudy and Earnest sat in the middle of the row of chairs with their mother, who looked as if she hadn't slept. At their feet were the crates of journals and a canvas drawstring bag.

The Goatman stood by an open window, yawning. Boyce was wandering around the room examining the woodwork as if he'd never seen it before.

"You didn't bring the dog?" Medford asked.

"She's back at the house," Boyce said. "Stinking up the hearth rug."

"She's a nice dog," Medford said.

"Glad to hear it," Boyce said.

Deemer swept in, wearing a dry Council robe, and his second-best tricorn. He acted as if no one else were there, just went to the Book's safe and unlocked it.

Ward followed the Councilor in, carrying a crate full of Medford's carvings. He and Bailey arranged the carvings on the Council table.

With Boyce's Alma figure so fresh in his mind, Medford thought his own carvings looked awkward and stiff, especially the Prudy head. Why was that? The figures were perfect; he'd even measured them. So why was that Alma figure so much livelier?

Unnameable thoughts again.

Ward pulled the Goatman's sash out of the crate and took it to him. "Ah," the Goatman said. "At la-a-ast." He put it on and blew his nose on it.

"Bailey," Ward called. "I'm just going downstairs to wash my hands."

Councilor Comfort Naming walked in, followed by Councilor Freeman Trade. The two ignored each other, eyes trained in opposite directions, and ignored Medford, Twig, and Boyce, too. They sat down on opposite ends of the Council table.

Councilor Grover Physick headed straight for Medford when he came in. He clasped Medford's hand and shook it hard. "Courage, boy," he said, his round, pink cheeks glowing with goodwill. "Whatever happens. Courage." He nodded to Boyce and made his way to the seat beside Comfort.

Head Councilor Verity Welfare entered last, stony-faced as usual. She stalked to the Council table, breaking stride only briefly when she caught sight of Medford's carvings. She took the center seat at the Council table.

"Master Runyuin, Masters Carver and Carpenter," she said. "Wilt thou be seated, please. 'Tis eight of the clock."

"Nobody's here," Medford whispered as he, Twig, and Boyce sat down next to Clarity and the journals. Boyce grabbed the canvas bag and stuffed it under his seat.

"They'll come," Twig said. But all of a sudden he looked as tired as his wife.

Clarity barely noticed their arrival, she was concentrating so hard on Medford's carvings, on the edge of her chair as if she wanted to be as close to them as possible. She looked sick, but Medford didn't think his carvings were making her that way.

"Bweh-eh-eh," the Goatman said, clip-clopping over to the front row of chairs.

Verity looked up at that truly Unnameable sound and froze, mouth open. Medford had to admit that hearing about a goatman was nothing compared to seeing him lope in your direction. Verity probably could smell him, too.

"I fa-a-are well," the Goatman informed her, and sat down next to Boyce, leaning forward on his staff to relieve the discomfort of sitting in a chair. Boyce eased himself toward Medford to avoid touching the Goatman's robe.

"Let us proceed, Councilor Learned," Verity said faintly, and got up to help Deemer carry the Book from its safe to its lectern.

Deemer leafed through to a page near the back, then he and Verity bowed to the Book and returned to their places. Verity sat down while Deemer stood at her side.

"We are gathered," he said, "to consider what is to be done about young Master Medford Runyuin, who hath embraced the Unnameable in secrecy among us. The proof of his misdeeds be on the table before us." He indicated Medford's carvings. His fellow Councilors dutifully contemplated them.

"Further, young Master Runyuin hath brought into our midst a . . . a creature, a manlike thing with the hooves of a Lesser Horned Milk Creature and horns like, well, like nothing else." The Goatman waved at the Council and hastily put his hand down, one eye on the treetops outside. "And that creature hath made a great wind to the danger of all. Never hath this island seen such a creature."

Grover made a rumbling sound, clearing his throat. "In introducing the subject matter, Master Learned, 'twould be best to avoid words like 'misdeeds' and 'danger.' Thy fellow Councilors might think thou hadst made up their minds for them."

"This subject, Councilor, hath little to do with physick."
Deemer gave Grover one of his jumble-toothed smiles.

"The tone," Grover said, beaming back at him, "hath
little to do with justice."

Deemer raised his hand in a ceremonial way, as if declaiming from the Book. "Master Runyuin's actions imperil a society that hath proved itself fruitful and pleasant
for more than three hundred years. This Island took him
to its bosom from the unknown, and yet he hath broken
our laws and endangered our very lives."

He walked to the lectern. "The Book makes it plain,"
he said, and read out: "*If it hath no Use, it needeth no Name,
and wilt do thee no Harm. Turn thy Back and 'tis gone. Beware, lest thou stare at the Nameless thing for too long. Thou,
and only thou, canst Transform the unnamed to the Unnameable. And then in Truth thou shalt be Gone.*"

There it was, Medford thought. The text he and Prudy
figured had banished Essence. The text they'd waited for
Deemer to explain in class and he never did.

Well, Medford had spent most of his life staring at
Nameless things, from seabirds to carvings. He was as
good as gone.

"Perhaps the Councilor would be kind enough to say
what that passage means," Grover said. "Nobody ever did
explain it to me. Even thy mother in Book Learning. I
asked her once, but got no satisfactory answer."

"We shall leave my mother out of this discussion,"
Deemer snapped. "Councilor, this passage is a powerful

warning against the Unnameable, one which the merest child could grasp if he had a mind to it."

"Oh, aye?"

"Councilor, is a seabird Nameless?" Deemer asked.

"Aye, 'tis."

"So a gray seabird that floats on the ocean is a Useless object and a Nameless one." He picked up the seabird bowl from the table in front of him. "But this seabird, this . . . object, this is beyond Useless, thou wilt agree."

"Well," Grover said, "I have to admit I'd have a hard time eating stew out of that."

Comfort tittered. "Eat stew out of such an object! Imagine!"

Grover ignored her. "'Tis Useless, no arguing about that. And 'tis surely Nameless, because we've never seen anything like it before, so we haven't had a chance to name it. But I don't know about Unnameable."

"I wonder," Deemer said to Verity, in a tone that made Medford shiver, "whether Councilor Physick questions the very concept of Unnameability."

"Nay, I do not question it," Grover said, unruffled. "But I do keep saying, just because a thing is new . . . Well, I don't think we need to be hasty. We let Clayton off with a week on the Barrens after he put the sugar paste on the muffins. Why banish Medford?"

"Councilors, we live on an island in a cold sea," Verity said. "Our survival dependeth upon the work of our hands. Instead of carving bowls and other items that would aid our survival, Master Runyuin hath wasted precious time on these objects here on the table. They are Useless, we all agree. Master Learned makes a convincing argument that they be Useless to the point of harm. Looking at them distracts us from more Useful pursuits."

"And that, in my opinion, transforms them from the Nameless to the Unnameable," Deemer said.

"Hear, hear," Freeman said.

"There is no question, of course, that the horned man be dangerous and must leave," Verity said. "The only question is Master Runyuin."

"If it helps, Mistress Head," Deemer said, "there is the matter of Master Runyuin's wanton behavior last night. Setting aside his other infractions, the fact that he secured the release of this creature shows how little he values our safety."

Medford kept his gaze on Deemer, determined to keep his face bland even though he could feel each Councilor's gaze boring into him.

"A Trade voyage is due to depart at eleven o'clock," Deemer continued. "Two hours from now. Councilor Trade"—he bowed to Freeman, who graciously bowed back—"says the boat can take passengers. I suggest we send Master Runyuin and his creature off today, after trussing up the creature so that he cannot call the wind."

"Bweh-eh-eh!"

"Best place for him," Freeman said heartily. "Such horned men, of course, be commonplace on Mainland."

"Oh, aye?" Comfort Naming said. "Then why have I never heard talk of them?"

Freeman chuckled. "Mistress Naming is aware of little beyond the end of her needle. As the acknowledged expert on Mainland matters, naturally I would know—"

"Acknowledged expert on Mainland matters, my foot," Comfort said. "Why hast thou never talked of horned men all these long years?"

"I had no wish to cause distress," Freeman said.

"Pah," Comfort said. Medford couldn't help agreeing with her.

"He's telling a tanner," the Goatman said softly. "Heh. These flatfoots will believe a-a-anything."

"What exactly *is* a tanner, anyways?" Boyce murmured.

Medford shook his head, trying to follow what was happening.

"Mistress Head," said Grover, "is it wise to send Master Runyuin off with so little discussion? After meeting almost in secret, with so few present? I must say, the fate of Master Learned's daughter doth haunt me. We never heard what she did wrong."

"I have told thee before, Councilor, my daughter was my responsibility, to dispose of as I wished," Deemer said. "Dost thou argue with that?"

"She was young, I admit," Grover said. "But she was past Transition, and was therefore subject to the Council more than to her father."

"I appreciate your concerns, Councilor Physick," Verity said. "And yet I think Master Learned is correct as to Master Runyuin's fate. We are in peril as long as the creature remains here, and Master Runyuin certainly harbors him and aids him. Master Runyuin's carvings show us that he is ill-suited for our society, so I see no injustice."

"I move," Freeman said, "that Master Runyuin be gone with the creature."

"Too soon," Twig muttered.

"I second Councilor Trade's motion," Deemer said.

"All in favor?" Verity said.

Everyone except Grover raised a hand.

"Done," Deemer said. "Done."

"We didn't get a chance to say anything!" Prudy wailed. "We have things to say that might change your minds."

But did they? What, after all, had they learned last night? That the Learneds kept secrets, that others before Medford had made Unnameable Objects and been banished. Those things told them why Essence had been sent away, probably, but would they save Medford from the same fate?

Medford didn't think so.

He wondered if they'd let him take his carvings. They might insist on burning them. He thought about grabbing his favorites and . . . and what? Hide them like Cordella Weaver had? He didn't have time. He had only two hours left of his life on Island.

He imagined himself on a Mainland beach with the Goatman, watching Violet Waterman steam away home.

How would he survive? Would he have to live with the goatfolk? How would his nose survive?

The Goatman's staff caught his eye. Goatfolk carved, didn't they? Those goat heads were pretty good—not as good as Boyce's Alma figure, perhaps, but he could learn something from the Goatman's uncle.

Unnameable thoughts.

Well, why not? His life was going to be one long Unnameable thought now.

A door banged downstairs. The building began to creak and slam and thump.

Voices murmured, more voices than Medford had ever heard in one place before. It sounded like a storm on Gravel Beach.

Chandler Fisher was the first through the auditorium door. "Well, well, well!" he thundered. "What have we here? A secret meeting of Council, Carvers, and Carpenters? Might a Fisher sit in?"

"And a Waterman or two," Cooper said. "A Pickler, a Cook, and three Bakers. A Tanner. Two Sawyers."

In they trooped: Mylon Smith. Irma Cobbler. Foresters, Candlewrights, Millers, and Farmers. Enoch Shepherd, his two sons, and his daughter, who'd come to Town for branding irons and news at Smith's Forge. Cartwrights. Weavers. Shearers. Spinners. They packed the auditorium and spilled out into the hallway.

More could have fit inside but nobody wanted to get too close to the Goatman. The Shepherds and Shearers, who were nearest, left a circle of clear floor around the Goatman's chair, pretending to talk to one another while keeping an eye out to make sure he didn't do something Unnameable or smelly while they were standing there.

Nobody wanted to get close to Medford's carvings either, whether for fear of contagion or for fear of knocking them over, Medford couldn't tell.

"Only one row of chairs?" Chandler boomed. "Why, Councilors, were we not expected? You folks by the door, start handing chairs in from that stack in the hall. Move them desks out of here, too. The rest of you cram up to the walls so we can make some nice neat rows here."

Verity put her hand in the air like a Learned. "Canst thou not stand, Master Fisher?" she shouted over the tumult. "The Council's business is nearly concluded."

"I stand up all day at my ovens," Clayton Baker yelled back. "I can't stand up here, too, and expect to get any thinking done."

"Yep," Chandler said, winking at Twig. "I believe we can take the time to set this place up proper." With a start, Medford remembered that Twig had wanted the meeting to last until ten o'clock. Why was that?

Verity knew defeat when she saw it. "The Council will be in recess until the chairs be set up," she said. She, Deemer, and Freeman forced their way out through the crowd and down the stairs. Grover kept his seat and chatted amiably with Comfort.

Medford relieved the Shepherds and Shearers by

taking the Goatman over to an open window to air him out a bit. He could use a little fresh air himself, truth to tell. His brain felt like it was rattling around loose in his head. He looked at the clock over the map of *Island and Surrounding Waters*. Twenty-five minutes past nine o'clock. An hour and a half left on Island. He wished he could see his cabin one more time.

Arvid sat down next to Prudy, smiling at her. Medford found he didn't care that much, his mind already on the boat to Mainland. She'd need a friend when he was gone.

Twig chatted his way through the crowd, slapping shoulders, bending in to exchange a word, ducking the chairs being handed in from the hall. He caught Medford's eye and waved. Then he disappeared out the door . . . going where?

Against his better judgment, Medford's heart lifted. Maybe Twig had something up his sleeve that would help.

Hope dies hard.

CHAPTER TWENTY-FOUR

Twig's Surprise

I think often of poor Cordella, my dearest friend since childhood. I sit on the beach and try to see Mainland. Is she well? Is she happy? Is she even alive?

—*Journal of Amalia Carter, 1836*

WHAM!

Everyone jumped.

"Wa-a-asn't me," the Goatman said.

Over in the front row of chairs, Arvid was on his feet, his chair fallen over. "Wilt thou let it be, girl?" he yelled, and stalked out of the auditorium.

In case Prudy looked at him, Medford turned to the window and stared out.

"Why are you smi-i-iling?" the Goatman asked him.

To Medford's surprise, Prudy came right over. "Arvid can be a little short-tempered," she said. "But he's not as bad as we thought."

Medford didn't know what to say to that. With unusual wisdom, he kept quiet.

"Anyways," Prudy said, "I think there be hope."

265

"I know," Medford said. "Your pa—"

"I don't know about Pa. I was thinking of Clayton Baker."

Medford thought about Clayton Baker, too. "You mean the muffins?"

"Arvid says if you promise to stop fancy carving they'll have to let you stay. They'll just put you out on the Barrens for a while."

Medford ran out of wisdom. "Arvid says that, does he?"

"Thou never givest Arvid a chance," Prudy said.

"A chance to what, kick me into the bog?"

"He's been very pleasant to me since Transition."

"Oh, aye?"

"Pleasanter than thee." How *did* she get her back so straight? "Of course we know now that thou wast lost to us all because of those . . . those Unnameable . . ."

"Why don't you go talk to Arvid some more, Prudy. He being more like yourself and all."

"Just what is that supposed to mean?"

"Why don't you ask Arvid? If he ever comes back, that is."

"I thank thee. I believe I will." She stalked off, braids hanging straight.

He watched her go, feeling miserable. That might have been the last conversation he would ever have with Prudy.

Or could he make a deal with the Council, like Clayton Baker? Did he want to?

He imagined himself swearing not to do any more fancy carving. Going home without the Prudy head, the squirrel bowl, and the rest, which the Council would burn.

Filling his root cellar, finishing Twig's bowls. Walking out to smell the sea.

And instead of that, what? Off for a bone-chilling boat ride, never to return.

Life didn't have to be difficult and frightening. He could do this. He straightened his shoulders, drew in a lungful of air, let it out.

"Aye," he said, more to himself than anyone. "I'll promise to stop."

"Bweh-eh-eh." Medford hadn't realized a bleat could sound so disapproving.

The chairs were set up in neat rows, the Councilors back in their places. The clock read fifteen minutes before ten o'clock. He had an hour and a quarter left on Island.

What if he could stay?

He'd stop at Merchant's and Cook's on the way home, get supplies for the cabin. And the next day . . . *Twig's bowls first,* he thought, walking back to his chair.

But when he neared the table full of carvings, his imagination hit a snag.

It felt like his brain opened up—he could see where he'd gone wrong on the Prudy head. He'd been so busy perfecting each individual feature that he'd missed what Prudy was like as a person. *"Ma-a-aybe you should stop practicing and just do it,"* the Goatman had said.

Huh.

Even one cocked eyebrow would help. Never mind whether it was perfect. Then the forehead would wrinkle, maybe one end of her mouth would lift—

Medford shuddered. It was a sickness.

Boyce sat down, face as blank as the Prudy carving. Had Boyce ever looked cheerful? Medford couldn't remember.

The Goatman was staring out the open window, one finger tracing a pattern in the air. Outside, dry leaves swirled on a light breeze, making an S curve, then an eight, then a complicated swooping loop, following the Goatman's fingertip.

Uh-oh.

Whup!

A slap of wind rattled the window. The Goatman's purple robe billowed. But then it was over, as if nothing had happened. Islanders taking their seats near the windows looked up, thinking they'd heard something, then went on talking.

The Goatman clopped over to his seat, shaking his head. "I ca-a-an't hold on to it," he told Boyce as he sat down.

"Glad to hear it," Boyce said.

"The Council will reconvene," Verity announced, rapping on the table.

Twig wasn't back yet. Medford didn't know what to

do. Should he stand up now, promise not to carve any more Unnameable Objects?

But Chandler Fisher was up first. "Before the Council moves on, Mistress Head, we want to know what we missed before we got here."

Verity's mouth looked so much like a fissure in granite that Medford thought she'd refuse to tell Chandler anything. But she said, "This Council hath voted to banish Master Runyuin for his Unnameable carving and for exposing Island to danger. The horned man will leave with Medford."

"Bweh-eh-eh!"

Chandler had his mouth open to say more, but the Goatman's comment had thrown him. It was now or never.

Medford stood up. "*Ungh*," he managed. That wasn't what he'd meant to say.

Mistress Head eyed him with curiosity. "Master Runyuin?"

"*Armf*," Medford said. Through a haze of terror, he saw ten raised eyebrows, two per Councilor.

"What're you doing, boy?" Boyce whispered, tugging his sleeve. "Sit down."

He had to say two words: "I'll stop." Medford thought about daybreak behind his cabin. Tea on a crisp morning. Prudy.

Boyce tugged again. Medford looked down at his foster father's tired, unhappy face. *A lifetime of spoons.*

He looked at the Prudy head. The squirrel bowl. The Bog Island view.

They were his. They were him.

"I won't stop carving them," he heard himself say. "I don't think they're Unnameable at all."

"We thank thee for making that plain, Master Runyuin," Verity said.

Medford sat down because his legs wouldn't hold him up anymore. What had just happened? Why was his heart so much lighter?

"Was that supposed to help, boy?" Boyce whispered.

"Master Runyuin may go or stay as it please thee, Mistress Head," Chandler said. "What I want to know is, what about them journals we ain't supposed to see? Medford read to us from one this morning, told us all about the original Naming and there being no Capability C. Craft and—"

"No Capability C. Craft?" Freeman said. "What in the Names do you mean? He wrote the Book, says so right on it."

"'Tisn't anyone's real name," Prudy said. "'Twas an unscrupulous printer and information from Wolley and Murrel and Old Wives."

"Wherever didst thou hear such a thing, Mistress Learned?" Verity asked.

"From Medford. He read it in a journal from the Archives."

"I continue to be amazed that anyone believes what

Master Runyuin tells them," Deemer said. "'Tis true, he and the creature broke into our Archives last night and stole extremely valuable records from our history. It pains me to say that Mistress Learned and Master Earnest Carpenter were there, too, although perhaps they wished only to protect the Archives from destruction."

"As a matter of fact," Earnest said, "Prudy and I let Medford out of jail and I took the lock off the Archives door."

"Thy father's influence, no doubt," Deemer said. "But that is neither here nor there. The point is that Master Runyuin hath misread a journal and misinformed those around him. This is why there be a lock on the Archives and Learneds to guide the reader."

"Oh, aye?" Chandler thundered, making Deemer's voice sound like a Honeybug by comparison. "Why, then, do the precious Learneds never guide us up there? Why can't we read them journals? Why ain't they part of Book Learning, hey?"

"If thou object to my teaching practices, Fisher, I invite thee to suggest improvements," Deemer said.

"I'm no teacher and maybe I don't care about going upstairs to read every day like you do. The point is, if I did want to, why couldn't I?"

"From what the real Mistress Learned tells me," a voice said from the doorway, "I think that is exactly the point."

"I go by Mistress Cook these days, Twig," a second voice said. "Essence Cook, they call me on Mainland."

Earnest jumped up so fast his chair fell over like Arvid's.

"Hullo, Earnest," Essence said. "Still taking things apart, I see."

Earnest blushed. "Hullo, Essence. Where'd that hair come from?"

Medford thought Earnest had asked a good question—he'd never seen hair of such a shade, bright red as autumn leaves and hanging down to Essence's waist. She had on a sweater in colors nobody on Island had ever thought of before and also some kind of skirt, if you could call it that. He'd never seen so much bare leg, except his own in a bath, nor such shiny black boots with such tall heels.

She had a woven bag hanging from her shoulder, stuffed with papers. It swayed as she walked in on those tall heels. She walked like the Goatman except she didn't have a staff to lean on.

Earnest, grinning like a Farmer at harvest, gave his seat to Essence, who crossed her legs and waggled a shiny black foot at the Council.

"Hullo, Pa," she said. "Thou lookst bummed." The only color on the Councilor's face was the purple, green, and yellow lump Medford's fist had put there.

"Who is tha-a-at?" The Goatman tried to whisper but didn't.

Essence glanced over to see who was talking. Her eyes went round.

"I fa-a-are well," the Goatman said.

Essence swallowed hard. "Another one," she croaked.

"Pardon, Mistress . . . er, Cook," Grover said. "Did I hear thee say 'another one'?"

Essence swallowed again. "I never thought to see one in the flesh," she said.

"Thou has seen one *not* in the flesh?" Grover asked.

"Aye. And so have Earnest, Prudy, and Medford. At least I hope they have."

Cordella's cloth man. How could Essence know about that? Medford craned his neck to look at Prudy. Her back was rigid and one braid was straight up and down.

The other braid was in her mouth.

"I never saw any horned man not in the flesh," Earnest said.

Essence frowned. "Earnest, I know you got my message. I can see Pa's crates right there on the floor beside Prudy. Didn't you find my grandma's journals in there?"

Earnest looked at Medford, who looked at Prudy, who refused to look at anyone.

"Your grandma?" Earnest said.

"Constance Learned," Essence said. "The 1963 one is the best, but there be others."

Medford had been a child when Constance Learned had died, but Islanders still talked of her in reverent tones. In thirty years as Head of Council, she never wavered on matters pertaining to Island Ethics.

Everyone said she had brought up her son in her own joyless image.

"Fellow Councilors, I regret to say my daughter appears to be raving," Deemer said. "My mother kept no journal after 1955, as the girl knows full well. Constables, please remove Mistress Essence Learned from this room. I will decide her fate later."

The crowd made a throaty sound, almost a growl.

"Mistress *Cook* is a year and a half past Transition," Grover said. "Thou decided her fate last year and 'twas over before we could stop it. But she was an adult then and she is one now. I believe this be a Council matter. And so I ask thee, Mistress Cook, what in the Names art thou talking about?"

Essence stood up. "Councilors, I left a note up in the Archives," she said.

"Not a ve-e-ery good note," the Goatman interjected.

Essence blinked, then persevered. "I hoped Prudy would find my note—I could see when I left that she'd be my pa's next apprentice. Councilors, Pa sent me away so I wouldn't tell about things I learned in the Archives. Before I left he packed up the important journals and had the Constables take them to his house so no one else could read them and threaten him as I did. My note said where the journals were and I know Prudy found them because there they are."

"I looked at all the journals in both those crates this morning," Earnest said to Essence. "There wasn't anything by a Learned."

"Two crates?" Essence asked Earnest. "Where's the third one?"

And Deemer said, "I see nothing wrong with a Learned, a *descendant* of Learned upon Learned, taking our ancestors' journals home for contemplation before the fire."

Prudy took the braid out of her mouth.

"Before the fire?" she said. "*In* the fire, more like."

❧

CHAPTER TWENTY-FIVE

Constance Learned

As my life wanes I worry about my journals. I should burn them, but 'tis a Learned's charge to preserve such records of our past. Can I fail in that duty now?

—Journal of Constance Learned, 1981

*I*N THE FIRE, Mistress Learned?" Grover said. "What dost thou mean by that?"

"Do not answer, Mistress Learned," Deemer snapped. "'Tis not the time for public discussion. As Master Physick himself hath said, this be a Council matter."

Prudy ignored him and spoke directly to Verity. "Master Learned was burning journals, Mistress Head. Medford saw him through the window. And the Goatman lured Master Learned away so we could go in and rescue the journals that were left."

"Still more lies from Master Runyuin—," Deemer said.

"Bweh-eh-eh," the Goatman said. "Carver Boy doesn't tell tanners."

Verity raised an eyebrow at Medford. Boyce elbowed him in the ribs.

"Ah," Medford said. "The Goatman has decided to call . . . uh . . . tales . . . well, he calls them after Master Tanner. He calls them tanners."

"Not ta-a-ales," the Goatman said. "Lies."

"Hey!" Dexter Tanner said. A wave of chuckles swept across the audience.

"Very ingenious, Master Goatman," Grover said. "But we name a person after what he does. We do not name the product after the maker, apt though the name may be."

"Hey!" Dexter said.

"Why not?" the Goatman said.

"Because we don't," Grover said.

"Anyways," Prudy said, getting back to the subject, "Medford does not lie."

Deemer pointed at the seabird bowl. "No? Didst thou know about these carvings, Mistress Learned?"

Prudy went pink. "He didn't lie about them. That is, not so much lie as . . . not say."

"Pa," Essence said. "Tell me you wouldn't burn your own mother's journals."

"My mother kept no journal after 1955," Deemer repeated, his face expressionless.

Essence flung herself to her knees and burrowed into the crates of rescued journals. She flung them out onto the floor in a jumble. "Comstock, Mitchell, Weaver,

Constable, Spinner, Carpenter . . . ," she muttered. "Nay, no, nay, nay, nay."

Prudy knelt beside her and straightened the discarded journals into neat stacks.

Essence pulled the last journal from the second crate and stared at it as if it had just spoken to her. "They're not here," she said. "They must be the ones he was burning."

"I told you," Deemer said, his face gleaming in triumph. "My mother kept no journal in her later years."

"Burning thine own mother's journals . . . ," Essence whispered, white-faced.

"They were not my mother's—" Deemer stopped short, took a breath. "I was not burning journals and no one can prove that I was."

Prudy said nothing. What could she say? They couldn't prove it, could they?

"Begging Mistress Head's pardon," Bailey Constable said. "I got something in my hankie you might want to see."

Verity didn't look as if she wanted to see what Bailey had in his hankie. Bailey did not let this bother him. He pulled his handkerchief carefully out of his pocket, unwrapped it, and carried it to the Council table as if it were a bird's nest with an egg in it. He placed it gently in front of Verity. The other Councilors got up to see what it was.

Verity took something out of the hankie and examined it closely. "What is this, Constable? 'Tis all burned up."

Bailey loomed over the table, pointing with a huge

finger. "Not all of it, Mistress Head. See there? Red leather, like the covers of them journals upstairs. Got it out of Master Learned's sitting room stove this morning."

"You went through Master Learned's stove ashes?" Grover asked, amused.

"Them journals be Island property," Bailey said stiffly. "Nobody has the right—"

"Nobody has the *right* to enter my house without permission," Deemer said.

"That's true, Councilor," Verity said, squinting at Bailey's charred object. "But why is there burnt red leather in thy sitting room stove?"

"'Tis not leather," Deemer said. "'Tis bark, altered by the flames."

Grover contemplated his fellow Councilor. "One hates to jump to conclusions, Master Learned, but burned-up bark never looks that way in *my* stove." He turned to Verity. "Are there no other crates where the missing journals could have been . . . er, secured? Mixed in with town records, perhaps?"

"There be no missing journals," Deemer said, glaring at Grover.

"All town records are in the Council office," Verity said, "and I know the contents of every box."

But not all town records were in the Council office, Medford reflected. There was that crate outside the jail cell, wasn't there? One lonely crate. Odd.

Hardly knowing what he was about, Medford stood up. ("Not again, boy," Boyce whispered.) Medford gave Ward a look. Ward gave it right back. They started for the door at exactly the same time.

"Master Runyuin!" Verity called after him. "Constables! Stop the boy!"

"The boy seems to have a Constable with him." That was Grover Physick.

"Just a notion, Councilors!" Ward yelled as they ran for the staircase. "We'll be right back!"

The crate marked TOWN RECORDS—NOT FOR TRADE was in the corridor outside the jail cell, where Earnest had used it for a seat the previous day. The slats on top were nailed down. "Ward," Medford said, "we need . . ."

But the Constable already had a prying bar in his hand, and in seconds he had the top off the crate. It was packed full of brown journals. Medford removed a top layer written by Hazel Learned in the late 1800s, a second layer by Wilfred Learned, early 1900s. And there, in the very next layer, he found . . .

Constance Learned, 1965. 1970. 1959.

And 1963.

THE QUIET IN the auditorium was so intense Medford felt his skin tingle as he walked to the front and handed Essence her grandmother's journal.

"Essence," Deemer Learned said. "I beg thee to think before acting."

"I've had ten long months to think, Pa," Essence said. "'Tis not for the Learneds to decide what people know."

Islanders were leaning forward in their chairs. Some of them might have been about to walk out. A person could take only so much in one Town Meeting.

Essence faced the crowd, hand in the air like a Learned. "Many of you remember my grandmother," she said. "She was an impressive woman but difficult to know. 'Twas only after she died, when I saw her journals, that I felt I could love her."

Deemer moaned and covered his face with his hands.

"Although he wouldn't say so himself," Essence said, "I like to think my father feels the same. I hope that's why he couldn't burn her journals. But then, you didn't burn any Learned journals, did you, Pa? You'll burn the thoughts of Weavers and Constables, but never the Learneds."

She flipped pages, found the one she wanted, cradled the journal open against her chest. "My grandmother's journals described her life in detail, down to what her fellow Councilors wore under their robes. But she also did this."

Essence showed the journal first to the Council. Deemer did not look at it. As Essence was about to show it to the crowd of Islanders, Freeman grabbed her arm so he could look at the journal closer. Then he sank back in his chair, blinking hard.

Watching Essence walk past the crowd was like seeing a woodpile collapse after you'd removed the wrong log.

Clarity and Prudy whispered to each other as Essence drew near. They leaned in close when Essence held the journal up to them. They goggled, reared back in surprise, leaned in to confirm what they'd seen. Prudy clapped her hand over her mouth.

Finally, Essence held the journal out for Twig, Medford, and Boyce.

The left-hand page was covered with spidery writing in brownish-black ink, just like the journals Medford had seen upstairs. But the right-hand page was like nothing Medford had ever seen before.

It was a sketch in soft lead, but not like the sketches Medford had seen Twig do when they were planning his cabin. This wasn't rafters and windowsills. This was a person, a man, frighteningly alive.

A man with horns and hooves, hand raised to call the wind.

"There be more drawings like these, in this book and others," Essence said softly. "She sketched everyone on the Council, her family, other Islanders. They're quite good, most of them."

Essence moved on to show the journal to the Goatman and the Constables. Medford contemplated his Prudy head again. It looked even stiffer to him now. A sketch first would help, maybe.

He watched Ward Constable prod the figure in Constance Learned's journal as if it might be round and breathing. "Look at that, Bailey," Ward said. "Another horned man." To Medford's astonishment he clapped a hand on the Goatman's shoulder. "Almost like our own."

The atmosphere had changed, although Medford couldn't figure out exactly how. His brain could only suggest that this would be a good time to sit down and stare at nothing. So that's what he did.

At the Council table, Comfort was muttering to herself and shaking her head. Grover was whispering with Verity, looking as if he wanted to laugh. Freeman got up to join them, not laughing at all. Deemer just sat, blue-tinged.

"Bweh-eh-eh," the Goatman said softly. "When wa-a-as that goatman here?"

Medford got his brain working. "One dead grandfather ago," he said. "Maybe one and a half."

Essence set her grandmother's journal on the table with Medford's carvings.

"Mistress Head," she said, "thou wilt agree, I think, that Medford is not the first Islander to create . . . well, for lack of a better term we'll call them Useless Objects. And, unless I'm much mistaken, he won't be the last, either."

Deemer lunged to his feet. "An aberration!" he cried. "Every generation has them. 'Tis our responsibility to cast them out. Though it be my own family, my own mother, I will not allow her weakness, her Unnameable—"

But now Boyce was up, too. He dragged the canvas bag out from under his chair and undid the drawstring.

He thumped it down on the Council table. The bag fell away to reveal its contents: the Alma carving.

"Another of Master Runyuin's objects, Master Carver?" Verity asked.

"Nope," Boyce said. "'Tis mine. 'Tis Alma. Made it years ago. Couldn't burn it like the others."

"Boyce," Clarity said. "Oh, Boyce." And she stood up, pale as a Learned.

"Go on," Twig whispered. "'Twill be fine."

"I make little clay figures almost like that Alma carving but smaller," Clarity said, talking fast. "I've made them for years, at night. I have some my grandpa did, too. They're tied up in a box, a lot of them, out in the woods." She faced Medford, sad-eyed. "I'm sorry I didn't say, Medford. I was afraid of . . . I don't know what." She sat down.

Prudy burst into the loudest, most wailing tears Medford had ever heard, and buried her face in her mother's lap. Clarity stroked her hair. "There, my brave girl," she said.

"How could you?" Prudy sobbed. "How could you?" With a moan, she pulled herself away from her mother and slid back onto her chair. She hid her face in her hands, shoulders shaking.

Clarity folded her hands in her lap. A tear ran down her cheek.

But now Prosper Weaver, Comfort's husband, was standing up.

"No, Prosper," Comfort moaned. "No, husband."

But Prosper ignored her. "I weave in colors, so did my ma, and she taught me," he said. "Sometimes they come out as figures like Constance Learned's, sometimes not. They're under the bed. Eats me up but there it is."

Medford was beginning to wonder if half the beds on Island weren't hiding—

"Abomination!" Deemer's eyes looked like they might pop out of his head. "Every confession tells us why we must avoid, why we must cast out the Unnameable from our midst!"

"What will you do, Deemer, banish half the island?" Twig called to him.

Deemer headed for Twig. When he came near, though, he changed his mind and lunged for his mother's journal. He held it up, open to more sketches of Constance's fellow Islanders.

"Behold, all ye who would embrace the Unnameable." Deemer was whispering, but Medford was sure even those in the back could hear. "Behold a corruption of the Useful, a thing without Use. Unnameable, because what name could suffice?"

He ripped a page out of the journal, crumpled it in his hand. Then he wheeled and hurled the journal at his daughter. She ducked and it sailed over her head.

"Thou hypocrite!" Chandler Fisher roared, on his feet now. "Banishing this boy when thine own mother—"

The crowd erupted, shouting, stomping, shaking fists. Somebody kicked over a chair. The Constable brothers bellowed for quiet, Council members held up their hands in a plea for calm, but no one paid them any mind.

"We better move," Boyce said. "Seen nothing like this before."

"Bweh-eh-eh-eh," said a windy, grassy voice behind Medford. "Bweh-eh-eh. Bweh-eh-eh . . ." The sound got one Islander's attention, then two, then ten.

"*A-a-a-ahhh hoo-o-o-o,*" the Goatman said. He stood up, raised a hand, twitched a finger.

Through the open window came . . . a leaf. One perfect leaf from a Tanningbark tree, golden brown and dancing on a breeze.

A delicate line of Honeybugs followed the leaf as it looped and swooped across the ceiling, dipping occasionally to within a foot of some Islander who gaped up at it, mouth open, eyes wide, voice silent. The air buzzed, but the noise wasn't from the insects. It wasn't even entirely noise. It was some combination of the senses: a sound, a scent, honey on the tongue, a caress on the cheek, a lifting of the spirits.

Medford felt himself . . . well, not exactly cheering up, but something like that. His fears and worries didn't go away but were diminished by something broader and wilder, which swept past him without caring whether he was worried or not.

"Ahhh," the Goatman breathed. "Tha-a-at's the wa-a-a-ay."

The breeze went calm. The leaf dropped to the floor. The Honeybugs completed one last loop and flew in a line out the window. The Goatman lowered his hand.

Whup! A sharp blast of wind rattled the windows. Everyone jumped.

The Goatman shrugged. "Not ba-a-ad," he said. "Almost kept it."

"I am glad I saw that," Boyce said. "I thank thee, Master Goatman."

Grover Physick sat down heavily and groped for his handkerchief. "Whew," he said, mopping his brow. "I was afraid we'd have bloodshed. Now that, Master Goatman, is what I call a Useful gust of breeze."

The Goatman threw back his head. "Bweh-eh-eh-eh," he caroled at the ceiling. "If it's so Useful, wha-a-at would you name it?"

"Eh?" Grover said, startled.

"Wha-a-at would you name it?" the Goatman said. "If it's Useful, it has a na-a-ame, right?"

"A name for a gust of breeze?" Deemer said with a bitter laugh. "Might as well name those abominations of my mother's. Or the foul things on this table."

"Why not? You could na-a-ame it the Goatman's Useful Gust," the Goatman said.

"Ah, but Master Goatman," Grover said, "that would

be naming the product after the maker. And we don't do that, as I told thee before."

The Goatman gave Grover a goatish look. "A use may not always have a na-a-ame. But sometimes a name has a use. Those ca-a-arvings on the table have both, if both they must ha-a-ave."

He looked down at Medford, his eyes blue and kind. His grin was so wide every stumpy tooth was visible.

"On Mainland," the Goatman said, "they're called run-yuins."

CHAPTER TWENTY-SIX

❧

A Runyuin and a Carver

Connor Farmer hath petitioned the Council to add the name Shepherd to the Book. He would bring sheep in by Trade, as well as two dogs. The Council agreed to change his name if the sheep survive the voyage.

—*Journal of Nell Learned, 1819*

I F A FLY HAD wandered into the auditorium at that moment, it would have had plenty of open mouths to buzz into.

And everyone would have heard it, because no one was capable of sound.

Chandler Fisher's voice splintered the silence. "Well, that solves that."

The room began to murmur, progressing quickly to pure jabber. "Always said Runyuin could be a name," Jeb Pickler told Cooper Waterman. "I did, too. You remember, that time we was talking about creature names . . ."

Deemer sank to the floor, his face in his hands. Essence retrieved her grandmother's journal and returned to her seat, giving her father a wide berth.

Somewhere in Medford's brain a tiny, compressed voice was chanting, "Once a Runyuin, never a Carver." He leaned past Boyce to get at the Goatman. "They're called runyuins, really? Why didn't you tell me?"

"Just ca-a-ame up with it," the Goatman said, beaming. "It's a tanner."

"Oh. You mean it's not true."

"Not yet."

Rap-rap-rap. The crowd ignored Verity. *Rap-rap-rap.* The crowd looked up at the Council table, annoyed, and saw that it wasn't Verity doing the rapping. Verity was sitting in her chair, looking like something you'd thought was a rock but then it melted.

It was Grover Physick who was on his feet, rapping his knuckles on the table. Out of curiosity, everyone stopped talking to listen.

"Seems to me," Grover said, "that we have a proposal for a new name and a new craft. That right, Master Runyuin?"

Medford, caught off guard, managed to nod.

Verity roused herself. "I cannot preside—"

"Then don't," Violet Waterman called to her. "Let Councilor Physick do it."

"For what it's worth, I have seen carvings like this on Mainland," Essence said. "People like to look at them and they trade for them."

"Then I have a question," Comfort said, "for our acknowledged expert on Mainland affairs." Freeman eyed Comfort as if she were a barrel of root beer about to explode in his storeroom.

"I should like to know, Councilor Trade," Comfort said, "why thou saidst nothing all these years about a possible meaning for Master Runyuin's name. In thy dealings with Mainland Traders, surely thou hast heard them speak of runyuins?"

She raised her eyebrows at him and waited.

Freeman rose slowly to his feet. Medford was still trying to come to terms with his salvation resting on . . . well, on a tanner. Now he realized that his salvation was only going to last a minute or two. Now Freeman was going to tell everyone that Runyuin meant no more on Mainland than it did in Town Hall.

Freeman's Council robe, fresh that morning, was soaking wet in the armpits. "Councilor Naming," Freeman said, sweating, "thou ask a worthy question."

Comfort's smile went stale. This was not the reaction she had expected.

"I . . . I assumed . . . that all knew such items existed. I saw no need to mention them because . . . because we do not make such things. Now it appears that some of us do make them and perhaps the things be less . . . well, they may be more Useful than we thought."

Medford tried to sort out where tales ended and tanners began. He gave up.

"In any event," Freeman said, "Mistress Essence suggests these runyuins may have some value in the Trade. Perhaps, in time, we may come to understand their Use."

Trade his carvings? Watch some stranger walk away with the Prudy head? *I'd rather burn them*, Medford thought.

"Say nothing, boy," Boyce whispered. "Let it work itself out."

Grover nudged Comfort with his elbow and addressed the room. "Perhaps we should rely on our very excellent Councilor Naming to preside at a later meeting," he said. "Discuss whether we can add the name Runyuin to the Book."

"Aye," Comfort said slowly. "Aye, perhaps we should."

From his seat on the floor, Deemer directed his cold pewter glare at her.

She ignored him. "As Councilor Naming, I call a hearing for the twentieth day of the Hunter's Moon to consider the addition of Runyuin to the roster of Island Names and Employments. Medford may stay on Island until that time."

"And, most likely, beyond," Grover said, smiling at Medford.

Comfort forged ahead. "Any who wish to testify—"

"I will testify," Deemer snapped, standing up.

"So will I," Grover said.

Freeman gave Comfort a half bow from his seat. "And I."

"And now," Grover said, "if there be no other—"

"Wait," Prudy said. "What about the Goatman? What becomes of him?"

All the Councilors turned to Councilor Welfare. Medford held his breath.

"He must be gone, of course," Verity said. "He is most unsafe."

"Bweh-eh-eh!"

"No!" Medford stood up, feeling he'd be more persuasive that way. "He's not dangerous. 'Tis just . . . he's just learning to control himself."

Verity considered the Goatman. "We could be blown out to sea whilst he learns."

"He did all right with that leaf," Twig said. "Give him a chance."

"There ain't been a bad wind the whole time he's been in jail," Ward said. "He just has to keep still and 'tis fine. Ain't that right, Bailey?"

Bailey eyed his brother as if he didn't know him. "Looking at them carvings must have addled your brains, Ward. What if the fellow gets mad? We've seen how windy he can get."

"Well, he ain't gotten windy today," Ward said. "'Cept with that leaf, which I liked."

"But he smells bad, Ward, almost as bad as that Herding Creature last night." Bailey addressed the Council. "You folks can't smell it because you're over there. But I been standing here and my nose is ruined for life. I ain't never smelled anything like it."

"Sme-e-ell!" Deemer yelled. "Contagion! Contamination! Abomination!"

Before anyone could stop him, he grabbed Medford's Boyce bowl from the Council table. He lifted it high above his head, then smashed it onto the floor with all his strength. Chips of nose and chin flew sideways.

"Bweh-eh-eh-eh!" the Goatman yelled, leaping to his hooves, arms waving.

Whup! Whup-whup-whup!

The Goatman whirled around, a panicky eye on the world outside the windows.

"Oh," Medford said. "No."

A blast of wind slammed into the side of Town Hall. Several people screamed.

The world screamed back.

Dead leaves spewed through the open window. The window slammed shut and its glass shattered, along with every other windowpane on that side of Town Hall.

The entire Shepherd-Shearer clan jumped up and bolted for the door. Farmers, Cobblers, and Watermans stood and shouted. Glazers, Weavers, and Candlewrights hunkered down on their chairs and covered their heads with their arms.

Deemer gave Medford a full, jumble-toothed grin. Then he stalked out the door.

He was no sooner out of sight than the world went quiet again. Islanders stopped shouting when they noticed that the wind was silent and the broken windows were the only damage. For a Goatman-induced breeze, Medford thought, it wasn't much. But a glance at the Council table confirmed that the timing couldn't have been worse.

Three and a half bloodless faces confronted him. The half belonged to Comfort, who had her arms up protecting her head.

The crowd had had enough. No one who was standing sat down again. Everyone who was sitting stood up. "Get rid of that thing," Millicent Brewer called out.

Verity's mouth was a fissure across her face. "I agree," she said. "I move that the horned man spend tonight in the jail. Tomorrow morning he shall board the boat he came in and be towed to sea to find his way to Mainland. All those in favor?"

She raised her hand. So did the other Councilors. Even though their votes didn't count, most of the Islanders in the audience raised their hands, too.

"Done," Verity said. "Medford to stay, the horned man to go, the name Runyuin to be considered. I move we adjourn."

Chairs scraped. Floorboards creaked. Fishers, Watermans, Shepherds, and Shearers crowded to the door. Twig joined them and so did Boyce, the Alma carving cradled in his arms. Clarity tried to talk to Prudy, who got up and walked away. Clarity stared after her for a minute, then put her arm around Essence and steered her toward the door.

Numb from brain to toenail, Medford sat down and watched them all go. He should be elated. He could stay. He—and his carvings—belonged to Island now. But he owed it all to a smelly man with horns.

Who would be towed to sea in the boat he came in.

"Guess we gotta take this fellow down to the jail now, Medford," Ward said, grabbing the Goatman's arm. "I'm sorry about it all." Ward's eyes were red and watery.

"I'm spending the night in the jail, too, Ward," Medford said.

"Me, too," Earnest said. "And Prudy will, too."

CHAPTER TWENTY-SEVEN

ᆓ

Risk and Beauty

I am right pleased with the wall I built for Mistress Farmer.
We seldom talk of Beauty, but that's what this is: Fitted for
its Purpose, each Rock in its proper Place.

—*Journal of Birch Mason, 1799*

*B*AILEY SHUT the door to the jail cell, but he didn't
lock it.

The Goatman made himself a nest of blankets and fell
noisily asleep. Medford, Prudy, and Earnest sat down and
stared at one another.

"I forgive you, Prudy," Medford ventured at last.

"For what?"

"Tuh. For betraying me to Deemer."

"I didn't." She'd never lied to him before. Had she? He
tried to think.

"I didn't," Prudy insisted, looking like she might cry
again. "I decided not to, but I couldn't live with *two* secrets. So I went to tell Deemer about Cordella's Unnameable Object. But he already knew about you, so I didn't tell
about Cordella after all."

"But . . . Earnest said you told Deemer . . ." Medford tried to think what Earnest actually had said. *"She went to see Deemer Learned this morning. She didn't tell Pa she was going."* Nothing about what she'd told Deemer, as a matter of fact.

"I did tell about the Goatman," Prudy said. "That wind came up and knocked everything over and I thought . . . well, I thought it was best."

"I might have done the same," Medford said. "But who told about me?"

"I don't know. I thought it might have been Arvid; maybe he'd seen something when he visited you. But I pressed him hard when the chairs were being set up and I truly don't think he did it. What in the Names is wrong with you, Earnest?"

Tiny screwdriver in hand, Earnest was attacking his pocket watch in a fever. He had the cover off and was detaching a wheel. "I did it," he told the watch innards.

"Did what?" Medford peered down at the watch.

"Told Deemer. About your carvings."

They stared at him as he pulled out the wheel and palmed it.

"Sorry," Earnest said.

"Earnest," Prudy said. "What were you thinking?"

A tiny metal coil took flight from Earnest's watch. He retrieved it. "I wanted to find out what happened to Essence," he said. He tried to fit the coil back into the watch but it took flight again.

"What do Medford's carvings have to do with Essence?" Prudy asked. "Earnest, stop fooling with that thing and look at me."

Earnest rescued the errant coil and gave her a patient-elder-brother look. "Prudy, if I'd said, 'Let's break into the Archives and find out what happened to Essence,' would you have done it?"

Medford had to admit Earnest had a point.

"With Medford in jail, we had a way in and a reason to go up there," Earnest said. "And see how well it all turned out."

"Medford could have been banished!"

"But he wasn't, was he? And now he'll carve what he wants to and Essence is back and . . . all's well." Earnest set to work reinstalling the coil.

"By all the Names, Earnest," Prudy said, "you took us apart just like that watch."

For dinner, Ward and Bailey brought vegetable stew, biscuits, and late corn from Cook's. Ward woke up the Goatman and sat down to eat with them. Bailey took his portion down to the Constables' room.

"He feels bad that he said the Goatman smells," Ward explained, then lowered his voice so only Medford could hear. "Also, he liketh not the smell."

While they ate, Medford and Prudy tried to think

up ways to keep the Goatman on Island. None of them made much sense, since they all involved the Goatman hiding and not calling down any blasts of wind and no one thought he could do either for very long.

The Goatman was silent and broody, although he did manage to eat everyone's discarded corncobs as well as all the napkins.

They napped and talked, talked and napped all afternoon. The Goatman plucked some of the taller grass blades growing outside the window and played a slow tune, lilting but lonely. It sounded like winter.

When everyone else was sleeping, Medford's brain kept revisiting the moment when he'd tipped over Boyce's kitchen table, sent Alma flying. He imagined himself stopping first, yelling at Boyce but not destroying the carving. *Why didn't I do that?*

He knew he should go over and make sure Boyce was all right, share his anguish over the carving. But he told himself Boyce would want to confront this alone and in silence, the way he confronted everything. *What could I say to him, anyways?*

"Hoo," Prudy said. "What's that smell?"

"Sti-i-inky!" The Goatman sat up.

"No argument here," Earnest said.

Everyone crowded to the window. They took turns standing on the bench to pat the dog and have their faces licked.

"I'll let her in," Medford said, heading for the door.

Prudy sniffed her hand. "I wouldn't," she said.

The dog seemed content to lie down next to the window, gazing in at them. "She's a very smart dog," Prudy said. "We took her over to the Fishers' bait shed and she knew just what to do."

"Smells like she did it again," Earnest said, coughing.

Medford lay down again, trying not to think about the Alma carving. Instead, his brain skipped to . . .

"Earnest, how did Essence get here this morning?"

Prudy and Earnest exchanged a glance. "Remember the light we saw in the radio room last night?" Earnest said. "That was Pa. He radioed the Mainland Traders in the middle of the night, asked them to bring Essence over this morning."

"But why?"

"Pa thought she should tell what she knew," Earnest said. "Good idea—I would have done it if I'd thought of it."

"'Tis so unlike him," Prudy said. "Don't you think so, Earnest? He never actually does anything. Usually all he does is talk."

"And usually to someone who already agrees with him," Earnest said.

"You sound as if you don't approve of him," Medford said.

"I love him," Earnest said. "I like talking to him and

I like listening to him. He's smart and he's good to have around. I don't think of him acting on his words, that's all."

"Until now," Prudy said.

"Maybe," said her brother.

Medford had always envied Prudy and Earnest their lively, interesting father, especially after growing up with silent Boyce Carver. Yet Boyce had had that Alma carving hidden under his bed all these years.

And now Medford had broken the Alma carving, perhaps beyond repair.

He had to see Boyce. Now.

"I'll be back," he told the others.

He found his foster father in the workshop, doggedly sanding spoons. Alma was on a table in the corner with a new chin.

"Don't touch her," Boyce said. "The glue's drying."

"She looks good," Medford said. He meant it—you could hardly tell she'd been damaged unless you knew what to look for. But he knew that for Boyce—and for him—that carving would never be truly whole.

"What will you work on next?" he asked.

"Bowls," Boyce said.

"That's all? Bowls? You can carve what you like now."

"If you mean Unnameable carvings, no, I can't. I promised Alma. She'd hate that I taught you to carve the things."

"You didn't. You always told me to avoid the Unnameable."

"I don't know, Medford." Boyce put his sandpaper down in the exact place where he always put it down. "I don't know."

"Truly, Boyce," Medford said. "I started seeing things in the wood, that's all."

Boyce shook his head. "I saw you with that seabird wing years ago, and I thought, 'Oh, the Book, I made him see that.'"

"You told me things were beautiful for their Use," Medford said. "That's all."

"Maybe I shouldn't have said 'beautiful.' 'Tis a dangerous word. But maybe just being around me made you do it. Maybe 'tis a contagion after all."

Medford had a startling thought. "Is that why you made me move out? You thought you were teaching me wrong?"

"Didn't do much good, did it? Look at all them things you carved."

"I think Alma'd say 'twas all right now," Medford said. "Now that they're runyuins."

"No, she wouldn't," Boyce said. "And one Runyuin in the family is enough."

Medford was back in jail and snuggled under his blanket before he thought about Boyce using that word, "family." He'd never used it before and might not again.

Once was enough.

CHAPTER TWENTY-EIGHT

૭

Another Useful Gust

When a Neighbor is to embark upon a Voyage, 'tis Right
and Proper to provide such sustenance as thou canst spare
from thine own Larder and Stores.

> —*A Frugall Compendium of Home Arts and Farme*
> *Chores by Capability C. Craft (1680), as Amended and*
> *Annotated by the Island Council of Names (1718–1809)*

THE MORNING dawned clear and chilly. Ward brought
biscuits with butter and honey and ate with the
group. At the end of the meal he collected the napkins
and gave them to the Goatman.

Medford wasn't breathing well. He thought about
what his life had been like before the Goatman arrived—
just five days ago. The sick feeling in his stomach every
time he carved something Useless. The fear that someone
would find out. The loneliness.

"Where will you go now, Master Goatman?" Prudy
asked.

"Ba-a-ack he-e-ere," the Goatman said, goatish.

"Thi-i-is time I'll go to those barrens you ta-a-alk about. I'll hi-i-ide and practice on the wi-i-ind."

Medford could see from Prudy's face that this wasn't the answer she wanted to hear. "The first wind that comes up they'll all turn out to find you," she said. "I don't know what they'll do then."

Medford envisioned the Goatman trying to make his way back to Island over a late-autumn sea. Or foraging for himself on snowy Mainland, still exiled from his home.

They met Boyce, Twig, Clarity, and Essence at the wharf. Chandler had towed the Goatman's sailboat over from the beach below Medford's. Everyone stood on the float, silent, while Chandler tied the sailboat to the Trade motorboat for towing out to sea.

Myrtle Cook bustled down the ramp and handed Medford a covered basket. "For thy friend with the horns," she said, eyeing the Goatman from a safe distance. "'Twill last him to Mainland, I think."

Astonished, Medford peeked under the cloth. The basket was half full of cheese biscuits. Freshly laundered cloth napkins filled the other half. "That-that's nice of you, Mistress Cook," he stammered.

She blushed. "Ward says he's a nice enough fellow. Just . . . funny-looking and windy, and he can't help that. And we know things we didn't used to. That ain't all bad."

Millicent Brewer arrived next with three bottles of root beer. She handed them to Chandler, who stowed them in the sailboat. Prosper Weaver arrived with blankets. Freeman Trade strutted onto the float and handed Boyce an imported compass. Boyce handed it to the Goatman, who sniffed it.

Comfort Naming brought a sun hat with the brim cut out on the sides and ties added for each of the Goatman's horns. She gave the hat to Medford, glanced sidelong to see where Freeman was standing, and turned away from him, only to run into the Goatman. She jumped backward with a squeal, and Chandler caught her before she tumbled into the water.

"Best get this voyage under way," Chandler said, steering Comfort toward the center of the float. "Don't know how much more of this we can take."

More Islanders arrived. So many of them tried to crowd onto the float that Chandler posted Bailey at the top of the ramp to block latecomers, who then lined the wharf and shore instead.

Finally, all was ready. A hard lump formed in Medford's throat. He hoped he wouldn't get teary in front of everyone. The dog came over to lick his hand. He knelt down to scratch her ears and chest, breathing through his mouth.

"Ca-a-arver Boy," the Goatman began.

But then Verity let out a yell that could be heard from

one end of a hayfield to the other. She pointed to the shore.

On a bluff over the rocks stood a lone Pitch Tree that, unlike most of its kind, had large branches perfectly spaced for climbing. Ever since anyone could remember, Island children had dared one another to climb to its top, where the trunk would bend under their weight some thirty feet above the ground and at least forty feet above the rocks.

Hazel Forester was up there now, an arm's reach from the top. Hazel had grown more than she realized and the trunk was bending more than usual. Verity's sharp eyes had seen what Hazel did not: After years of abuse, the tree was about to give up.

There was a loud crack. "Ma!" Hazel yelled as the tree-top began to topple.

"Hazel!" screamed her mother, Sarah Candlewright, standing on the wharf.

"A-a-a-hhh!" yelled everyone else.

"Bweh-eh-eh! No-o-o!" The Goatman flung up his hands in horror.

Whup!

Before anyone knew what was happening, a blast of east wind flung itself at the falling treetop. The wind caught the branches and, with Hazel aboard, the treetop took flight. It sailed out over the rocks, over the shallows, over the floats. Girl parted company with tree and plummeted into deep water, three feet away from a dinghy where Rufus Fisher was gutting harbor fish. Hazel emerged on the surface, flailing.

Rufus adjusted quickly to the novelty of young girls falling out of the sky. He grabbed Hazel by the scruff of the neck and hauled her into the dinghy, where she lay gasping amid fish guts. The treetop plunged into the water thirty feet away and bobbed to the surface. Rufus gaped at it, then at Hazel. He looked to the crowd on the wharf for guidance. White-faced, everyone on the wharf gaped back at him.

"Well, I'll be," Ward said.

"That," Verity said, "was a Useful gust."

"Mistress Head," Grover Physick said, "I believe the Council should reconsider its vote. This creature may have redeeming qualities."

The Goatman had frozen in place, but now he lowered his hands.

"Did you do that on purpose?" Medford whispered.

"Don't know," the Goatman said.

"Maybe we can say you did."

The Goatman raised his eyebrows. "Ma-a-aybe it's not true."

"Not yet."

Rufus hoisted Hazel onto the float, soaking wet and covered in fish slime. Her mother hugged her, weeping. Then, hands on her daughter's shoulders, Sarah propelled Hazel toward the Goatman.

Hazel hesitated, gazing up into the Goatman's blue eyes. The Goatman reached out a hand and showed his stubby teeth. Hazel threw her arms around him.

The Goatman patted Hazel's head. His nose wrinkled. "She sti-i-inks," the Goatman said.

CHAPTER TWENTY-NINE

꠸

The Unnameable

To cleanse the air of Offensive Smells, pick Lavender flowers when the Dew has just dried. They can be Strewn, en-
closed in a Pomander, or dried and crushed.

—*A Frugall Compendium of Home Arts and Farme
Chores by Capability C. Craft (1680), as Amended and
Annotated by the Island Council of Names (1718–1809)*

ESSENCE STAYED with Clarity and Twig for almost a
week. When she finally left for Mainland, she took
Earnest with her.

"More things to take apart," Earnest explained, not
meeting anyone's eye. "And I can come back if I want."

Clarity wept as Earnest chugged away on the Mainland
harbormaster's boat. "He'll be back," Twig assured her. But
he was as solemn as Medford had ever seen him.

Two days after Earnest left, Twig attended a Council
meeting to propose that all Islanders—adults and young
ones alike—be given history classes in the Archives. He
refused to leave until he got his way. He became a regular
at Council meetings, and made himself such a nuisance

that Grover started hiding behind the nearest Fleabane Shrub when he saw Twig coming.

Since no one really believed Earnest would come back, his departure presented Prudy and the Council with a puzzle. Now Twig was the one without an apprentice.

Fortunately, Hazel Forester chose that moment to sneak up to the Archives on a non-Book-Learning day. She was discovered poring over a collection of Forester journals.

"The girl shows an interest, Master Learned," Comfort Naming said at the next Council meeting. "See how she fares, and in time perhaps thou might release Prudy back to her father."

Deemer eyed Hazel with distaste. Hazel straightened her back and tried not to giggle.

"I'd still come up to the Archives to make sure all's well," Prudy told Deemer. "Even if I be a Carpenter." Medford wasn't sure if that was reassurance or a threat. He could see that Deemer wasn't sure, either.

Prudy agreed to stay a Learned long enough to put the Archives back to rights—no one trusted Deemer to do it. As far as Prudy could discover, more than a dozen journals had gone into the Councilor's sitting room stove, including two by Cordella Weaver, one by Jeremiah Comstock/ Weaver, and three by Jeremiah's father, Jacob Comstock/ Potter.

Other than ordering that the lock stay off the Archives door, the Council did nothing to punish Deemer for his infractions. "'Twill be punishment enough that we know all his secrets now," Prudy told anyone who would listen.

She also organized the testimony on Medford's behalf when Runyuin became an official name, written in the front of the Book just like Carpenter and Tanner.

"That girl's for the Council someday, Raggedy," Grover whispered to Medford.

"Raggedy" had become a friendly nickname, although not one Medford would have chosen for himself. It took Arvid several weeks to realize that other people were using it affectionately. He and his father immediately stopped using it. That was something.

To Arvid's further displeasure, exchanging runyuins was becoming a popular way of marking anniversaries and special occasions. While no one would have called them exactly Useful, their owners admitted they weren't unpleasant to have around. Islanders began stopping Medford to ask what he was working on, and managed not to look horrified when he told them.

"Ma's going to sell some of her runyuins at Merchant's," Prudy told Medford as they walked to Bog Island one day in Hunter's Moon. "Fine with me. Get them out of the house."

Although she was doing her best to adapt, Prudy's attitude toward runyuins was inconsistent. She could pore over Medford's carvings by the hour and even asked one or two questions about technique. But she still hadn't forgiven Clarity or Medford for all the years of secrecy, and made a point of ignoring the little clay figures that dotted every flat surface at home.

Medford had traded the Prudy head for one of Clarity's pottery runyuins, a charming rendition of a spring lamb kicking up its heels.

"Did you feel anything when you got the idea for this?" Medford had asked Clarity. "A . . . hum? Or a buzz? Fresh air in your brain?" Clarity had looked at him as if he had his breeches on his head.

"Surely you must feel *something* when you make these," he added in desperation.

She thought for a minute. "I'm happy. Is that what you mean?"

Prudy and Medford still hadn't been back to Bog Island. But so many people wanted to see Cordella Weaver's cloth man that Boyce finally withdrew his opposition.

Medford wasn't sure that was a good idea. He still turned red at the thought of all those courting rumors— although that did not prevent him from wanting to spend every possible waking minute with Prudy everywhere else.

She was his best friend, he told himself as they scuffed through the bronze-colored leaves that covered the path. You didn't court your best friend, even if her cheeks were shell pink and her hair smelled like grass.

Not yet, anyway.

They'd asked the Goatman to join them, but he was on the blueberry barrens practicing wind control. He had been up there every day since the Council withdrew his banishment. Islanders were learning to grab something solid and hold on when they heard a *whup* coming in from the north.

So far, the winds hadn't been bad. "I fa-a-are well," the Goatman reported proudly to Medford.

Bog Island looked almost the same as it had a year ago, and Cordella's cloth man was right where Medford had buried it. "We'll take it to Prosper Weaver," Prudy said. "He's probably related."

As they neared Prosper's shop, however, Deemer Learned was pacing down the sidewalk in Council robe and dented tricorn, on his way to Town Hall. "Why art thou not in the Archives, Mistress Learned?" he asked when he was in earshot.

"I had other business," Prudy said. Deemer's face tightened at the lack of respect in her voice. His manner did not improve when Prudy unfurled Cordella's woven object.

"This is what Medford and I found buried on Bog Island last year," she explained, "and now we take it to Master Weaver, since its maker was a relative."

"Such an object belongs in the Archives," Deemer said. "'Tis part of our heritage and must be kept safe."

"We'll see what Prosper Weaver thinks," Medford said. "Perhaps he will agree. But perhaps not."

Deemer's stare would have frozen Medford's blood a month ago. But Medford stared right back. Minutes ticked by, then a century or two.

Whup-whup-whup! Medford and Prudy flung themselves to the ground as a blast of wind rocketed in from the north. Their hair lifted from the backs of their heads. Dry dirt from the street swirled around them.

But in the next instant all was quiet again.

"That wasn't bad," Prudy said, getting up and dusting herself off. "Worse than yesterday, though."

"Abomination," Deemer Learned muttered, on his knees clinging to Irma Cobbler's fence post. "Ruination of us all."

Medford put out a hand. "Let me help you up, Master Learned."

Deemer stared at Medford's hand for a long minute, then turned away and heaved himself up without it. "Thou and thy Unnameable Objects," he said, "will hasten the decay of all we hold dear."

A door slapped shut across the street. Freeman Trade and his nephew, Matthew Merchant, stood on the porch at Merchant's Store, unfurling a banner that read: RUN-YUINS BY CLARITY POTTER, STARTING NEXT WEEK.

Deemer snorted and stalked off toward Town Hall.

Watching him walk away, a lone black-clad figure looking neither right nor left, his fellow Islanders passing him by with no cheery call or wave, Medford was surprised to feel a twinge of sympathy.

Just what Prudy said, he thought. Master Learned had not escaped punishment.

When he got home, the Goatman was insulating the porch with evergreens so he and the dog could sleep under there all winter. The dog was hunkered down gnawing on something. Medford didn't look close to see what it was.

"I lost the wi-i-ind," the Goatman said when Medford peered in to see what he was doing. "I was be-e-etter yesterday."

"You'll get it," Medford said. "Is that whoosh you feel slowing down any?"

"Yes. No. I don't know. I don't wa-a-ant to talk about it."

"I wish I knew what to call that feeling I get when I'm carving, that hum or buzz or fweeee."

"You ca-a-an't call it anything," the Goatman said. "It's Unnameable."

He probably was right.

Acknowledgments

IT TOOK A VILLAGE to bring Medford and friends to print. For the most part, that village was Brooklin, Maine, but sometimes its borders stretched to New York and beyond.

Kathy Dawson, my editor, is the person above all others whose judgment and guidance gave Medford a book worth living in. I wouldn't have met Kathy without the talent and energy of my agent, Kate Schafer, and I wouldn't have met Kate without the intervention of Genie Chips Henderson and her husband, Bill Henderson. I wouldn't have met Bill if Doris Grumbach hadn't asked me to her birthday party . . . but I could keep this going forever, so I'll stop now.

Shelly Perron, best friend for life, was Medford's first editor. Her son, Graham P. Nelson, broke it to me that the original first chapter dragged. The Foul-Weather Writers Group (Tania Allen, Deborah Brewster, Maggie Davis, Becky McCall, Gail Page, Kim Ridley, and Zoe Sullivan) was generous with insight and moral support.

Other readers, listeners, and advisers included Rob Shillady (six drafts!), Cynthia Voigt, Sosha Sullivan, Oliver Sullivan, David Sullivan, Matthew Allen, Oliver Gellerson, Alorah Gellerson, Jill Knowles, Paul Sullivan, Henry Sullivan, Mary Catherine Dunn, Sherry Streeter, Eric Jacobssen, Anita Jacobssen, Sarah Pavia, Alice Wilkinson, Stephen Fay, Dorothy Booraem, Abigail Booraem, Holly Meade, and Lisa Heldke. Cynthia Thayer and the Peninsula Writers Group (Bettina Dudley, David Fickett, Annaliese Jakimedes, Paul Markosian, and Thelma White) delivered a well-timed kick in the breeches.

Island's language and culture were informed by Samuel Pepys, William Wycherley, the King James Bible, Lydia Maria Child (*The American Frugal Housewife*, 1832; reprinted by Dover Publications, Inc., 1999), Liza Picard (*Restoration London*, Avon Books, Inc., 1997), and the websites of Plimoth Plantation, Old Sturbridge Village, and Colonial Williamsburg. I borrowed a couple of Book phrases from *Rules of Civility & Decent Behaviour in Company and Conversation*, as transcribed by the teenage George Washington in 1744. Myriad facts, minor and major, came my way via Brooklin's Friend Memorial Public Library, and librarians Gretchen Volenik and Stephanie Atwater.

Medford and the Goatman originally appeared in paintings by my partner, Rob Shillady, who cheerfully let me steal them.